"A delicious story generations of Texans have fervently wanted to believe"

Bob Tutt
The Houston Chronicle

"Electrifying . . . Educational . . . Emotional"

Beola Sales
"The Beola Sales Show"
Houston Access Cable

"A wonderful love story"

Fred Kuehnert
Producer
"The Buddy Holly Story"

"From a scrap of history, Anita Bunkley has created an absorbing novel"

Sally Dooley
Editor, *Texas Review of Books*

"Bunkley's debut an inspiration"

Paul Harasim
The Houston Post

Emily, The Yellow Rose

Emily, The Yellow Rose

by
Anita R. Bunkley

Rinard Publishing
Houston, Texas

ISBN: 0-9624012-0-X
Library of Congress Number: 89-62840

Cover Design by Eric T. Seaholm

Published by Rinard Publishing
P.O. Box 821248
Houston, Texas 77282-1248
United States of America

Typography & Printing by
D. Armstrong Co., Inc.
Houston, Texas

Dedication

To

My daughters, Angela and Ramona and my husband, Crawford, and to all my family and friends who have shown interest and support in the writing of this book.

THE YELLOW ROSE OF TEXAS
Original Lyrics

There's a yellow rose in Texas
That I am a going to see
No other darky [sic]* knows her
No one only me
She cryed [sic] so when I left her
It like to broke my heart
And if I ever find her
We nevermore will part.

Chorus:
      She's the sweetest rose of color
      This darky ever knew
      Her eyes are bright as diamonds
      They sparkle like the dew
      You may talk about dearest May
      And sing of Rosa Lee
      But the yellow rose of Texas
      Beats the belles of Tennessee.

      Where the Rio Grande is flowing
      And the starry skies are bright
      She walks along the river
      In the quite [sic] summer night

She thinks if I remember
When we parted long ago
I promised to come back again
And not to leave her so.
Oh now I am agoing to find her
For my heart is full of woe
And we will sing the song togehter [sic]
We sung so long ago
We will play the banjo gaily
And will sing the song of yore
And the yellow rose of Texas
Shall be mine forevermore.
                Anonymous

*Original spelling

Preface

There were approximately one hundred fifty free Negroes living in the Mexican Province of Tejas during the time of the Battle for Independence in the mid-1830s. Most left little record of their time spent in the frontier, fading silently into the history of the society they helped build. But one of them, Emily D. West, did leave a sketchy trail of her existence, surrounded by a mysterious tale of two doomed lovers who ultimately inspired a folk song. Much more is known of Emily than her unknown lover, who created the ballad which inspired a legend. This tapestry of historical figures and fictional characters creates the legend of *Emily, The Yellow Rose.*

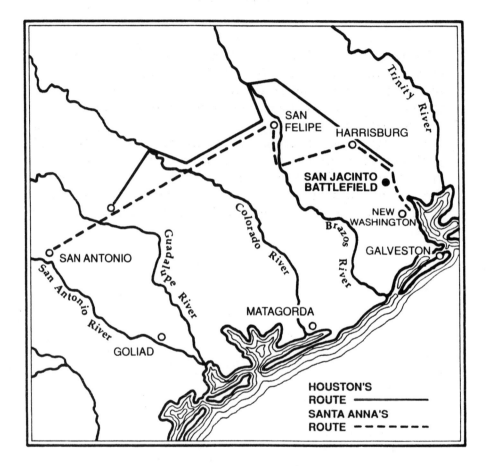

SAN
FELIPE

HARRISBURG

**SAN JACINTO
BATTLEFIELD**

NEW
WASHINGTON

GALVESTON

Trinity River

Colorado River

Brazos River

Guadalupe River

SAN ANTONIO

San Antonio River

GOLIAD

MATAGORDA

HOUSTON'S
ROUTE —————
SANTA ANNA'S
ROUTE – – – – –

Chapter One

When Emily stepped onto Texas soil, she felt immediately . . . she was home. The schooner, *Exert,* docked at Anahuac at high noon after carefully maneuvering sand bars in Galveston Bay. As the *Exert* stood anchored at the primitive harbor, Emily realized for the first time just how far from civilization she was.

So . . . this is Texas, the Mexican province on the verge of becoming an independent republic. "Texas," she murmured to herself, feeling her spirits lift with the sound of the word. Two months after leaving New York, she was here at last, in the wide frontier where, hopefully, a woman of color could live in dignity and freedom.

She shifted her single bag from one hand to the other, lifting it high to balance its weight against her hip. The scorching Texas sun seared her face, and humid, swampy air closed in around her as she looked at the crowded harbor. Seeing the other Negroes who had made the trip with her standing to one side, she instinctively understood the order of things and took her place with them. Not lifting her eyes at the group of settlers who had come to watch the ship's unloading, she tossed her bag to the ground. Grouped together tensely, the Negroes clutched their ragged bundles possessively. No one spoke. They only waited for someone to direct the last leg of their journey. Emily shook out her skirts, then stole a glance at Nathan.

No more than twelve years old, the young boy who had shared her cramped, dark berth during the voyage already looked like a man. The constant diet of cornmeal mush and fatty saltpork seemed to have sapped his strength and broken his spirit. Remembering Nathan's tortured cries from anguished dreams, she yearned to touch his arm, to comfort him in some way. But, instead, she pulled a gray bandana out of her pocket and tied it around her head. My God, she thought, would it always be so hot?

Holding her sleeve to her nose against foul body odors rising from the tattered congregation, Emily tried to minimize the stench. It was impossible. Perspiration soaked the back of her own cotton dress. Her dirty petticoats, two months unlaundered, stuck uncomfortably against her legs. At least the bandana kept sweat from running into her eyes and held her long, dark hair off her neck.

"Keep it moving! We ain't got all day to empty this ship," the loud voice of a soldier rose above the noise. "All you niggers heave to," he yelled, prodding the silent black men with the butt of his rifle. Under the burden of their heavy loads, the strong men kept their course, out of the hole, down the gangplank and across the dock to the waiting flatbed wagons. In an unending stream of moving cargo, the long-awaited contents of the *Exert* were delivered to the settlers of the Galveston Bay area.

Emily eyed the soldier cautiously as he strutted the length of the dock, the rakish tilt of his cowhide hat adding to his air of authority. The ever-present sun caught the smooth blade of his bayonet, reflecting its keenness toward her. She squinted against its brilliance, inwardly shuddering at the danger it represented, feeling sure that this man would use it if necessary.

Suddenly, he looked in her direction, narrowing his small eyes as he swung the rifle over his shoulder with confidence. Emily stiffened as he walked toward her and the group of Negroes on the dock. The sorting was about to begin. Soon, she would meet James Morgan, the man who paid her passage from New York and had bought her services as a house servant for the next four years.

"Clabe, all the Negroes going to New Washington in my wagon yet?" asked a tall man, dressed in a black broadcloth coat.

"No sir, Mr. Reese," answered the soldier. "I was just about to start gettin' them together. Some of 'em are goin' to Harrisburg, I think."

"Well, get on with it, then. I need to start to Morgan's place as soon as possible," Reese said, turning toward a stack of crates marked New Washington, Texas. He walked around, examining the cargo, while making notations in a leather bound book. His shiny black boots and starched white shirt told Emily he must be a merchant, a businessman, certainly not a farmer. Reese then sorted out a few of the smaller crates and took them into a log cabin set back from the dock. A handwritten sign on the door read, *Anahuac General Store.*

The soldier, Clabe, went down the line of Negroes, asking each one his destination. He spoke in harsh, rough tones, shoving them to one wagon or another. Emily's stomach knotted in fear as he approached Nathan.

"Where you headed, boy?"

"Harrisburg, sir," Nathan answered in a low voice.

"You got papers?"

"No, sir. I'm "dentured to Luke Clayton in Harrisburg, sir."

"Huh," Clabe snorted, "Luke Clayton's got a slick way of gettin' his slaves into Mexico. All right . . . over there, that wagon," he said, pressing Nathan's back with his rifle.

"Yes, sir," the young boy answered, giving Emily a parting glance before scurrying away from the dock.

Clabe turned to Emily, "You got papers?"

Quickly she reached into the deep pocket of her full skirt. The coolness of two silver coins met her fingers, then the roughness of a folded paper filled her hand. Taking it out, she extended her arm full length, offering the document to the soldier. He snatched it from her and read:

THE NEW WASHINGTON ASSOCIATION

The bearer of this letter, Emily D. West—a free, mulatto woman—has permission to pass into Texas on the schooner, *Exert*, to be given over to James Morgan for employment thereof.

> Given by
> Aquile Murat
> Vice-Council of
> U. S. of Mexico

"So, another of the colonel's free niggers?" He sneered as he spoke, poking Emily's full skirts with his bayonet. Circling slowly, Clabe examined her with lusty interest, running his eyes over her full breasts and narrow waist. Emily lowered her head, afraid to meet Clabe's mocking face, the kind of face which told her he could easily sell her into slavery for "disrespectful or unruly behavior," if she dared to provoke him.

"You carryin' any money? Any books? You know it's illegal for niggers to have them things."

"No, sir," Emily said, trembling where she stood. And as she shook her head in vigorous denial, the two silver coins in her pocket weighed heavily against her thigh.

"Maybe I should search you," Clabe taunted, raising his bayonet to her face. Emily braced herself as the vulgar soldier traced the edge of her bandana with the shiny tip of the weapon.

"Let's take a look," he laughed, his voice lowering to a gravelly taunt. In one swift movement, he ripped the gray cloth from her head, the keen blade slicing off a lock of Emily's long, dark hair, which clung magnetically to the smooth surface of the wicked knife. The rest of her hair fell in a silky mass over her shoulders, past her waist. The completeness of her beauty caught Clabe by surprise, stopping his harassment.

"*Dios Mío*," he whispered in a flat Texas accent. "Nothing like this ever got off a boat here before."

He had let loose the full mane of her hair, black as a raven, framing a golden, oval face. The disguised delicacy of her features now took full form: warm brown eyes radiated hidden glints of gold, high cheekbones blushed with a natural rouge, and her tiny mouth puckered like an unopened rose.

Emily finally raised her eyes, throwing back her head in anger. She hoped the hate in her eyes could convey the message of disgust she felt. This was the first time she had ever suffered public humiliation, and the control needed to hold back her words was making her sick. In New York, she had been generally overlooked, living silently within the prejudicial confines of the Northern system. She had always avoided any situation which might cause ridicule or attention.

Clabe pushed back his dirty hat, revealing equally dirty hair. "It's a good thing you've got papers," he said, untwirling her hair from his bayonet. "Otherwise you'd come home with me."

A wave of fear swept over Emily at the thought of this man's rough, calloused hands touching her body or his scraggy, whiskered face near her own.

"I think we'll be meeting again," Clabe went on, "I know where to find you."

Holding her breath, she watched him tuck her hair into his shirt pocket, the sound of her own pounding heart roared in her ears, blocking out his triumphant laugh.

"Here. Take your precious paper and get over there in that wagon," he said, throwing her document to the ground.

Biting her lips to keep control, Emily swiftly gathered her bandana and paper from the ground and fled to the waiting wagon.

Squeezed between huge sacks of rice and corn on the partially loaded wagon, Emily nervously twisted her hair into a bun at the nape of her neck. Tears of frustrated disappointment burned her eyes as she fought to keep them from spilling over. Trembling, drenched with perspiration, she wondered if she had made a mistake in coming to this wild, foreign place. She didn't understand these people, and it was so hot and damp she could hardly breathe.

Watching Clabe move the rest of the ragged immigrants from the tiny harbor, she pondered her situation. She saw little evidence of a settlement: no real streets, a few log houses, no carriages or shops. There was only a deeply rutted wagon path that led away from a large, open warehouse into a stand of oak trees about fifty feet away. Tall prairie grass covered the low, flat, land and on this September afternoon, not a blade of it was moving.

A far cry from what I had expected, Emily thought, remembering the picture painted for her by the Union Land Company man in New York. He had said that coming to Texas would be the answer to her dream for a new, free life. Her decision to come had been made when the man had said: "If you sign up to come to New Washington, the Mexican government will issue you a passport, certifying that you are free. This is more than the United States is willing to do."

A passport! Certification of freedom! Those two elusive documents denied her by the United States suddenly lay within reach. If she had to leave her own country to have those papers, she had been willing to do so. Emily had no real family, and the vision of a better life in Texas had given her the courage to sign up for the long voyage on the *Exert*.

Now, sitting in the sweltering sun, she fought the cloud of disappointment closing in on her so soon.

"You Emily West?" a voice from behind startled her.

"Yes," Emily answered jerking around to see the man who had been examining the cargo earlier.

"I'm John Reese, owner of the store here. I'll be driving this wagon out to the Morgan place." Without waiting for any response, he opened his ledger once more, flipped a few pages, then looked around.

"Supposed to be another Negra. A Diana Linnard. Know anything about her?"

"I boarded ship with her in New York, sir, but about two weeks out to sea she became very ill. The Captain took her out of her berth. I never saw her again for the rest of the crossing. I don't really know what happened to her, sir."

John Reese paid little attention to what Emily was saying, a frown of irritation creased his brow.

"Clabe! Clabe!" he yelled to the soldier. "Round up the rest of these darkies going to New Washington. Where's the two field hands picked up in New Orleans?"

"Right here, comin' now," Clabe shouted back, striding toward the wagon with two muscular men behind him. The heavy pine kegs on their broad, sweaty shoulders loomed high above their heads, and on Clabe's signal they stopped at the side of the wagon, waiting for further instructions.

"Says here on the list—Diana Linnard, female, Negra washer-woman, age thirty-nine. Did she get off the ship?" Reese asked Clabe, ignoring the waiting men.

"No. I got 'em all sorted out, on the right wagons. Didn't see nobody like that get off. Maybe she's still on board. Want me to go check?"

"No, I'll take care of this. Stay here and get this wagon ready to go," Reese said, turning impatiently on his heel.

As soon as the harried merchant had walked away, Clabe began giving orders.

"You," he said, prodding Emily with his rifle, "get up there in the front." He kept the butt of the weapon pressed firmly against her body, urging her forward. Its heavy weight forced her to move quickly.

"All right, now, load them kegs down there," he said to the field hands.

As the men started to roll the barrels into place, Emily scrambled faster to the front, managing to balance herself on top of a bulging bale of cotton. With her back to the three men, she positioned herself to view the *Exert*. With its sails secured and everyone off its decks, the sleek schooner looked naked, empty, but serene. She appreciated its beauty for the first time, but secretly hoped she would never again be confined to any vessel so long.

She kept her eyes on the narrow passageway which led up from the hole, anxious to know what had happened to her traveling companion. Suddenly, the Captain and Reese emerged, half dragging, half carrying a thin, lifeless body. Emily gasped and covered her mouth to keep from crying out at the sight of Diana's pitiful condition.

The woman's torn, filthy dress fell away from her shoulders, revealing taut, brown skin stretched over visible bones in her neck. The deathly, gaunt appearance of this woman bore no resemblance to the happy, jovial person who had started the voyage two months ago. As they came closer, Emily saw that Diana's eyes were glazed over in fever or fear and wide dark circles ringed her vacant stare.

"Y'all lift her up" the Captain ordered gruffly. "Lay her over there by that sack of flour."

Emily leaned over, touching Diana's forehead. It was hot and dry. The skin around her mouth was cracked and peeling, dried blood caked the corners.

"Do you have water?" Emily asked. "She's very hot."

"Nope, not here," Reese replied. "We'll be stopping for water soon enough. She can wait." He climbed into the driver's seat.

"Clabe, you gonna bring that other wagon out later?"

"Probably be tomorrow before I can get it loaded and out to Morgan's place."

"All right, I'll tell Morgan," Reese said, slapping the reins against the waiting oxen. The wagon started rolling, and as Emily jogged from side to side, she wrapped a comforting arm around Diana's frail shoulders.

"Everything's gonna be all right," she whispered into the sick woman's ear. "Don't you worry, you made it to Texas!"

Chapter Two

Tormenting mosquitos buzzed incessantly, biting and stinging with a vengeance Emily had never thought possible. The humming drone of the pesky insects filled the muggy air, rising above as the travelers headed westward out of Anahuac. Vast level lands stretched far into the distance, dotted intermittently with isolated trees which blended into sea-green hues with the verdurous hog-bed prairie. An azure sky, cloudless in its purity, pressed down over the earth, engulfing Emily and her companions in the boundless stretch of coastland.

Placing her shawl over Diana's exposed shoulders, Emily fanned wildly against the mosquitos' unrelenting attacks. Tucking her hands into the folds of her wide skirt, she huddled with Diana in the wagon. As the intruder into this swampy lowland, she resigned herself to its discomforts, letting the insects have their way with any unprotected flesh. Their torture continued until the group had forded the brackish, shallow Trinity River, gradually moving above the steep banks of Galveston Bay.

At least she was riding. Tom and Billy, the two field hands who had arrived with her, walked slowly behind the wagon, trudging ankle-deep in mud. Several times, when the wagon stuck in the soft, boggy trail, the two strong men put their shoulders to the cart and got it moving again. Emily looked into their expressionless faces, a wave of unspoken awareness passing between them, holding their attention for a second or two. Her thoughts went painfully back to the first time she saw them, chained together on an auction block in New Orleans, the last stop the *Exert* made before arriving in Texas.

The bustling Louisiana port had been fascinating to Emily; intriguing her so, she accepted the Captain's unusual permission to go ashore that morning. No one had paid much attention to her as she had moved curiously away from the crowded dock into the heart of the city. Absorbed in the sights and sounds of the French-speaking area, she stared openly at beautiful dark-eyed Creole women strolling leisurely over rough cobbled streets. The ruffled organdy dresses matched with delicate, tiny parasols were so exquisite and alluring, Emily could hardly take her eyes off them.

Winding along, past street vendors whose crates of freshly picked vegetables and tubs of bright red crawfish jammed together so tightly there was scarcely room to walk, Emily breathed deeply of an exotic mixture of scents mysteriously new to her. A tent-shaded table held fragile butter pastries, laced with rust colored raisins, offered to the passerbys with demitasse cups of thick chicory coffee or tiny cups of light wine. Firmly ripened melons of various colors and sizes lay sliced open for buyers to taste, and deep wooden tubs filled with oysters and shrimp were set back from the street for protection from the sun.

Emily felt sure this was Beauregard Square, the dense Negro section of New Orleans where traders and shopkeepers, vendors, and peddlers touted their goods to the throng of buyers passing through. Three kinky-headed little girls, their shirt tails flapping out behind them, skipped in a circle to the rhythm of a tune:

> "Milk in de dairy nine days old,
> Sing-song Kitty, cant you ki-me-o?
> Frogs and skeeters getting might bold
> Sing-song Kitty, cant you ki-me-o?"

Emily watched the youngsters, oblivious to the bartering of their elders as they lost themselves in play, their faces bright with the excitement of their own private world. Leaving the Quarter, Emily had rounded a corner next to a dark, brick building and followed a steeply sloped path down to the levee. At the foot of the gentle swell, in an open grassy area, stood a low wooden platform facing up the hill toward her. In an instant, Emily knew that she had come upon a slave auction in progress, and as her mouth went dry and her heart pounded fiercely, she looked around for a place to shield herself from view.

An old lean-to at the edge of the clearing provided a safe, protected station from which she could watch elegantly tailored bidders gather around the auction block. Southern gentlemen landholders spoke among themselves as they pulled off their kidskin gloves, waiting for the first slave to be offered. The human chattel, bound in irons, were all stripped naked to the waist; some of them were heavily greased with fat to disguise any marks or scars which might have lowered their value. Men, women, and children, their eyes staring vacantly over the heads of bidders, silently waited their turn to be cried off in auction.

"Now gentlemen," the red-faced auctioneer had started, "here's two hard workin' niggers . . . won't give you no trouble and never been under the lash. They're strong, black bucks who'll work like mules . . . how much am I offered for them?"

"One thousand," came an answer.

"Twelve hundred," countered another.

"Come, gentlemen," the auctioneer prodded, "each one of these bucks is worth that much. I'll not entertain any bid under two thousand dollars. Surely you can see the years of hard work you'll get in return for these two."

"Three thousand dollars," the Captain of the *Exert* offered.

"Three thousand dollars, three thousand dollars . . . who can top this bid?" goaded the loud-voiced auctioneer.

"Thirty-five hundred," a young, handsome gentleman put forth.

"Thirty-five . . . thirty-five . . . who will give me four?"

"Four thousand," Captain Ezell of the *Exert* threw out, eyeing his competition boldly.

"Four thousand dollars . . . four thousand dollars . . . going once, twice . . . sold to the Captain for four thousand dollars," the bidding was finished in a sing-song tone.

As Captain Ezell pulled out a wad of bills from his worn, leather pouch, the two solemn slaves were led from the risers and handed over to him. With this transaction over, the auctioneer had begun to cry off a middle-aged woman, whose talents at breeding were proudly proclaimed to the wealthy, potential buyers.

Rooted to the spot, unable to take her eyes off the spectacle unfolding before her, Emily leaned her head against the rough, splintered boards of the weathered structure. The usual proud jut of her fair-skinned jaw was lowered in deference to the degradation she witnessed.

Now, trekking over the Texas soil, these same two men in tow, Emily wondered seriously if their life out here would be much better than the one they'd left behind. So far, she had seen nothing to inspire her to believe that a fraction of the comforts of New Orleans existed in this crude, untamed settlement of the West.

The wagon groaned to an uneven halt, its front end leaning dangerously low. Emily grasped Diana in panic, unable to keep the sick woman's head from ramming against the wagonside.

"Damnit," John Reese cursed, climbing down to check the seriousness of the sink. Using a small branch snapped from a nearby shrub, he measured the hole's depth, then got back up in the driver's seat and urged the oxen forward. Nothing happened. The wheels were hopelessly mired down.

"Get out. We gotta lighten this load," Reese said. "Start taking off those barrels in front," he ordered Tom and Billy, the two slaves.

Emily shook Diana urgently, "We've got to get out. Can you hear me? We have to get down."

The weak woman opened her eyes and nodded in understanding.

"Hold on to me and try to sit up," Emily advised.

Diana struggled to raise up clutching at Emily as she managed to move forward, finally sitting up as Emily supported her back.

"Good," Emily said, "Now, I'm going to get down first, then I'll help you over. Try to hold the side of the wagon."

With a quick thrust of her strong, capable arms, Emily swung herself over the wagonside, down onto the muddy road. She then reached back into the wagon to help Diana over the rail. As the weight of her sick companion fell across Emily's chest, she lost her balance and both of them slid down into the soft, wet soil.

"Are you hurt?" Emily asked, rolling Diana onto her side.

"No, don't worry 'bout me," Diana whispered in a husky voice. "I'll make it." Pursing her lips, she grasped Emily's sleeve, and the two women crawled through the mud to the side of the trail.

Crouched on a vine-covered tangle of weeds and grass, Emily wiped mud from her arms and face while watching the men unload the cargo. Recent rains had left the ground so soft that it was oozing water all around, making it almost impossible to set the wagon free. The oxen strained once more against the weight of the heavy cart while all three men pushed from behind . . . nothing happened.

"All right," Reese yelled, "we need some logs to put under these wheels."

Taking his long-handled ax from beneath the wagon driver's seat, he strode intently toward the edge of the forest. After carefully examining several medium-sized trees, he quickly felled a sturdy live oak, which was soon reduced to four foot logs.

Emily estimated that they had traveled about five miles inland from the bay, she was thankful for the protective grove of oaks and pines where they had stopped. The mosquitos had completely disappeared, prevented from following their prey by tall, dense foliage. They were left to wait in anticipation for the next group of travelers to cross the open prairie. With the absence of sunlight in the secluded stand of trees, the forest's eerie dimness struck a cord of fear in Emily.

Since leaving Anahuac, the caravan had passed only two cabins. They were crudely built log structures, offering only shelter from the elements. The absence of civilization intensified the sense of isolation Emily was beginning to feel. No one had mentioned how long it would take to arrive in New Washington, but time was slipping past. The forest was growing darker, and it appeared to Emily that they might be forced to spend the night amidst the rank, humid underbrush.

"Having trouble with your wagon?" a man's voice floated through the still air behind her.

"What?" Emily said in surprise, reacting to the startling question by jerking her head around. She faced a broad-shouldered stranger whose striking bronze features captured her gaze with their angular lines. His honey-colored eyes locked with hers as he moved closer, speaking to Emily while emerging from the woods.

"You've got some problems with your wagon?" he asked again.

"Why, yes," Emily stammered, springing to her feet. "We've sunk in the mud, I'm afraid."

"Well, maybe I can give you a hand," he said, not taking his eyes from her face.

Emily didn't reply, but stepped slightly aside in a gesture to let him pass, shamelessly returning his curious stare.

"Joshua, hello," Reese yelled from the other side of the trail, signaling the stranger over. "You're just in time to help me get this wagon moving."

"Oh, it's you, John," Joshua called out in familiar recognition. "Looks like a pretty bad sink you got there."

"Yea, the road's in worse shape than I figured when I left Anahuac."

"Where're you headed?"

"New Washington."

"It's a bad time to travel, Reese," Joshua said, bending low to examine the sink. "The river's high and dangerous now, don't know if you can cross with that load."

"Well, we're gonna try. Come on, give me a hand with these logs."

Joshua swung his rifle down, leaning it against a tree by the edge of the woods. Straightening up, he glanced again in Emily's direction, undisguised interest filling his stare. When his taut, muscular frame turned from her, Emily saw that a small Bowie knife hung from a rope twisted around his firm, narrow waist. His slim, dark breeches tapered smoothly into worn, leather boots. As he bent to put a log under the wagon wheel, the wind caught the fullness of his billowing shirt sleeves and ruffled its coarseness against his bronze skin.

The logs finally in place, Reese slapped the waiting oxen on the buttocks, forcing them forward, successfully maneuvering the cart onto drier ground.

"O.K. Let's reload this wagon and get started," the wagon driver yelled.

"You're not gonna make the San Jacinto tonight," Joshua said, "You'd better make camp before dark."

"Guess you're right," Reese agreed as he and the field hands reloaded the wagon. "Where's the best place to put in?"

"About two miles south there's an abandoned Mexican camp, pretty well sheltered, where I think you could camp. I see you've got some women with you."

"Yeah, all goin' to Morgan's place. One of em's kinda sickly though . . . maybe you can take a look at her."

Emily caught her breath as Joshua walked over to her and Diana. He stopped directly in front of her and knelt down.

"I'm Joshua Kinney," he said to her.

"I'm Emily . . . this is Diana. You a doctor?"

"No, not really. I just know a little somethin' about medicine."

"Diana's real sick. I think she's been this way for a long time. We arrived yesterday on the *Exert.*"

"Let's see," Joshua said, placing a gentle hand on the woman's forehead, then, looking into her mouth and throat.

"She's dehydrated, that's for sure. Got any water?"

"The wagon driver says not."

Without another word, Joshua stood up, took out his own canteen, and knelt over Diana putting the round flask to her lips. After she had drunk sufficiently, he stripped off his handkerchief, wet it, and pressed it to her hot brow.

"She's probably got dysentery. It happens a lot to the settlers on the way out here. Would you like a drink?" he asked Emily.

"You sure it's all right?" she hesitated, anxious for the offer.

He smiled at her but didn't answer, and placed the canteen in her hand. Emily drank thirstily, watching Joshua over the tilted edge of the container. Finished, she handed it back to him, the accidental touch of his hand against hers sent shivers through her body.

"You goin' to work in the free colony at New Washington?"

"I'm to work for Colonel Morgan, in his home."

"Where'd you come from?"

"New York."

"New York? That's a far piece to travel, for a woman, I mean."

"Hum . . . maybe so." Emily was slow in her response, turning his statement over in her mind. "I'm hoping life will be better for me in Texas."

"Life in the colonies is not so easy, you'll see."

"It's not at all what I expected," Emily said. "Much more wild and unsettled than the agents in New York told me."

"You'll find New Washington better settled, probably fifty families out there by now."

"Is that where you live?" Emily was more than just curious about this handsome stranger.

"Me? No, not me. I move around a lot, always have. I have a little place on Redfish Bay, but I'm really not there very much."

"Where'd you come . . ."

"Let me put your friend in the wagon," Joshua cut off her question, lifting Diana from the ground. "I think Reese is ready to move on."

Surprised at how abruptly Joshua terminated their conversation, Emily observed him closely, noticing a slight frown on his forehead. She made no comment when he paused at the wagon, turning to say, "I'll stay with you 'til you cross the river," then he lowered Diana down into the wagon.

Settled once more in the heavy cart, Emily again used her bandana to wipe mud from her face and arms. She was exhausted, hot, and dirty. She wanted to hide from Joshua, shield herself from his unsettling stare. Why was her heart pounding so fast? Why did she suddenly want to know more about him? She asked herself these questions, realizing that at twenty-one, she had never felt this way before, never been so strongly affected by any man.

During the years when other girls had been flirting with boys at church socials, Emily had been carefully separated from her peers. By keeping their adopted daughter so close to them, her elderly parents had unknowingly instilled a fearful distrust of men. She had grown up proudly independent, but lonely, self-reliant enough to leave the only home she had ever known to search for a better one in Texas. With both parents now deceased, she felt no attachment to an oppressive Northern society which mocked her freedom. A society she had eagerly fled when the opportunity had come.

Now, pretending to protect her eyes from the glare of the sun, she put her hand over the top of her face. Under lowered lashes, she watched Joshua as he walked alongside the wagon, his leather hat hanging by a string around his neck, his dark wavy hair exposed to the final blush of the evening sun. She liked the way his hair curled so softly over his collar and wondered how it would feel in her fingers. As they slowly made their way westward, Emily secretly scrutinized every part of Joshua's tall, lean body.

The orange-red Texas sun, which had gradually lowered itself below the stark horizon, took the last light of dusk with it, leaving the travelers surrounded in darkness. They halted at a sharp curve in the trail which brought them out of the forest, standing in a circular clearing where others had camped before.

"This is it," Joshua said, up beside Reese. "We can build a fire over there in that pit, and if we post the wagon to the north, it should offer some protection."

"Suits me fine," Reese replied, circling the wagon on the edge of the campground.

Joshua immediately set about gathering wood to make a fire, while Reese unloaded the few provisions he had brought with them in the wagon. Tom and Billy wrapped dry pine needles and large brittle leaves around the ends of two sturdy poles, secured them with wiry vines, then set them afire in a crackling blaze of light. They staked them near the pit. Emily squinted against the brilliant light. In the velvety black solitude of their isolated position, the two golden fireballs shone like the piercing eyes of a prowling beast, crouched on the prairie, gazing at its prey.

John Reese, who had packed food for the journey, handed Emily a pouch of dried, dark meat which smelled pungent, a sack of parched ground corn, and a bucket of water. Saying no more, he went off to tend the oxen, leaving her to take up the task of putting together a meal. She sniffed the withered slab of meat, wondering what it might be, finally deciding she was better off not knowing, as there was nothing else to eat. Her tired, cramped stomach no longer knotted and rumbled in hunger, but settled into a silent acceptance of the long absence of food.

Emily peered into the darkness, unable to fix her eyes on Joshua, who had strayed far from the camp, completely out of view. He would be no help in deciding what to do with this meat. The two dark field hands squatted on rigid haunches, waiting, near the fire.

Common sense took over as Emily lifted a heavy iron kettle from the wagon, filled it halfway with water, and placed it in the fire. Then, she threw in the dried meat, piece by piece, moving it around with a knarled black stick. Soon the meat was turning over and over, rolling in a boil, sending the strong aroma of cooking flesh wafting through the camp. Next, she emptied the sack of ground corn into the rest of the water, and using her stick, stirred the mixture into a sticky, yellow paste. Scooping up handfuls of the tacky dough, she patted them into irregular balls and dropped them into the boiling pot, to simmer along with the meat. In a matter of minutes, Emily smiled to herself as she watched her first attempt at dumplings swiftly rise to the top of her frontier stew, bouncing around with stringy soft meat.

With the meal underway, Emily slipped soundlessly out of the circle of light toward the wagon where Diana still lay. The night air had taken on a damp coolness, and the tremor of a breeze stirred the prairie grass. Crossing the space from the fire to the wagon, she glanced upward at the pitch black sky. An incandescent crescent moon, bordered by twinkling, pin-point stars, hung glimmering in the heavens, a symbol of constancy which reassured Emily.

Joshua emerged suddenly from the darkness, approaching on her right, walking easily and steadily toward her. He held a bushy, gray mass in his arms.

"You can use this to make a pallet," he said, dropping the load in a heap beside the wagon.

"What is it?" Emily asked, picking up a long, soft strand of the delicate vegetation.

"Spanish moss," Joshua answered. "Haven't you seen it hanging from the trees?"

"I didn't know what it was," she said, fingering, smelling and tugging at the unusual growth. Its tentacle-like structure was dry, with no odor, and made a spongy ball when compressed.

"Smells like you've fixed something to eat," Joshua noticed.

"Only some meat and boiled cornbread," Emily muttered, both proud and unsure of her first attempt at frontier cooking. Looking toward the campfire, she saw that Reese, Tom, and Billy were hungrily eating the stew from wooden bowls, expressions of relief on their solemn faces as they ate.

Joshua handed Emily an armload of the moss, "Why don't you make your friend a place to sleep in the wagon and I'll get her something to eat." He walked away as she kept her eyes fixed on his back, wondering where this gentle, concerned man had come from.

Padding a narrow space in the wagon with moss, then covering it with her heavy woolen shawl, Emily worked on her hands and knees, preparing a bed for Diana. She could hardly concentrate on what she was doing. Her mind was on Joshua, caught up in fascination with a man she knew nothing about, fastened on a desire to bind him closely to her. She had met him less than four hours ago, they had spoken very few words, and now, obsessively locked in a search to understand him, her mind sorted through a myriad of thoughts. Perhaps he was already taken, married to a fine woman, with beautiful children. Perhaps he thought her naive and shallow, unworthy of his attentions. But worse than that, could it be possible, he didn't think of her at all?

Shortly after Joshua had brought the two women steaming bowls of stew, he said good night, returning to the campfire, to huddle there with the men. After settling Diana in her bed, Emily knelt inside the wagon, intently watching Joshua as he stood and walked to the fire, poking at the burning coals with a piece of wood, speaking seriously to Reese. They spoke of the easiest place to ford the San Jacinto River the next day. Emily noticed how Joshua carried his muscular frame with confidence and strength, moving with almost cat-like gestures, a calculated sureness behind each motion. His rugged naturalness excited Emily, compelling her to acknowledge that he was the reason her face flushed warmly and the innermost source of her womanhood quivered. Had he come into her life to fill it with turmoil, or to show her a way of reckoning with its havoc?

Overcome with exhaustion, Emily crawled stiffly onto the lumpy pallet and lay down next to Diana, clasping her hands behind her head, staring up at the multitude of gleaming stars. Tomorrow, she thought, after we cross the San Jacinto River, would Joshua really disappear from her life as abruptly as he had entered? Would he say goodbye in his cool, casual tone and vanish back into the forest? The answers would come soon enough, she decided, pulling a worn, Indian blanket over her shoulders, anxious for escape into sleep.

＊-＊-＊--＊-＊-＊

Even before they reached its banks, the unmistakable sound of moving water had alerted Emily that the band of travelers were very near the San Jacinto. They had broken camp at the first signs of sunrise, trekking westward for more than five hours, reaching their destination just as the torrid midday sun touched the land with its blazing rays.

Now, standing on the edge of the chocolate-colored river, calculating the distance to the opposite shore, Emily was frightened by the powerful force of the water as she watched it rush downstream, dragging tree limbs and debris past her with a roar. The swollen, twisting river swirled toward the Gulf of Mexico.

Reese took charge of the crossing, ordering the two slaves Tom and Billy to swim the oxen over as he floated the wagon with Diana in it across behind them. Emily looked on, terrified that she would have to swim that treacherous span, unsure of both her strength and ability to make it to the other side. She raised her terrified eyes at Joshua, who was standing at her elbow. He moved forward and touched her arm.

"Ready to cross?" he asked gently, stacking his rifle and his large leather bag under a nearby tree.

"I think so," Emily answered, gathering up her full skirt to step off shore.

"You swim ahead and I'll follow close behind," he offered, laying his hat and buckskin jacket on top of his other things. "Don't worry, this is really a shallow river; it's running a little high right now because of all the rain we've had. There's no danger in crossing."

Emily waded into the water cautiously, moving further and further into the current. Cold water caressed her ankles, inching slowly up her legs, claiming the hem of her skirt. Suddenly the sandy footing underneath gave way. Emily cried out as she felt herself being swept into a pocket of deep rushing water. It pulled her under, sucking her into its flow, devouring her with watery jaws, making her helpless in its grip.

Flailing her arms in desperation, Emily fought the threatening pressure and managed to push to the surface, but unable to stay afloat, she submerged again, doubling over in the fast-moving current. In a panic for air, she concentrated on rising once more, stroking firmly into the resistent water. Her arms ached and her mind was numb, but she finally came up for air.

"Don't panic!" she heard Joshua yelling over the roar of the water. "Keep swimming."

On the brink of giving out, she sensed she was standing still, making no progress out of the watery trap. Heaving deeply to fill her bursting lungs, Emily gagged violently as water rushed unexpectedly into her mouth and nose. Frightened at the thought of being carried far downstream, Emily willed herself to stroke harder, not breathing at all. When it seemed as if her lungs would rupture, a floating log smashed into her side, throwing her clear of the current's strong grip, plunging her into much calmer water.

Her feet made contact with the sandy river bottom, confirming she had reached a shallow area. In stunned relief, too frightened to cry, Emily stumbled from the river, falling painfully onto shore. Joshua rushed up the slippery bank, kneeling breathlessly at her side.

"Emily, are you all right?" he grasped her shoulder, sliding one arm behind her trembling body, pulling her closer to him.

Emily nodded, shaking as she gasped. Her long dark hair, laced with sand, clung in a matted tangle around her face and cheeks. Joshua lifted its raven-colored strands from her olive skin, resting his cool, wet hand under her pointed chin.

"I never should have let you try to cross alone," he said in a low voice filled with guilt. "If I'd known there was a whirlpool in the river, I'd have carried you across."

"I'm fine," Emily whispered, lowering her lids against his intense gaze. "You can't blame yourself."

Joshua's hand moved smoothly along Emily's satin jaw, down her neck, stopping on her shoulder. "You're too fragile to be in this wilderness . . . it's not a place for a woman like you."

Although drawn to Joshua by his tender concern, a surge of strength flowed through Emily at these words.

"I'm here to live, Joshua, there's no going back for me. I'll make my own way out here. Don't worry."

Slightly annoyed, more at herself for bungling the task of fording the river than with Joshua's well-meaning words, Emily struggled to sit up, determined to keep going.

"Let me help you," was all Joshua said before sweeping her easily into his arms, carrying her to the wagon.

Emily let her head fall naturally against his chest, savoring the sweet, musty smell of his damp, wool shirt. An urge to press her chilled, tired body next to this stranger's warm, throbbing heart, made Emily go shamelessly limp in his arms.

"You'd better rest," Joshua advised, placing her next to Diana in the wagon. "Take care of yourself and your friend, I have to be on my way." His words were final, but he made no move to leave.

"Thank you," Emily murmured, searching his face for an unspoken promise that she would see him again. "You've been very kind," was all she could think of to say.

Backing away from the wagon, Joshua rubbed his hands awkwardly on the sides of his tight breeches, and never breaking his gaze from Emily, called out loudly to Reese, "I'm moving on, John. Good luck for the rest of your trip."

"All right, Joshua," Reese threw out, "thanks for all your help."

The afternoon heat peaked in its fury, and steam rose visibly from the flat bottomland. Rattlesnakes slept coiled under bushes, and huge thick-skinned alligators reposed undisturbed. Emily noticed none of these dangers, as she stared trance-like over the land. As the wagon lumbered southward toward New Washington, all disappointing thoughts of Texas were pushed from her mind, as the firmly etched image of Joshua Kinney took hold.

Chapter Three

There were two square windows in the main living area of Celia Morgan's split log house. Stark, without curtains, pine shutters thrown open to the sun, their eastward position funneled morning light across bare wooden floors. A brass handled hutch, made of dark cherry wood, faced a pair of high backed chairs with woven rush seats. A small plush settee, overlain with a handsome set of white lace doilies, arched its gracefully curved back under a fading portrait of a uniformed man. With an arrogant gaze of righteousness, the stern-faced captain looked down from his place on the hand-hewn wall at the simply furnished quarters of James Morgan's home.

"These came all the way from Ireland," Celia Morgan said, running her blue-veined hand over the delicate webbed doily on the arm of her sofa. A faraway look came over her face as she fingered the raised pattern. "I got them as a wedding gift from Mrs. Mallory, the pastor's wife in my hometown church. I'll never forget how she used to talk and talk about her trip to her parents' home in Dublin. I often wonder how she's doing. I don't get many letters out here."

It was apparent to Emily that her new employer took a great deal of pride in her home, striving to make it as comfortable as the one she had left in North Carolina five years ago.

"And this chair," Celia went on, "was hand carved from cherry trees on the Morgan plantation at Durham County; most of the furniture in this house was made there."

"It's lovely," Emily said, touching the tufted velvet back of the richly carved rocker. "I've never seen anything like it . . . everything in your home is beautiful, Miss Celia. Did it all come from North Carolina?"

"Yes, I brought all my furniture from the old place out here when we left, and although James said it would be easier to get furnishings out of New Orleans, I wouldn't dream of leaving the family pieces behind . . . makes it seem more like home."

Letting the starched bit of lace fall from her translucent fingers, the slender, serious woman moved to rearrange a grouping of four brass candleholders sitting on an ornate sideboard. Pausing, she glanced into a gilded *trompe l'oeil* mirror centered evenly above it. Distorted by curved glass, her reflected image clearly showed a woman whose age could not easily be measured. Skin too delicate for the harsh Texas sun, had succumbed to its rays in a premature network of wrinkles and lines. Hair which had once glistened with tiny threads of gold, now fell in ashen wisps across a furrowed brow. Primitive frontier living had taken its toll on Celia Morgan, but her dauntless spirit and love for her family gave her the youthful courage to face each day.

Speaking more to herself than Emily, she whispered, "I miss the Carolinas a lot, but after so many years on Galveston Bay, I'm about to start calling myself a Texan." She moved through the wide, airy room into an open breezeway as she talked. "Let's go to the kitchen now, Emily."

Walking behind her mistress' straight and willowy frame, Emily noticed how her brown cotton skirt fell in wide gentle folds over her hips, emphasizing a leanness which indicated strength, not weakness. Celia was a woman of her own mind, Emily felt sure, a woman who ran her house with a firm but generous hand, expecting things to be done correctly, with little supervision.

Even before the sun had pushed up over the cypress trees along the bay, a gentle tapping on Emily's cabin door had awakened her this morning. A young black boy, barefoot and wide-eyed, had peaked through the crack in the door, straining on tip toes to see past Emily, as she stood in half sleep at the entry.

"You Miss Emily?" he had managed to say at last, still not looking directly in her face.

"Yes," Emily had replied slowly coming more fully awake.

"De Missus be wantin' you up ta de house."

"Now?"

"Yes'um. She say, 'Go tell dat new gal Emily to come up here so's I kin meet her'. Dat's what she say."

"I'll be right there," Emily said, almost closing the door on the boy's curious nose which had carefully been inching its way forward. She opened her big cloth bag, shaking out her only other dress; a thin blue wool trimmed with bands of gray cotton at the neck and wrists, wrinkled deeply from staying so long in her valise. She wished she had time to air it, but knowing the mistress of Orange Grove waited, she quickly splashed a handful of water over her face, smoothed back her hair which she twisted into a knot, and quietly slipped out of the cabin, leaving Diana sleeping soundly.

Her initial conversation with her new employer had centered around Emily's qualifications for the job as house servant.

"It is correct you finished a free school in New York, isn't it?"

"Yes ma'am," Emily had answered, "I understood that was one of the qualifications for the job."

"That's right. You'll be working mainly in the house, cooking, serving, helping with the children. I don't want field help working in the house."

Emily had said nothing, standing perfectly still as the mistress of Orange Grove looked her over, then gave her approval.

"I think you'll work out fine," was all she had said before starting to explain the necessary details of Emily's new position.

Now, crossing the open breezeway, Emily paused, looking out over a smooth expanse of emerald green grass surrounding the house. Giant twisted oaks defined the Morgan property, casting somber lacy shadows on the ground. Already warmed by an early morning sun, the wind, which swept over Emily's face and neck, carried the faint-sweet smell of jasmine.

Running a hand over her tightly knotted hair, she stepped down from the porch into the square, spacious kitchen on the opposite side of the house. Completely separated by the airy passageway, the dirt floor kitchen was the hub of the plantation.

A deep, smokey fireplace dominated the room, and heavy iron pots lined its unusual bricked hearth. An adjustable crane, equipped with a handle, suspended a steaming black kettle over coals, while a domed adobe oven, adjacent to the fire, stood ready for baking. An assortment of flat, long-handled spades hung nearby.

"Morning, Hanna," Celia called out to a young girl who looked to be no more than fourteen. Busy kneading dough at a narrow wooden table in the center of the kitchen, the girl flashed a bright smile at her mistress, then answered, "Mornin' Miss Celia. How you be dis mornin'?"

"Fine, Hanna, just fine." She stepped aside so Emily could face the busy cook. "Hanna, this is Emily, she came in last night from Anahuac. She'll be working in the house with you."

"Lawd knows us needs some help 'round here," Hanna said matter-of-factly, pumping the dough more vigorously. " 'Tween cooking for you, Massa Morgan, and de chillen, ain't no time left for all dem soldiers been comin' tru here." Hanna's mouth was set in a firm, straight line, puckering her smooth brown cheeks into dimples on each side. Her girlish face was framed by a kerchief tied over her ears at the back of her neck, in the fashion worn by her elders. Almond shaped eyes, wide set and darkly lashed, left no doubt that she was far from her prime. Patting and shaping as she listened to her mistress, Hanna's nimble fingers plied the mound of dough with expert movements.

"Not much we can do about that, Hanna, seems like there's going to be soldiers coming through Orange Grove for some time yet." Turning to Emily, she explained, "Many soldiers stop here in New Washington on their way to join Ben Milam and his men who are fighting the Mexicans around Goliad. The least we can do is give them a good meal and a decent place to sleep for a day or two. It's a long march to Goliad."

"How dangerous are the Mexicans?" Emily wanted to know.

"We haven't had any trouble around here, but further west, the soldiers are putting up a pretty good fight to keep the Mexicans out of the settlements," Celia Morgan said, a ring of pride in her voice.

"Many people live out there, further west from here?"

"Oh, yes, it's much more settled than New Washington. San Antonio's a busy place, lots of trade goes on."

Emily watched the expression on her mistress' face as she talked of the possibility of war. It was evident she hoped it wouldn't touch her life, but the imminent threat was with her at all times.

"Maybe we'll be lucky and be spared any part of the fighting if it comes," Celia finished, pressing her hands together, fingers laced, in a tense, prayerful gesture. "Now," she went on, "Hanna will show you where everything is, and I'll let you get started with your work."

After Celia Morgan had left the room, Hanna stopped her rhythmic kneading, wiped floured hands on her stiff white apron, and looked questioningly at Emily.

"Where you come from?"

"New York," answered Emily.

"Yeah? New York? My, my, dat's a long ways off."

Emily nodded in agreement. "Two months by boat, that's how long it took."

"You free or 'dentured?" Hanna asked, her eyes round with interest.

"Free . . . I was born free, lived all my life in New York."

"If you's free, why'd you come all de way to Texas? You can live free in de North." She leaned back, lifting her round chin high, propping dusty white hands at her waist. "Iffen I was you, I'da never left de North, all my life I been a wanting to head up north, but all I git is being brung down here to Texas."

"I guess I was looking for a better life than New York," Emily told the puzzled young girl, remembering all the worried days and sleepless nights she had spent while making her decision to leave.

"Life out here's hard," Hanna warned. "Iffen de mosquitos don't eat you 'live, de mud and de rains gonna suck you under. Last time de big rains fell, put knee-high water in my cabin. Took four days to git it down. Never had no mess like dat back in Carolina."

"Did you come out from North Carolina with the Morgans?"

Nodding as she resumed kneading absently, she said, "Sure did, long time ago. Back in Carolina I was a slave, but seen' as how dey don't 'llow slaves in Mexico, de Massa made us all 'dentured servants so's us could come out here. Guess it's better'n bein' a slave, but it still ain't de same as bein' free." She stopped and thought for a minute. "But de Massa promised me, iffen I's ever ta marry, my chillen gonna be free. Now dat's somethin', ain't it?"

"Sure is," Emily smiled at Hanna, whose own wide smile creased her chocolate face.

"I already got me a fella," Hanna confided, "Sam . . . he be workin' 'round here mosta de time, helpin' Miss Celia move furniture an' all. Seems like all dat woman do is move dat ol' furniture from one side o' de room to de other. Massa Morgan don't care nothin' 'bout dat ol' stuff she dragged all de way out here from Carolina. But it sure makes her happy, fiddlin' wid it all day. You'll see . . . you gonna be cleanin' an' polishin' it most every day."

"Your fella, Sam, is he free?"

"Sam? Naw, he's 'dentured like me and come next summer, after I turns fifteen, us planning to jump de broom. Den us gonna have our own cabin an' lotsa free chillen." A dreamy shadow of happiness played around Hanna's eyes as she spoke of the future she hoped for. "You got a fella?" she asked Emily.

Emily wished she could say, "Yes, I have a fella." Instead, she could only recall a tall, gentle-spoken man whose mysterious touch seems to hold the power to not only calm but excite her, a man whose presence had stayed with her like a cloak since she bade him goodbye on the shores of the San Jacinto River. Ashamed to admit she had never even kissed a man other than her father, Emily hedged the questions, mumbling, "Not really."

Hanna raked Emily with a suspicious glance, cocking her head quizzically to the side. "Now dat's hard to believe! Considerin' how you looks, and Lawd how you talks, I figgered you ta come out here wid a husband right behind."

"I came alone," Emily stated firmly, trying to keep hidden tremors of doubt which threatened to show in her voice.

"Dere's more men dan women in Texas. Won't take you long 'fore you find yourself a fella. But be careful, stay 'way from dose Islanders what lives on de Bay. Crazy as loons an' don't speak no English. Bolt your cabin door come night an' don't neber be walkin' 'round late."

"What do you mean Islanders? Where are they from?" Emily asked.

"Most people figger dey was dropped here from Barbados, a spell ago, been livin' down on de rice fields ever since. Don't nobody go near 'em, just like savages dey is. But every now and agin one of 'em come up here ta de house, beggin for water or somethin' . . . I just shoo 'em off like dogs," Hanna threw back her head in laughter, "an after I shake my broom a couple o' times, dey more 'fraid o' me dan I is o' dem."

Emily raised her eyebrows at Hanna's final words, the mere thought of savage Africans roaming about made her nervous, but under it all, she felt the young girl was more than likely exaggerating.

Hanna smoothed pale mounds of dough into deep square tins, then slipped them into the oven, expertly placing the metal containers over the heat from the coals.

"Here," she said to Emily, handing her a stiff white apron like her own, "put dis on, us got plenty bakin' ta do dis mornin'."

Emily worked alongside Hanna mixing, cutting, peeling and

tasting, and by late afternoon, a long wooden table was laden with baked sweet potatoes, peach pies, roasted pork and fried ham. Stoneware bowls, covered with white cotton cloths, sat waiting full of rice and corn.

With the bulk of the day's cooking behind her, Emily rested for a moment at the kitchen window, which faced southward from the house. A clear blue sky permitted the sun's baking rays to penetrate the sodden earth, making the quagmire of a wagon path running in back of the house a little more passable. Mud-caked mules and dirty carts moved along the path, driven by men whose workday included many trips up and down the trail.

The sugar cane harvest, nearing its end, drew every able worker into the fields to slice the remaining stalks with sharp keen machetes.

Fragments of a conversation, carried on in a familiar voice, drifted over to Emily from the western end of the house. Leaning out the window, she saw Captain Ezell speaking earnestly with James Morgan.

"Took on some damage comin' into the Bay," the Captain said in clipped, blunt tones. "I'll need at least a fortnight in port to ready the *Exert* for another trip up the coast." In the manner of a man not accustomed to being rushed, he tugged his pointed graying beard and waited for Morgan's response.

"I just received a letter from Samuel Swartout, you know, he's chairman of the New Washington Association. He's been able to secure more funds for the Texas Navy. Now we can get on with this fight with the Mexicans."

James Morgan, whom Emily had met on her arrival last night, looked much taller in daylight, and also less stern. A man of average height, whose thick brown hair stood stiffly around a bony face, his only striking feature was his direct and forceful way of speaking. He had a take charge attitude which immediately captured followers.

"The ranks of my crew have thinned greatly since setting sail this last trip," Captain Ezell said, "I lost two in New Orleans who abandoned ship there, and four more to bilious fevers during the voyage, but we'll do what we can to get the *Exert* ready to leave by the first of December."

"I've plenty of good workers here, and I can spare a few to go back with you to Anahuac," James Morgan offered. "We'll be needing all the arms, ammunition, and supplies you can bring back. This war is on the brink of breaking and our forces are far from matching the Mexicans."

The seriousness of this conversation frightened Emily. The reality of an impending conflict between the Texans and the Mexicans was suddenly very real and imminent. She had traveled more than two thousand miles to find herself at the center of this approaching revolution.

Shoving his hands deeply into his pockets, the portly Captain Ezell looked at the ground as he spoke, "The Mexicans outnumber us tremendously. You know, our only hope is to make each shot count."

"That's true, Ezell," James Morgan agreed, lips set in a firm straight line. "If Mexican forces move this way, I fear we'd lose and lose very badly. We're just not ready to defend the coast. We need more men, ships, and ammunition."

"What about Ben Milam, up in Bexar County? Heard he's got more than three hundred men under his command, all eager to get on with the fighting," Captain Ezell said.

Morgan laughed under his breath, surprised at Ezell's statement. "Three hundred men . . . that's a drop in the bucket in comparison to what Mexico will send this way. Why, the Mexican dictator, General Santa Anna himself, commands a troop of five thousand which he's vowed to lead into Texas any day."

"But," the Captain persisted, "Mexico's own civil war is using up those troops, and unless they can get some order to their own government, they'll be spread too thin to make a good stand against us."

"That's a point," Morgan conceded, "but we can't depend on that to lessen the fight. I want every able-bodied man in Texas to join in this fight. That's why I'm feeding and supplying as many as I can, to keep their spirits up."

"I want the *Exert* to sail no later than mid-December or she'll be of no use to us," was the last thing Emily heard as the men rounded a curve and left her sight.

✦·✦·✦··✦·✦·✦

Glowing like a red-hot coal under traces of thin white clouds, the setting sun cast a warm rosy hue over the land as Hanna and Emily left the big house after a long day's work in the kitchen. Emily's

shoulders ached from bending over big iron kettles of boiling water
and her hands were red and raw from washing dish after dish with
harsh lye soap. She had never felt this tired before, this kind of
work was new to her.

Living in a free state had afforded Emily the privilege of
attending free colored schools where she learned to read and write.
Her work as an assistant to the colored teachers in over-crowded,
under-staffed city schools did little to prepare her for work as a
house servant in the primitive Texas frontier.

Muscles cramped in the calves of her legs as Emily crossed the
grassy yard toward her cabin. She thought about the steaming
baths she used to take at the Colored Public Bath House in New
York City. She had hated going there with her mother, having to
undress with strangers all around while standing in line for her turn
in the large wooden tub. Her mother had turned a deaf ear on her
childish protestations and laughed out loud at Emily's spoken vow
that someday she would have her own private house with its own
private bath.

Now, with the prospect of soaking in warm water so far removed
from her current situation, Emily's long-standing dislike for the
bath house faded and she would have welcomed any opportunity
to bathe.

"Where's your cabin?" Hanna asked, shortening her long stride
to fall back with Emily.

"Over there, that one near the well," Emily pointed out.

"Oh, de new cabin. I was wonderin' who gonna git dat one.
Onliest cabin built high offen de ground, an' I seed inside de
window dat deys beds in dere. How you manage dat?"

"The beds?" Emily asked, referring to the crude wooden frames
strung tautly with ropes which held straw mattresses. "Don't you
have the same?"

"Naw, us jus sleeps on de floor, got me an ol' blanket I throws
over some straw, dat's all." Hanna didn't seem to be complaining
about her situation, only curious why Emily's cabin had two beds.

Hurrying along, Emily shook her head at Hanna's statement "I
don't know why," she finally said. She was anxious to see how
Diana was doing, having left her alone all day in the cabin. This
morning when she left, her friend had looked a little better, able to
get up and move around.

Approaching the cabin, Emily realized for the first time that it did appear new. It was constructed of freshly cut logs, set off from the other structures in the quarters, and built on stakes which kept the floor off the ground. Four walls and a roof, one window and a door, it gave her shelter and privacy, nothing more.

Emily mounted two planks for steps, pushed against the cabin's rough pine door, and entered the dim, stuffy room which was the extent of her home.

Besides the two beds, a square plank table with two straight-backed chairs were the only other furnishings in the room. A mud and stick fireplace, pushed up against the house dominated the wall directly opposite the door. One wall held pegs for hanging clothes and the other harbored a single window, its light cut off by a wide board covering.

As her eyes adjusted to the darkness, Emily made out Diana's still figure lying motionless on her bed. Going immediately to her side, followed closely by Hanna, Emily leaned over the sick woman and shook her gently.

"Diana. Diana. Can you hear me?"

Diana moved slightly, eyes fluttering open, then closing calmly again.

"Who's dat?" Hanna asked, peering over Emily's shoulder, curiosity and apprehension on her face.

"This is Diana, she came in last night with me. We came from New York on the same ship, but she's been sick for a long time. She's burning up, her forehead is so hot . . . feel her," Emily asked.

Hanna stepped cautiously over to put her hand on Diana's cheek.

"She be hot, all right. I seed people like dis before. Dey don't neber git better, jus' git sicker an' sicker 'til dey pass on."

Emily wet a rag in water and passed it over Diana's feverish brow as she talked. "We met a man named Joshua on the way out from Anahuac. He looked at her, gave her some water, but didn't say for sure what might be wrong."

Hanna stepped to the side and looked directly into Emily's face. "Joshua? Joshua Kinney? Where you seed him?"

"On the way here . . . our wagon was stuck, he helped us get out." Emily's chest tightened, and her hands shook, as she tried to speak calmly of Joshua. She couldn't help asking, "Do you know him?"

and bit her tongue trying not to show much interest in Hanna's reply.

"Know him? Lawd, gal, don't nobody know Joshua, I recollect his face and I's seed him come 'round here, but he don't say nothin' ta most folks. But, I 'spect iffen Joshua Kinney don't know what's ailin' dis woman, den nobody does, 'cause he's de nearest thing ta a doctor 'round here. Probly figgered wasn't nothin' he could do, you know? Best ta jus' let her alone."

Emily continued wiping Diana's face and neck. "How do you find Joshua? Do you think he'd come and look at her again?"

"Usually he be wanderin' from Anahuac ta Harrisburg, helpin' wid de sick folks, playin' his banjo."

"He plays a banjo?" Emily asked.

"Sings, too," Hanna replied, "reckon he's one o' de best singers in deese parts, folks come from all 'round when us sometimes has a meeting iffen day knows Joshua gonna be singin'."

"Do you know where he's from?" Emily was curious.

"Joshua was livin' on dis land when I come here wid de Morgans, an' far as I knows he ain't neber told a body where he come from. De story is dat he's a runaway, hidin' out in Texas from de bounty hunters. He ain't got no free papers an' he ain't got no massa, dat's what I hear 'bout him."

The cup of water Emily was holding to Diana's lips slipped, spilling water over the sick woman's chin. Joshua, a runaway slave? She stiffened at this thought. In the black space of a second, Joshua's image flashed before her, a flawed apparition she had mistakenly embraced. This cannot be true, she told herself, but I would like to hear it from him.

"Can you help me find him?" Emily wanted to know.

"I can put out de word, maybe in two, three days it catches up wid him," was all Hanna could offer.

"Please, do," Emily urged, sponging Diana's skin gently.

"I's gonna tell Sam right now, he know how ta git de word circulatin'," Hanna said, moving to the door.

"Thank you," Emily said to the young girl as she left the cabin and stepped into the deepening shadows of an approaching dusk.

Wearily, Emily pushed herself up from the floor, moving to sit on the edge of her bed. Hanna's words hung in her mind and she fought them in disbelief, not wanting to admit that the man who had caused shivers to run down her spine and who had captured her thoughts for the last two days, was a hunted man, a man on the run. As much as she yearned for his touch, craved for his presence, she feared entanglement with him. What future could there be for a free woman and a hunted runaway slave?

Chapter Four

The fitful sleep, which finally captured Emily's whirling thoughts, was punctuated with nightmare scenes of being chased by brutal, howling dogs. It seemed as if her legs were banded in irons. She couldn't move, and as the landscape changed from prairie grass to shadowy swamp-cypress trees, a frightened Emily scrambled faster toward salvation from the vicious hounds.

Hazy dawn light filtering through a paneless window caught Emily wide awake, lying rigidly on her lumpy bed. She stared at the rough wooden beams stretched above her. She knew exactly where she was and how she came to be there, but still a voice within her questioned: What is this place and why am I here? An urge to push this unfamiliar feeling from her mind, coupled with a fear of the future, heightened her state of distress. Coming from their own mournful source, tears of loneliness gathered at the corners of her eyes, draining wetly down smooth satin cheeks to disappear under the collar of her gown.

The sense of isolation she had lived with all her life, now took the form of a yawning cave, ready to pull her in. This longing sensation made her arms ache in such a yearning that she wrapped them tightly across her chest, tucking cold hands beneath her shoulders. Emily forced final tears from her eyes, and inhaled deeply to clear her mind to get up and start the day.

A gentle tapping at her door surprised Emily, but thinking it was Hanna, she sat up under her Indian blanket and called out, "Who's there?"

"It's Joshua. Joshua Kinney," a voice she had memorized answered.

Wrapping the blanket Indian style around her shoulders to cover her muslin gown, Emily padded quickly over the rough floor to the door. Opening it slightly, she saw the unmistakable silhouette of Joshua Kinney framed in gray misty light.

"You came," she said, both surprised and puzzled, happiness openly showing in her eyes. "How did you get word to come so soon?"

Now it was Joshua's turn to give a puzzled stare. "I got no word," he answered, "I came on my own. I've brought some medicine for your friend, she's really very ill."

With a smile of relief, Emily opened the door wider to let him enter.

She lowered her gaze, fixing it on his boots as he brushed her gown in passing. A thick coating of mud clung to his dark and soaking wet boots. They were soft and fringed, and the soft tops hugged his breeches tightly.

Joshua talked in lowered tones as he placed his worn leather bag on the floor.

"When I met you in the forest, I had no medicine with me, but since then, I've been able to get a powder I think might help your friend. I'll need some fresh water. Do you have any?"

"I can get some," Emily said, grabbing her dress from the foot of her bed, pulling it hurriedly over her head.

Pausing at the cabin door to pick up a pail of dirty water, Emily watched Joshua as he knelt at Diana's side, tenderly lifting her head to see more clearly into her eyes. He spoke to her.

"I've brought something for you. It will make you feel better. I'll stay with you until you do," he promised as Diana nodded her head weakly in understanding. He glanced in Emily's direction, catching her watching him. The space between them thinned, narrowed by a magnetic force Emily knew would draw them closer, pushing aside any differences they had brought to this rare meeting.

"I'll need a cup and some clean rags, too," Joshua finally broke the silence, still not breaking his gaze.

Without a word, Emily grabbed the pail, sloshed the dirty water out the door, and started swiftly toward the well.

Unable to see more than a foot ahead, Emily moved cautiously through the dense fog rising mistily from the damp ground. She wanted to break into a run, reach the well as soon as she could to get Joshua whatever he needed to make Diana better. He had come on his own. He was a good man, a gentle man, Emily told herself.

Despite any danger to himself, he had been willing to come to Orange Grove to help save Diana. She pressed her hands against her stomach to still the selfish emotions that flooded her. The memory of Joshua's embrace created a yearning for him which diverted her thoughts from Diana's grave condition.

The moss-covered side of the well was slippery green and cool against Emily's arms as she leaned over. Attaching her bucket to the iron hook, she smoothly lowered it down. It hit the water with a dull thud. Using both hands to turn the crank, she stiffly raised the full pail to the rim of the well, splashing herself as she unhitched it. Straining with its weight, Emily swung the pail to the ground. Drying her hands on the hem of her blue woolen dress, she hefted the water up and started back.

Blurry golden patches of sunlight broke through the fog, illuminating the unfamiliar path for Emily, who hurried along balancing the water, anxious to get to the cabin. A rooster's morning reveille wafted across the barnyard, signaling the start of another day to all parts of the sleeping plantation. Hanna was probably getting up, Emily thought, helping the younger children dress before starting out for the big house. Realizing that there wasn't much time before she, too, had to be in the kitchen, Emily took wider steps to quicken her return to Joshua as he waited in the cabin.

"I wish I could stay here with you, but I've got to go up to the house," Emily said, stepping through the door.

"Don't worry," Joshua replied, "there's nothing you can do here. I'll be giving her this powder through most of the day. We'll just have to wait to see if the fever breaks."

With a bent-handled spoon, he deftly measured a level dose of snow white powder into a tin cup of water, mixed it slowly with an even stir, and offered it to Diana. Half conscious, she drank thirstily, spilling much of the liquid down her chin. Giving up in weakness, her head fell heavily on Joshua's arm. He lowered her onto the bed.

Emily touched Joshua's shoulder, lines of worry tightening the skin around her mouth, an anxious gaze flickering in her eyes, and she said, "Thank you for coming, Joshua."

He didn't reply, only returned her look with one of unspoken understanding and gently clasped her hand, squeezing it firmly as he told her, "Go tend to your work, don't worry, I'll be here when you return."

Joshua's gaze remained fixed upon the closing door as Emily stepped through it into the damp morning air. For him, being with Emily brought back feelings that he thought would never return. The warm softness of her hand made an impression that touched him deeply.

Joshua became overwhelmed with recollections of another woman whom he had befriended many years ago. Joshua's attempt to suppress the unhappy memories of Lucinda's senseless and tragic death spoiled the hopeful mood that was created by seeing Emily again. He had met Lucinda many years ago as he, too, had traveled to Texas. He, on the run, and she, a slave for settlers on the same ship bound for Texas.

✦✦✦✦✦

Now, fog was gone and a breeze from the bay drifted through the plantation carrying the sweet smell of cane. The sun was steadily rising, promising to deliver another hot day. Cane choppers swung their heavy machetes in a dull thudding rhythm, hacking tall stalks to the ground, and Emily stepped across the muddy wagon path, making her way to the big house. Her mind was not at all on the day's work ahead, but filled with worry about Diana.

Her booted foot sank deeply into soft spongy grass which bordered the path on the side of the house. As she turned the corner, about to enter the kitchen door, the sound of mules braying and the noisy clanking of a heavy wagon made her stop to see who had arrived.

She froze in her tracks at the sight of a soldier sitting in the driver's seat. It was Clabe, the soldier from the dock.

Ducking behind a stand of oleanders near the kitchen doorway, Emily waited until he had climbed down. With his back to her, she quickly slipped up the steps, unnoticed, and entered the airy kitchen.

"Mornin' Emily," Hanna called out, turning from a fire, blazing, completely out of control in the hearth.

"Morning Hanna," Emily answered distractedly.

"How'd you pass de night? Sure was hot, wasn't it?" Hanna asked.

"Yes, it was," Emily agreed, "and I didn't sleep very well."

"Don't know how a soul on de place slept las' night wid all dem dogs a howlin' and carryin' on. Must be somebodys died or fixin' ta, dat's sure."

Emily pulled the cotton strings on her apron tautly, staring at Hanna in surprise. "What do you mean?"

"Oh, Lawd, Miss Emily, I didn't mean nothin', I's sure your friend gonna be fine real soon." Nervous regret kept her talking. "Ol' tales like dat git talked 'round de quarters, you know . . . dey don't mean nothin' at all. I's shuttin' my mouth for de rest o' de day."

Emily walked over to the fireplace, adjusting her apron in front. "That's fine, Hanna . . . but what about the dogs. Were there really dogs howling last night?"

"Either dogs or wolfs, dey both sound 'like to me," Hanna verified.

"I thought I was dreaming," Emily said, almost to herself, "the howling woke me up, but I thought I was dreaming."

"Naw, dey was for real, all right, dey wasn't no dream."

"I woke up," Emily started, "and soon after, Joshua came. I don't remember hearing them after Joshua arrived."

"Joshua Kinney's done come ta Orange Grove?" Hanna's voice was full of disbelief.

"Yes, he arrived on his own with medicine for Diana, he's with her right now," Emily explained.

"Now dat's somethin'! He don't usually come lessen he been sent for. Musta been powerful urged ta come out dis way, musta walked all night."

Emily set a basket of potatoes on the table, her mind on Clabe's arrival at Orange Grove, not Joshua's. Hanna went on.

"Well, jus' you count you blessings, if Joshua's here all you kin do is trust in him . . . and de Lawd, of course . . . and wait."

Slicing curved brown peelings in paper thin rings, Emily pared a potato in the palm of her hand. Hoping against another confrontation with Clabe, Emily fought to keep from looking out the window to see where he had gone. The last words he had spoken stuck in her mind: "Don't worry, I know where to find you."

"Hanna, where's Sam?" Celia Morgan rushed into the kitchen, a sheaf of papers in her hand. "There's a wagon full of supplies here from Anahuac and I need him to help unload."

"He be down at de stables wid Massa Morgan, tryin' ta board up dat stall Ol' Tucker kicked out yesterday. Seem ta me y'all outta git rida dat mule, he too mean and don't neber do nothin' but cause work for Sam."

Celia laughed. "Mules are scarce right now, Hanna. We need Old Tucker." She walked over to the window and looked down the path. "I'll go get Sam. Emily, when Clabe comes in, show him where to put everything." Before Emily could say a word, Celia Morgan was off to the stables.

"You know where the supplies go?" Emily asked Hanna.

"Sure," Hanna answered, "but Clabe more'n likely knows where ta put 'em. You jus needs ta unlock de door. De key's over dere hangin' next ta de door. Be sure an' lock it up after he done finished, Miss Celia's real particular 'bout keepin' dat door locked."

A familiar voice boomed across the room, "Don't know why Morgan trusts you free darkies so damn much."

Horrible memories of her arrival in Anahuac surged through Emily as she looked once more into Clabe's sneering face.

"Well, well, look who's here," he said, squinting narrowly at Emily. "You gonna be kind enough to unlock the door, Missy?"

Fumbling on tip-toes to reach the large iron key, Emily bit her lip so hard she felt the skin break, and after securing the key she nervously unlocked the storage room door. In the span of a moment, Clabe crossed the kitchen floor. Emily felt his hot breath on the back of her neck. Without turning, she pushed the wide door open, then stood to one side to let him pass. He didn't move.

"This is a sack of dried corn. Now just where you want me to put it?" the soldier asked mockingly, first leveling his eyes with Emily's, then, staring directly at her full bosom. Trembling, Emily stepped deeper into the dark area, its musty odor closing in around her.

"I think this shelf will be all right," she said, pointing to the closest one.

"Naw, I don't think so. Seems to me Miss Celia likes her corn stored further back." He still didn't move.

Glancing back at Hanna, who stood with her back to the storage room poking at the fire, Emily smoothed her apron nervously and stepped deeper into the dim space. Her eyes searched the shelves.

"Over there," she tried again, "this looks all right."

"Anything you say, Missy," Clabe replied, sauntering past her, kicking the heavy door shut with the thrust of his boot. It slammed Emily into total darkness with a dreaded, dull thud.

The sack of corn hit the floor. Emily turned around in fright. As she moved toward the door, she ran directly into Clabe's snaring arms. They closed vice-like around her waist, painfully squeezing her breath away. Clabe smeared his lips over hers, parting them with his foul tasting tongue. Bristling whiskers raked Emily's skin, leaving burning pinpoints all over her face. Unable to scream, she dug her fingernails into his side, pushing against his thick, course frame, fighting as his calloused hands went under her skirts, tugging and tearing at her thin muslin slip. When Emily sensed his rough fingers along her thighs, she raised a knee, trying to wedge it between them, but this was useless and only angered him more. He pressed more firmly to her. As his hand slipped under her panties, making its way over her buttocks to the soft, sensual mound of her virginity, Emily suddenly bit deeply into Clabe's upper lip and pulled her face away.

"Hanna! Help me!" she screamed. "Please, open the door!"

"Shut up, nigger," Clabe hissed hoarsely, slapping her face with his free hand. "It's time you learned how things is done down here."

He rammed her with the full weight of his body until she lost her balance and fell crashing to the floor, hitting her head on the corner of a rough wooden shelf. Skin tore away from her cheekbone, leaving an open jagged wound. Emily tasted blood in her mouth as she struggled under Clabe's pressing body. Twisting her fingers into his tangled, dirty hair, Emily yanked his head backwards as hard as she could.

"Goddamn you bitch," Clabe yelled, hitting her across the wound on her jaw.

The pain of his slap shot through her head like white-hot fire, blinding her to any more pain, forcing her to surrender unwillingly to the soldier's brutal force. From faraway, the sound of tearing fabric and panting breath floated to Emily on black waves of horror, and she steeled herself for his assault. When Emily felt the hot firmness of Clabe's now-erect manhood between her legs, she dug her heels into the hard dirt floor, propelling herself upward, screaming as she slipped out of his reach.

"Hanna! Hanna! Please, open the door."

The door burst open, light filled the room, and Emily saw that Celia Morgan, not Hanna, had interrupted the vicious attack.

"What's going on here?" she snapped, unable to believe the sight before her eyes. "Clabe, what's going on?" she repeated, her tone rising in anger.

"Just remembering this nigger who's boss 'round here," Clabe laughed as he hitched up his pants.

Celia Morgan's eyes glowed with rage. "Well, it's certainly not you," she threw out. "You leave my help alone, you hear?"

"Anything you say, Ma'am," Clabe said mockingly as he pushed past Celia.

Celia yelled after him, "After you finish unloading the wagon, you get off my place, and I don't want you around here again." Her words fell on empty space as Clabe strode unruffled to his wagon.

"Emily, your face," Celia said as she watched blood running down Emily's jaw. "Come out here, I'll get some ointment."

The side of Emily's face began to swell; burning and painful, it doubled in size. Clabe's vengeful look was seared into her memory, along with its promise to finish his aborted attack.

Emily knew he wouldn't give up easily. How many more times could she successfully escape his traps? In this wild open territory, men wielded their power over land and women, animals and slaves, taming any natural resistance with a controlling hand.

Later, Emily sat while Celia Morgan wiped the wound with a stinging ointment. The flaming pain of the cleansing swab temporarily wiped out her anger. She looked over Celia's shoulder at Hanna who stood shaking her head from side to side, a plea of understanding pouring from her eyes, a plea which Emily quickly recognized as one which had often passed over her mother's face in a doleful reminder that silent endurance was, and forever would be, the key to a Negro's survival.

+-+-+-+-+-+-+

Agitated and uneasy, Emily didn't lift her face skyward to watch a huge covey of squawking geese, noisily flapping southward in the fading light of day. Wings spreading dark shadows over the plantation, the soaring birds merged and separated several times before settling into an arrow straight column headed directly for the coast. She touched the burning line of her wound from the edge of her right eye to the center of her swollen cheek. Tears pressed the backs of her eyes, threatening to rush forth in a burst of fear, not pain. The wound was only a surface cut, quick to heal, perhaps without a scar. Fear of Clabe affected Emily deeply, leaving her with a sense of foreboding.

Joshua, sitting on her cabin stoop startled Emily at first, for she had completely forgotten about him and Diana in the midst of her preoccupation with Clabe's eventual revenge. From the expression on Joshua's somber face, Emily could tell that he, too, was lost in the private world of his own troubling thoughts.

Nearing the cabin, apprehension seized Emily as Joshua's face became clearer. He definitely had a worried, tense appearance which she hadn't seen this morning. At the sound of her steps, he turned in surprise, breaking his gaze from the geese overhead, leveling it easily on Emily's approaching form.

She stood directly in front of him, waiting for news of Diana.

"What happened to your face?" were his first words to her.

Running her finger once more along the swollen area of her jaw, Emily replied, "Nothing serious, an accident in the kitchen, that's all."

"What kind of accident? What happened?" he insisted.

Emily hedged, "I fell against a shelf in the storage room . . . it doesn't hurt . . . Miss Celia put some ointment on it." She couldn't tell Joshua about Clabe's brutal assault and take the chance that he'd seek revenge on her behalf. It would be a dangerous thing to consider, for if Hanna's story about Joshua were true, he couldn't risk attacking any man.

In a smooth, swift movement, Joshua rose to his feet, towering closely over Emily, the sweetly acrid smell of his suede and leather clothing filled Emily's nostrils.

"Let me see," he said, taking her face in his hands, examining the reddened flesh intently.

Emily raised her eyes to meet his, only inches from her own, and the familiar clarity of their golden brown hue had the same unsettling effect on her now as when she had met him two days ago. His gentle, patient manner cloaked her in a protective way symbolizing for Emily all that was trusted and safe.

Joshua kissed the smooth curve of Emily's jaw, brushing his lips lightly over her skin with a touch she barely felt. Leaning away, he said to her, "It's not very deep, it shouldn't leave a scar, . . . at least I hope not. A face as lovely as yours should not be marked."

He let her go.

Stepping aside, Emily turned to enter the cabin. Abruptly, Joshua grasped her arm, and with a puzzled stare, she raised her chin, nostrils flaring slightly in question.

"Don't go in," he warned.

Emily waited for him to continue. Her throat closed.

"Diana died . . . about an hour ago. I'm sorry, I did all I could," he faltered, voice cracking.

Without moving even her eyes, Emily stayed rooted, with Joshua's powerful hand clenched on her arm for several seconds, not wanting to believe his words.

"That's so unfair," she hoarsely whispered, "that's so unfair. She went through too much to get here . . . to have it end this way." Tears which Emily had fought to control too long now spilled out freely, shedding her disappointment in Texas, her fear of Clabe, and her misery at Diana's death together in one stream.

"A chance at a new life," Emily said through her tears, "that's all she ever talked about, and now she's gone."

Joshua clasped the back of Emily's neck drawing her head to rest on his shoulder, her dark hair fell loosely through his fingers, across his arm. "I know what you feel," he comforted, "I know. But just before she died, she gripped my hand with all the strength she had left and asked, 'Am I really in Texas?', and when I assured her she was, she laid back and closed her eyes, a smile on her lips. I'm sure she found some satisfaction knowing she was here."

Listening to Joshua's words murmured so softly, with such understanding, she knew what he said was probably true, but it did little to lessen her pain.

"I'll need to tell Morgan that she's dead," Joshua said, stroking Emily's head. "He'll have to make a coffin."

"Where will they bury her?" Emily asked, tilting her face to his.

"Most likely behind the quarters, over there," he pointed with his free hand.

Emily raised her head from his shoulder, looking in the direction he had indicated. A deeply shadowed grassy area, surrounded by huge china trees, lay south of the cluster of mud- daubed cabins which served as houses for the black laborers of New Washington.

Twenty crude structures lined the plain leading down to the bay, arranged in a semi-circle, their backs to the incoming winds. Among the cabins she saw the people of the quarters gathered in the early evening twilight, spending time together. Glad to rest after a long day's work in the cane fields, they passed their time in pleasantries, smoking pipes and whittling, trading gossip and laughing.

"I'd like to have a last look at her," Emily said to Joshua.

"All right," Joshua agreed, "go on in, I'm going to find Morgan and arrange for a coffin."

After a long quiet look at Diana, Emily pulled the cover over the woman's now serene face, then sank wearily onto her own bed. Thank God Joshua had been with her at the end, she thought. Hopefully, Joshua's gentle manner had been a comfort to Diana. Emily was grateful to him for arranging the details to put her friend to rest.

Through the small square window set high on the wall, Emily saw that the sun had sunk almost completely out of view, its fiery orange glow receding quickly into the horizon. A late autumn breeze blew through the cabin gently erasing the heat of the long afternoon, and as the room grew darker, Emily began to wonder if she would have to spend the night with Diana's body in the cabin.

Lying stretched on her bed in numb exhaustion, her cheek throbbing once more in pain, Emily had just closed her eyes when the darkness was suddenly penetrated by a smokey yellow fire at the entry. Emily sat up, looking curiously at a shriveled black woman standing there holding the torch in one hand and a wad of white cloth in the other. Her head was carefully bound in a deep red bandana, and her plain black dress hung loosely on her frame.

"Is dis where de dead woman be?"

Emily squinted into the yellow light, then swung her feet to the floor.

"Yes," she told the skeletal-like visitor, "the dead woman is in here."

"I's Wilena," the woman said, staking her torch at the cabin doorway, "I's come ta wrap de body."

In the flickering firelight of the cabin, it was difficult to see Wilena's face, but Emily did notice that slack and wrinkled jowls held a puckered toothless mouth.

Emily went to the fireplace, poked up the coals, and threw on another log for more light. Wilena shuffled to the bedside of the dead woman, knelt down in the semi-darkness and began her ancient ritual.

Lifting off the woolen blanket, she stripped Diana's body naked, then pulled a coarse sack-like shift over the corpse's head, ending this preparation by binding Diana's arms at her side with strong lengths of grapevine. Next, shaking out a long piece of white rough cotton, Wilena started at the head and began wrapping it around the body. Emily watched as the woman's black, stick-like fingers pulled and tugged at the winding sheets, making sure each turn was snug and tight. As Wilena lifted and wrapped, lifted and wrapped, she never raised her eyes from the body, but grunted in crude satisfaction at the completion of each turn until finally winding the sheets to a final tuck around Diana's feet. She sighed proudly, her task finished, the body encased, then pushed herself on thin bony arms up from the floor to her feet.

"Dey gonna be right along now wid de coolin' board. Den dey takes de body down ta de shed ta wait for de buryin' in de mornin'. In dis heat, dey don't be waitin' long ta put 'em in de ground."

Emily stood by silently, not sure what to say. She had never witnessed anything like this before, but nodded in understanding that the body was to be removed tonight.

"Dis is de first time I seed you," Wilena said, moving closer to Emily to have a better look. "Where you be from?"

"I came from New York . . . yesterday . . . we, the dead woman and I, came together."

"Don't talk like no slave, chile," the wise, old woman observed.

"I'm free," Emily explained, almost apologetically, "I went to school in the city."

"Um-hum," Wilena mused, shaking her head up and down as she gathered her things.

"A white woman used to come to the school," Emily went on, "teaching the students how to speak. She was a good woman, but many people hated her for the work she did in our school."

"I reckon dat's de truf." Wilena walked toward the door. "Well, maybe dis life out here gonna treat you better dan de rest o' us, it's sure been hard startin' up in Texas. Done wrapped six o' us'n dis month . . . dropped dead from de fever an' de runs, it gits 'em for sure . . . jus like it got dis lady here." The body wrapper moved to look down at Diana, her creased face fell slack and somber.

"She's gone ta Glory, yes sir, gone ta Glory where de Lawd's gonna give her de peace she been awaitin' for."

Chapter Five

Welcome Gulf winds, which had tempered the heat of summer, suddenly blew cool and rainy, preceding the long awaited change of seasons. Pine needles began to carpet the dense forest while a sprinkling of yellow-brown leaves gently fell in various parts of New Washington. Without drastic changes in its subtropical foliage, the tiny colony on Galveston Bay slipped quietly into Autumn. As the days grew shorter and nights much longer, Emily soon discovered that her day wasn't finished when the sun went down.

On a damp, blustery evening in October, Emily hurried out the back door of the big house, wrapping her woolen shawl tightly around her shoulders. Three bleached-muslin petticoats, worn one on top of the other, did little to prevent the damp winds of Autumn from penetrating her heaviest cotton dress. As the wind whipped towering oleanders almost to the ground, she quickened her pace, trying to get home before the rapidly moving rain clouds opened up.

Rumbles of thunder echoed across the planation as Emily reached her cabin doorway. Pausing on the steps, looking up into the ominous sky, a silent chill of fear ran through her body, a sensation of dread about the approaching storm. In the wide, flat, Texas lowlands, everything seemed so near, so real, so . . . touchable. Surely, if she stretched her hand high above her head, Emily felt she could touch the heavy, dark clouds hanging over the land. There seemed to be little between her and the nearing thunderstorm.

Lifting the rusty, iron latch of her door, Emily let go a sigh of relief as she entered the dark, stuffy cabin. The smell of smoldering wood greeted her, a reminder that she had been wise enough to bank the coals this morning. Although no heat emanated from the dark fireplace, she knew it wouldn't take long to get a fire going. Throwing her shawl on the rough, plank table in the center of the room, she took up the poker and shoved the coals around until a spark appeared. Picking up a long piece of straw, she lit it in the coals and ignited an oil lamp hanging above the fireplace. Tossing a small log onto the struggling fire, Emily then removed the rough board covering the cabin's single window. She stood there looking out, putting aside the need to tend further to the fire.

She was lonely. Since Diana's death, she had remained in the cabin alone. She missed her friend, the only person who had fully understood what her move to Texas had meant. Most of the people in the colony had been slaves before coming West, laboring for their masters under the cruel system which had kept them locked in ignorance. Now, in this free colony, they lived their lives much as they had in the States, still without control of their futures, working from dawn to dusk to create a town where only marshland had been before. Her life had been so different, it was hard for her to identify with them.

Emily folded her arms across the window sill, and placed her chin on them. Watching darkly silhouetted trees bend and sway in the force of the winds, she began to hum the spiritual which had been sung at Diana's funeral. The familiar song had been a comforting way to say good-bye to the short-lived friendship they had shared. Emily started singing softly to herself.

> "My mother prayed in the wilderness,
> In the wilderness
> In the wilderness
> My mother prayed in the wilderness
> And then I'm a-going home.
>
> Then I'm a-going home
> Then I'm a-going home
> We'll all make ready, Lord,
> And then I'm a-going home."

A knock at the door startled her. She crossed the room swiftly and peeked out. It was Joshua, the first time she had seen him since the funeral many weeks ago.

"So, you're here," Joshua exclaimed, holding his lantern high to see Emily better. "I thought the cabin was abandoned when I first approached. No light in the window, no smoke from the chimney. What happened to your fire?" he went on, entering the cabin. "Do you need wood?"

"No," Emily said, just now realizing that the lantern and the fire had gone out. "I just got in . . . I was just now getting it going," she lied, moving quickly to shut the door. She leaned back against it, watching Joshua as he put two large pieces of wood in the hearth. Then, he turned up the wick of her flickering lamp and hung his next to hers. With his back to her, she took her time observing how his soft, buckskin jacket hugged the breadth of his wide shoulders and his supple, leather breeches showed the muscular outline of his legs.

"Now, that's better," he said, turning to face her. The fire blazed brightly behind him, and as warm flames cast their golden glow around his handsome face, Emily marvelled once more at Joshua's striking, masculine beauty. In an abrupt change from her melancholy mood, she longed to lay the palm of her hand against the angular jut of his jaw.

As Emily ducked her head to try to wipe her face without Joshua noticing that she had been crying, a crack of thunder pierced the silence, and the rushing sound of pouring rain quickly followed. The storm had begun.

"Oh, the window," Emily remembered, hurrying to fasten the boards in place. The wind was now blowing the rain directly into the room and Emily struggled to move the wide plank over the opening. The front of her dress was quickly soaked by the time she had secured the window. She wiped her hands on the hem of her dress and walked toward the fire.

"Sit here," Joshua said, pulling a small three-legged stool close to the heat. "You're all wet."

Emily laughed as she sat down. "This looks like the kind of rain that Hanna says 'will leave four foot of water in my cabin by mornin'. If what she's told me is true, maybe we'll have to move to higher ground."

"There isn't any," Joshua said. "You're probably on the highest ground between the Gulf of Mexico and the San Jacinto River. This cabin is built pretty high, but the ones closer to the Bay are probably taking in water right now."

Emily spread her dress around her feet and leaned closer to the fire. She was suddenly conscious of her soaking wet bodice which clung tightly to her full bosom. Joshua pulled up one of her two straight-back chairs and sat above her, looking down. The drumming staccato of falling rain grew louder as Emily became more uneasy under Joshua's consuming stare.

"How have you been? Are you doing all right?" he asked. "I've worried about you since I left here . . . wondered how things were going."

Emily gazed into the flames, afraid to speak. Her throat was tight and dry.

"I'm fine," she finally managed to say, running a hand over the front of her hair. She realized for the first time that it, too, was very wet.

"Why don't you let it down?" Joshua said, referring to her tightly knotted tresses. "It may dry faster if you do." His tone was soft, urging.

Emily lifted her head and looked at him. Neither of them spoke for several long seconds. She fingered her hair, unable to bring herself to let it fall free, caught between her urge to do it and her fear of the magnetic force which Joshua radiated. Still holding her gaze with his honey-colored eyes, Joshua leaned over and gently loosened Emily's hair, laying its black, silky mass over her shoulders.

"You're very beautiful," he said, his hand still entwined in her hair. "You remind me of the fragile, yellow roses which bloom here in Spring. They're Miss Celia's pride and joy. No one dares touch them but her. You're special, too, like a yellow rose."

Emily's hand moved to touch his and Joshua knelt, sitting at her feet, taking her face in his strong hands. His eyes searched hers seeking permission to create a reality of the smoldering desire he carried. Emily answered by closing her eyes in an unspoken acceptance of the request he had made. Joshua pulled her closer, his lips covering hers in a burst of warmth and urgency which sent unfamiliar vibrations of pleasure through Emily's trembling body. The very center of her soul seemed to explode as Joshua's kisses, coming one upon the other, smothered Emily with an intense hunger to taste the beauty of her eyes, her cheeks, her neck. Locked in the strong circle of his embrace, she yielded to his possessive touch, aroused to a response by the sweet, masculine smell of his body next to hers.

Joshua's fingers moved across the wet fabric of her bodice, leaving a burning trail of sensation on the cool swell of her breasts. Pausing to look once more into Emily's face, to affirm her desire for surrender, he then swept her into his powerful arms and carried her to the feather-quilted bed on the far side of the cabin.

Emily lay still as Joshua unbuttoned her dress, slipping it easily over her slender hips. He placed one hand on her shoulder, then slowly moved it over her firm breasts, across the slight swell of her stomach, down to the inner warmth of her velvety thighs. She moaned in pleasure while lacing her fingers through his dark, wavy hair, and gave herself up completely to this floating, passionate journey. Releasing herself to the intoxicating beauty of the moment, Emily reveled in the sensation of abandon Joshua aroused in her. She feared it, yet craved it. The mutual satisfaction they gave one another in response to their liberated longings, moved to an exhilarating climax which was both unknown and natural to Emily.

When she lay sheltered and naked in Joshua's arms, the soft flickering light of the fire playing shadows on her body, there was no embarrassment, no shame, no regret. The joining of Emily and Joshua had come as naturally and easily as Autumn had come to New Washington.

Throughout the night, Emily listened as torrential rains pummelled the cabin roof and she snuggled deeper into her feather-lined quilt with each new howl of the wind. Languishing in the warm cocoon of Joshua's protective arms, she drifted in and out of a peaceful sleep, laced with wakeful moments of watching Joshua slumber at her side. The musical rhythm of his breathing lulled her into a wondrous feeling of security for which she had unknowingly been searching.

Emily rubbed the side of her face against the soft skin on the crook of Joshua's arm, then lay quietly. Joshua's arrival this night had confirmed that the attraction she had first felt on meeting him was mutual, and although he had openly shown his desire for her, she sensed he would not easily reveal much more of his soul.

Emily didn't want to admit it, but Hanna's story that Joshua might be a runaway slave nagged at her. If this were true, what future could there be for them? How long would it be before he had to move on or be caught? And even more frightening, what would his punishment be if captured? She had heard stories from runaways who made it to New York, about their companions and families who had not been so lucky. Runaways who were caught were either hung or shot. Emily squeezed her eyes shut to stop her whirling mind. She only wanted to make the happiness of this night last forever, shutting out any thoughts which might spoil it.

Numerous cracks and crevices between the cabin's mud-caked logs allowed the first signs of daylight into the room. Anticipating her day as she dressed, Emily moved silently, trying not to awaken Joshua. She buttoned up the front of her dress, now completely dry, and brushed out her long, dark hair, then twisted it once more at the nape of her neck. The room was cold. The fire had dwindled down to a few smoldering embers in the hearth, but she sat near what little heat there was to lace her sturdy leather boots. With her skirt above her knees, concentrating on the hooks and eyes, she was caught off guard by Joshua's voice from the other side of the room.

"You have very pretty legs. You should show them off more often."

"Why, Joshua," Emily said, yanking down her skirt, "how long have you been watching me?"

"Long enough to wish you didn't have to leave."

"Well, I do," Emily stated primly, finishing her laces with a yank. "There've been a lot of soldiers at the house lately, that means twice as much cooking and washing as the day before."

"They only come to Morgan's place to catch a glimpse of you," he teased, propping himself up on one elbow.

"I don't think so . . . they've got more important things on their minds than me."

"Yeah? Like what," he continued his teasing.

"Like war," Emily finished seriously, remembering the heated discussion she had overheard just yesterday about the position of the Mexican Army. "All they talk about is how big the Mexican Army is and how hard it is to get more men."

"That's a fact," Joshua agreed. "Sure looks like there's gonna be a war. A large shipment of guns and ammunition arrived in Anahuac last week. It's supposed to be delivered to Harrisburg by now. Andrew Stephens is holding it at his store for Morgan."

Emily walked to the side of the bed where Joshua lay, a frown of concern on her face.

"If there's a war, will you fight?"

"Sure. Why not? Texas has been good to me. If Sam Houston will have me, I'll fight."

"I wouldn't want you to go," Emily said, touching Joshua's face gently. "War's such an awful thing, you might not come back."

"Oh, I'd come back all right," he laughed, reaching up to catch her hand in his. "It'd take more than a little 'ol war to get the best of a guy like me. I've been through worse things than fighting a few Mexicans."

"Like what?" Emily prompted, hoping he would unveil one layer of his mysterious past.

Joshua tightened his grip on Emily's hand, suddenly becoming very serious. He pulled her fingers to his lips and kissed each one individually.

"Nothing we should talk about now . . . not now." He let her hand drop slowly, in a signal that perhaps he had already gone too far.

Emily knelt beside the bed, laying her head on the soft quilt.

"I hope there won't be any war."

"But, my sweet," Joshua said, stroking her hair as he talked, "now is the time for Texans to strike. I've been here long enough to see there is no choice but war. Mexico will not relinquish this territory without a fight and as much as President Jackson denies it, the United States is anxious to get this rich and profitable land."

Emily raised her head from the bed, looking into Joshua's eyes.

"You speak as if you know something of politics," she probed.

"I listen to the people talk . . . the soldiers, the speculators, they're all alike. They have a lot to gain from a war right now. I travel over Texas, from Harrisburg to San Antonio, and the talk's the same all over. The Mexicans cannot control the Texans much longer. Independence is the only answer."

"Can you read?" Emily was suddenly curious, impressed by Joshua's ability to express the complicated situation in Texas.

Joshua only nodded his head.

"Can you write, too?"

Again he nodded.

"Who taught you?"

"I taught myself, a long time ago, before I came to Texas."

"Where'd you come from?"

Joshua brushed his lips lightly across the top of Emily's head. "Enough questions for one day," he cut her off, masking the curtness in his voice with a wide smile. "I have to be on my way. Morgan's got a couple of sick mules in his stable I'm supposed to look at this morning. I had every intention of checking on them last night until I was so pleasantly distracted." He placed his hand under Emily's chin and tilted her face toward his. When his lips met hers, Emily once more felt the heated rush of yearning she had experienced the night before. There was no question in her mind now, a life of loving Joshua was what she wanted most. It suddenly made little difference that she was unable to fathom the shrouded enigma of his past.

"When will I see you again?" Emily asked, allowing herself to be gathered up in the loving circle of his arms.

"You never need to ask that question," Joshua said, kissing the tip of her nose. "When you need me, I'll be there, you can count on it. Now you run along and start your work before Miss Celia sends Hanna looking for you."

Flustered, realizing that she was already very late, Emily grabbed her shawl and smoothed her hair into place. Although she wanted to know if Joshua would be in the cabin that evening, she cautioned herself not to press him further. It was apparent that his independent spirit could not be tamed so quickly, nor his self-protective nature penetrated too easily. But after kissing him goodbye and stepping through the door, Emily instinctively knew she would find the key to holding Joshua's love forever.

✦-✦-✦--✦-✦-✦

"Sorry Ma'am, there's not a barrel of coffee in all of Harrisburg right now. Parched corn is about all I can give you," Andrew Stephens offered, apologizing for the lack of foodstuffs on the shelves of his general store.

"We've plenty of corn on the place," Emily said, "Mrs. Morgan was hopeful you'd have some coffee. We'd heard down on the Bay that a schooner was due in, and as soon as Mr. Morgan heard the news he decided to make the trip up and get some supplies."

"Yes. The *Flash* was supposed to have made it in by now, but some soldiers brought news from Anahuac that it's still laid up down there. Can't make it upstream. Since the storm two weeks ago, the bayou's been impassable, full of fallen trees and branches. More than fifty live oaks were felled around here that night."

The mention of the storm brought back vivid memories of Joshua. Emily's breasts still burned where he had left his indelible touch and the memory of his masculine smell assaulted her as if he were standing nearby. Although a little more than two weeks had passed since she had seen him, the impressions of that fateful night were so deeply etched on Emily that she felt she carried a piece of him in her heart at all times. While trying to keep up with her work at the house, she often lapsed into recollections of their night together and yearned for his return. Acknowledging the wanderlust in Joshua, Emily tried to keep from anticipating his arrival but usually found herself listening for his footsteps outside her door each and every night.

"Did you have much damage down on the Bay?" the bearded store keeper interrupted her thoughts.

"No, not much," Emily quickly replied, bringing herself back to the conversation. "We had a lot of high water, some cabins flooded, but there wasn't a lot of damage."

Emily moved toward the front of the dimly lit log structure, carefully examining stacks of dry goods heaped on broad wooden tables. There were ready-made white cotton shirts and waists brought down from New Orleans, heavy colorful Indian blankets woven by tribes in north Texas, and bolts of cloth of many colors ready to be cut into dresses and coats. A white lace mantilla, hanging on a peg with an assortment of hats and shawls caught Emily's eye. Gently, she took it off the hook and held it toward the light. With the sun behind it, the diamond-shaped weaving, bordered in rosebuds, took on the appearance of crystallized snow-flakes suspended in air.

Emily looked around. There was only one other customer in the store, a young girl whose deep-brimmed bonnet dwarfed her tiny face, and she was trying on a pair of leather boots with Mr. Stephens' assistance. Cautiously, Emily placed the mantilla over her head, adjusting the beautiful lace edges around her face. It fell softly over her shoulders, almost to her waist. She felt regal, elegant, important. Moving to position herself in front of a shiny new wash tub hanging from a pole, Emily searched for her reflection on its polished surface. The blurred apparition which emerged—the hazy picture of Emily's beauty ensconced in virginal white—made her smile, secure in the knowledge that some day she should wear this to marry Joshua Kinney.

"That's a beautiful piece, isn't it?"

Emily turned to face Mr. Stephens who had walked up behind her. He adjusted his steel-rimmed glasses as he spoke, eyeing Emily with interest.

"Hasn't been a wedding 'round here since Mary Asby and Tom Perry hitched up last spring. Many a young lady's come in here and dreamed over that tiny bit of lace. All the way from Mexico City it is, and no more like it are likely to pass through Harrisburg again. Juan Carlos used to come this way with goods from Mexico City, but he died of the fever this past July. A good merchant he was . . . bringing the ladies just the kind of pretty things we couldn't get from the States."

"How much is it?"

"Five dollars."

"Oh," Emily said softly, slipping the diamond patterned cloth from her head with the realization that it would take her some time to earn that much money. She thought of the two half dollars she had safely tucked away in her pocket, and took a chance.

"If I gave you half a dollar would you hold it for me? I work for wages and could pay for it in two months."

"Half a dollar, huh? Well, I don't know, maybe I'll be selling it soon, the preacher's due in these parts by Christmas. When he comes, usually there's two or three weddings at once."

Emily remained silent while the whiskered merchant considered her offer. He fiddled with a watch fob hanging below his protruding belly and looked again at Emily.

"Well, I think I could hold it for two months. That would put it right about the time the preacher's due." He reached in front of Emily and picked up the brilliant piece of lace. "I'll just wrap it up and put it in the back with your name on it. What'd you say your name was?"

"Emily. Emily West."

"Fine, Miss Emily," Mr. Stephens went on as he tore a square of brown paper from a wide metal holder and gently folded the mantilla into it, "you got yourself a weddin' veil. That'll be half a dollar."

Emily handed the storekeeper one of her silver coins and watched as he took the neatly tied package to the back room of the store. She was suddenly glad she had come to the store alone. At first, Celia Morgan had wanted to come along, then changed her mind, still too tired from the journey to leave the comfort of Ned and Priscilla Battle's fine frame home in Harrisburg to venture into the muddy, crowded streets of the city.

"Just some coffee or tea, whichever he has," Celia had told Emily as she pressed several bills into her hand. "It's been so long since we've had either. I'm not particular."

Remembering this conversation made Emily aware that she had forgotten to inquire about the availability of Mrs. Morgan's second choice.

"Do you have any tea?" Emily asked.

"Tea? Let me see. I'm pretty sure I've got a couple of two pound tins on the shelf over here," he muttered under his breath as he moved boxes and tins around. "Yes, here you are, some jasmine direct from New Orleans."

"Good," Emily said. "I'll take both tins for Mrs. Morgan with me now."

Emily paid for the tea, tucked the tins into her large cloth bag and left the store, promising Mr. Stephens that she would be back within two months to make final payment on the mantilla. Holding her purchases securely in her right hand, she stepped onto the crude but effective boardwalks running along either side of the muddy, main street of Harrisburg. Designed to protect pedestrians from the dirty mire of the frontier town, the wooden walkways connected a long row of shops, storehouses, and homes. Small, feisty mustangs, which Emily approached with caution, stood tethered at bars outside the buildings. Having witnessed for herself the strong inclination of these wiry horses to revert to their natural state of wildness, she circled them widely, staying out of their way.

In stark contrast to the sophisticated streets of New York, the traffic passing through Harrisburg was primitive and slow. There seemed to be three distinct classes of transportation, each one directly related to a settler's wealth and success. A big wagon hitched with six yoke of oxen rumbling through the streets caught everyone's eye, and quickly impressed upon them that a man of means had come into town.

The less fortunate but equally industrious settler brought his goods into town in an open cart pulled along by a team of mules. Bred and sold in Harrisburg, mules were cheap, dependable, and much more controllable than a mustang of the same size. Their availability made the teams of mules surging the streets greatly outnumber the yokes of oxen crowding the narrow passageways.

When a sleigh, fashioned in the same manner as the kind used for driving over snow passed by, Emily recognized the lowest class of transportation constructed in the colony. Hitched to either an oxen or a mule, the sleigh was a crude but serviceable device for moving men and goods.

Emily lifted her dress as she stepped over large holes of muddy water, making her way from the center of town to the two story house Ned Battles had built on the edge of the business district. Her hem was caked with dirt and her shoes soaked wet, but she paid little attention to this slight discomfort as she headed toward her destination.

She noticed a group of men gathered on the boardwalk about fifteen feet ahead where a painted board, swinging from chains overhead, read "Rubin Lazro, Dealer in Hides." The men, dressed in dark broadcloth coats and white starched shirts, smoked cigars or pipes as they stood around talking. A large, red-faced man, with mutton chop whiskers and a balding pate, seemed to be holding the center of attention, speaking with authority, waving his cigar to emphasize his statement. Emily lowered her eyes as she neared the men, not wanting to look at any of them. The closer she got, the more distinct the large man's words became.

"A man like that can cause trouble, you know. He moves too freely among the blacks."

"Oh, Joshua Kinney's no troublemaker. If it hadn't been for him, I'd have lost three oxen last summer. He's a little closed-mouthed, but he's all right," another man said.

Joshua! They are talking about my Joshua! Emily thought to herself. She slowed her pace to hear more.

"You're wrong, Roger," the balding man continued, "I think we should watch him closely or restrict his movements until this business of war is settled. If Joshua Kinney persuades the darkies to join up with the Mexicans, we'll have a hell of a fight on our hands."

"I think that's pretty unlikely, Martin," a thin man, the only one dressed in buckskin replied, "Joshua doesn't seem like the type to get too involved in politics. He's more inclined to play his banjo and sing for the troops."

"Don't let him fool you," Martin replied. "He's smarter than you think. I've heard he can read and write a legible hand . . . that's dangerous."

By now, Emily had stopped in her tracks, shocked at what she was hearing. This man, Martin, was convinced that Joshua could inspire the blacks to fight against Texas! What an absurdity! She knew Joshua had been speaking the truth when he had told her he was willing to fight if Sam Houston would have him. Surely all this was a grave misunderstanding.

"I agree with Martin," a man standing on the far edge of the group threw out. "If Joshua Kinney comes through Harrisburg again, maybe we'd better keep him here. Lock him up if we have to."

Lock him up! The words burned a hole in Emily's heart with their severity and lack of reason. She wanted to run, to get away from these narrow-minded, mean-thinking men.

She had to get to Joshua and let him know of this plot against him in Harrisburg. Instead of running, she took a deep breath, walked unnoticed past the agitated group, and set her mind to forming a plan to warn Joshua of this trap.

Chapter Six

Reeling from the vicious accusations she had just heard, Emily plunged blindly into the street, sloshing through yawning, muddy holes toward the large, white house where the Morgans were staying. Tensely folding her arms across her stomach, fists clenched, she weighed the validity of their accusations.

Could I have really misjudged Joshua, she wondered. His reluctance to speak of his past, and the rumored suspicion that he was a runaway slave, made Emily wonder if he had something to hide. Could he be a traitor? Would he use his freedom against Texas? The possibilities tumbled around in Emily's head. Her spirits lowered with each thought. No, she told herself, such ideas came from idle, prejudiced minds. She wouldn't be so easily swayed, so quickly convinced that the man she loved was a traitor.

Gray, fast-moving clouds swept toward the East, and the threat of more rain descended over the skyline. The dismal and depressing day shrouded the nervous anxiety Emily felt. She was worried, worried that in reality, she knew very little about the man who consumed her every thought. Worried, also, that Joshua was truly in danger and had no knowledge of it. She remembered his serious tone when he had said he would fight for Texas. There was no doubt in Emily's mind that Joshua spoke the truth. Until she spoke with him directly, she would believe what he had told her: that if Sam Houston would have him, he would fight.

In the wake of this decision, she saw her mission: find Joshua and warn him of the plot brewing in Harrisburg. She was smart enough to know that either proving his innocence or denying his guilt would be a much harder task once captured. But how could she find him? Where was he now?

In her concentration, Emily lost all sense of direction. She stopped to look around and realized she was at the turn-off leading into the spacious yard which fronted the Battles' place. Ned and Priscilla Battles, early settlers in Texas, took great pride in having one of the few frame houses erected in Harrisburg.

Three large oak trees rose up in front of the glistening white house, providing privacy and shade for a deep, covered porch. Six elegantly turned balusters supported its steeply angled roof under which there were nestled four tiny, square-paned windows. The highly polished front door, flanked by two narrow windows, faced onto an undeveloped, tree-lined street, while an outside stairwell afforded direct entrance to the bedrooms on the second floor.

Staring vacantly at the lovely structure, Emily hardly felt the light mist which had begun to fall as the sun retreated deeper into a swirling gray mass overhead. Listlessly, Emily circled the house, stopping to scrape some mud from her shoes as she entered the kitchen.

"Well, Miz Emily, I see you made it back," Dulcena, the Battles' cook spoke up, not missing a turn as she continued stirring cornmeal batter in an earthenware bowl. Bent earnestly over her task, straight black hair in her face, Emily was slightly surprised that the Mexican maid knew who had entered the room.

"You find eeny coffee?"

"No," Emily said, putting her damp shawl on a peg near the door. "Mr. Stephens says there's not any coffee to be found in all of Harrisburg right now. Seems like the schooner from New Orleans is still held up at Anahuac."

"No surprise to me," Dulcena went on in her heavily accented English. "Eeny time we have rain, nobody comes up the reever for weeks and weeks." With short arms propped on wide hips, the tiny rotund woman raised her tired eyes to Emily and said, "Maybe we have coffee by Chreesmas, eh?"

"Maybe so," Emily agreed, rinsing her hands in a bucket of water, then picking up a paring knife. Placing a straight-backed chair up to the hearth, she sat down with a basket of small squash in her lap. The heat penetrated her legs as she tried to relax while concentrating on peeling and quartering the multi-colored gourds. It was no use. Her hands were shaking nervously, and as she pulled the knife in jerky movements, she sliced her finger deeply. She put her hand to her lips, sucking to stop the blood, and her eyes filled with tears as she gazed into the fire. Its leaping flames reached out to pull her thoughts once more to Joshua's predicament. She would have to find him right away, to hear from his own lips that he was innocent of such accusations.

"Emily, Emily."

As if in slow motion, Emily dropped her hand from her mouth and looked to see who was speaking. Priscilla Battles stood in the middle of the airy kitchen, dressed in a black and white shepherd-checked gown. Her deep auburn hair was wrapped in two full coils over her ears. A white, starched collar fanned away from her neckline, framing a smooth, oval cameo which Priscilla fingered as she spoke.

"Dulcena says you didn't have any luck with the coffee?"

"No, ma'am. I'm sorry," Emily answered the mistress of the house.

"No tea, either?" a frown of dismay creased Priscilla's flawless complexion and her green eyes narrowed in concern.

"Oh," Emily uttered, remembering the two tins in her bag, "yes, the tea . . . he did send some tea. Let me get it." She hurriedly put the basket of squash on the floor, went to the peg and took down her heavy, cloth bag. Rummaging through it, she finally found the two small tins. "Here you are," she offered Priscilla.

"Ah, good, good. At least we'll have tea with dinner tonight. "Dulcena," she said, turning from Emily with a swish of her full, checkered skirt, "set another place, please. Luke Clayton's joining us this evening."

Luke Clayton! The familiar name caught Emily's attention. He was the man who had brought Nathan, the boy who had shared her berth aboard the *Exert*, to Texas. Her mind was quickly flooded with memories of Nathan's last days on board ship as he spoke of his future in bondage.

"If I'm to be a slave for life," Nathan had told Emily, "I count my blessings I'll serve Luke Clayton."

So, tonight she would meet the man who, against his better judgment, had converted his three hundred slaves into indentured servants to conform with Mexican law in order to work his vast empire of cotton and cane.

"Eenything else, ma'am?" Dulcena inquired of her fashionable mistress as she poured the last of her cornmeal batter into a heavy, iron skillet.

"No, that's all," Priscilla finished, moving to inspect the enticing array of meats, vegetables, and sweets laid out on a long sideboard far from the fire. A golden-brown turkey, stuffed with pecan and rice dressing, centered the table, while steaming bowls of dark collard greens and deep red beans emitted delicious aromas into the air. Honey-laced peaches floated in heavy amber syrup next to a tall, dark raisin cake of at least four layers. Priscilla lifted a tiny piece of venison from a large silver platter and popped it into her mouth.

"Delicious," she said, savoring the taste, "delicious as usual, Dulcena." Then, leaving as quietly as she had entered, the hostess swept out of the room to check on her guests.

❖·❖·❖··❖·❖·❖

Peeling, chopping and mashing, Emily absentmindedly prepared the summer squash for baking. As the hours of late afternoon slipped by, she and Dulcena put finishing touches on the evening's repast. Emily, in charge of readying the beautifully furnished dining room for the dinner party, carefully placed a vase of pale, silk flowers in the middle of the elegant Sheraton dining table. Surrounded by eight square-backed chairs of the same polished mahogany, it stood on a round, braided rug done in hues of rose and wine. Two elaborate, brass oil lamps positioned at each end of the long table, provided substantial light from their tall, glass cylinders. As Emily put Zinnia patterned plates in front of each seat, she was careful to check that each flower faced an upright position. Dulcena had warned her that Priscilla Battles became easily enraged if her table was less than perfectly set.

Emily glanced toward ceiling-high windows draped in gold brocade with velvet tassels, noticing darkening shadows of dusk descend over the trees. Moving away from the table, she lit two crystal sconces hanging on the wall and smiled as the room took on the air of an enchanted castle. Satisfied that everything was in order, she made her way back into the warm, pungent kitchen.

"The table is ready?" Dulcena inquired, tucking stringy hair behind ears hung with shiny, golden loops.

"I think so," Emily answered, looking down at the mud splattered hem of her dress. "I'm going to change now, what time will we serve?"

"Six o'clock sharp. The missus likes to eat on time, guests or not.

You'll see, six o'clock comes, everybody sitting down, waiting to be served. In thees house, we eat on time, *Gracias a Díos,* on time."

"It's not like that in the Morgan's house. With soldiers always coming through, I never know when I'll get done. Seems like the cooking never stops."

"I sorry for you," Dulcena sympathized. "No soldiers eat in thees house. No, no, only the Missus, Mr. Ned, and their friends what pass through. Miss Priscilla very particular about that. She very elegant lady, you know? Very . . . what you say? Cultured, that's it, cultured."

Emily was indeed aware of Priscilla Battles' reputation as a cultured, elegant woman. Celia Morgan had talked of little else during the trip up from New Washington. Celia had known Priscilla since girlhood in North Carolina, envying her friend who married the most eligible bachelor in Durham County and followed him west to help spend his family's fortune in the frontier. Unlike those who had come to Texas in search of wealth and opportunity, the stylish young bride had come comfortably endowed, wanting for little while setting up house on the bayou.

Stories, never verified, but coveted as true, still circulated about the lavish way the Battles lived aboard their own private schooner during most of '29, going back and forth to New Orleans buying furnishings for their two-story house. Priscilla personally oversaw the placement of each item, never consulting her indulgent husband who stayed busy erecting his own cotton gin.

"Thees man, Luke Clayton, who come to eat tonight," Dulcena continued, "many people say hees house more beautiful than thees one. Very rich man, he has many workers, I hear."

"How far away is his place?"

"Not too. Maybe half a day by wagon, out on the bayou."

"Have you ever been there?"

"Me? No, I don't know nothing but thees place here. Been here almost six years, suits me fine. I don't care nothing 'bout travelin' around."

"Does Miss Priscilla or Mr. Ned ever go out to visit at the Clayton place?"

"No, not visit much. Mr. Luke's a widow man, not much reason for Missus to go out there. One time I remember Mr. Ned went out to get some burning oil from Luke Clayton . . . that's the only time I know he visited the place. Why you so interested?"

Emily thought of telling Dulcena the truth; that she wanted to get on the Clayton place and try to find Nathan. However, not willing to reveal her motive, she decided against saying anything more.

"Just curious, that's all. I've heard his name before . . . " Emily's voice trailed as she let the conversation drop. Now she was looking forward to meeting Luke Clayton more than ever.

✦·✦·✦··✦·✦·✦

A hand-carved grandfather clock standing sedately in the parlor chimed six times as Priscilla Battles began seating her dinner guests at the gleaming Sheraton table. French crystal goblets and ornately cast silverware competed in their brilliance on the dark mahogany surface. Heavy Irish linen napkins, emblazoned with the letter *B* lay folded in cones at each place. In flickering, intermittent candlelight and the warm glow of oil lamps, the regal hostess reigned.

With a wave of her brightly jewelled hand, Priscilla indicated that her friend and guest, Celia Morgan, sit near the head of the table on her husband's right. Celia, dressed in navy linen, waned in dull contrast to her hostess as she took her seat with grace. Emily stood in pale blue cotton, her hair caught back in two ivory combs. She looked around the table; besides the Morgans and the Battles, there were two other men. One, a large, blonde man, not long into maturity, the other, an elderly gentleman who spoke with an accent. She wondered which one of them was Luke Clayton.

The kitchen door swung open as Dulcena entered with a steaming tureen of turtle soup which she handed over to Emily. Crossing the room to the head of the table, Emily stood silently beside Ned Battles as he ladled a generous portion into his bowl. He laid his large napkin over one leg and turned toward James Morgan.

"I've been hearing all about your work for the Texas Navy. Can we call you colonel yet?"

James Morgan smiled, wiping traces of turtle soup from his thin, graying mustache. "I'm still a little reluctant to call our fleet a Navy, but I work day and night to strengthen the ranks. We're under-manned and under-supplied, in desperate need of funds to have the ships necessary to defend the coast from an attack by water. However, if an attack should come soon, and if our forces are properly placed, what we have will serve us well."

The sure, firm tone of his voice left no doubt that he had faith and determination to make a credible Navy out of the fleet of reconditioned warships bought from the United States.

"And as to my title," he went on, "I expect it won't be conferred for some months yet."

"With war so close on the horizon, I doubt it will be long before you can put your fledgling fleet to the test," the large, blonde man spoke. Emily looked in his direction. He was a serious man, somewhat pallid in complexion, with less than striking features, but his deep voice was firmly resolute.

"So, Luke, are you finally conceding that a war with Mexico is inevitable?" James Morgan queried, raising an eyebrow in smugness.

Emily caught the reference, knowing now where Luke Clayton sat.

"You know I question the value of an independence secured by war," Luke continued, "I, as well as many others, have spent a considerable amount of time and money acquiring land and labor. The loss of life and destruction brought about by war are not easily overcome. Who knows how long such a struggle could last?"

"Too much time has already been spent in worthless negotiations with the Mexican government," James Morgan said. "There is no peaceful solution to this problem as we cannot trust their word. Without increased trade with the rest of the country, the colonists cannot survive much longer."

"But Morgan," Luke said earnestly, "we're allowed to import, duty free, whatever we need from the States. Our needs are . . . "

"What use is that liberty," Morgan interrupted, "if we cannot sell any of it for profit in Mexico?"

"Luke, I think Morgan has a point," the elderly man seated across from Celia Morgan entered the conversation. "We cannot rest comfortably on what we've gained so far, although for many it's an obvious temptation. We must consider the future of the colonies if these heavy taxes and trade restrictions persist. I, for one, could do better selling my hides closer to home than sending them by random schooners to New Orleans. Many times they lay in port for months waiting transfer to a vessel going north."

"But Rubin," Luke appraised, "the northern states line your pockets with their constant demand for furs and hides. A war right now would more than likely halt all shipping out of Texas, creating havoc with your trade."

"True," Rubin agreed, "the market to the east is a good one for furs, but if I could also sell my hides along the coast, into Mexico, I'd make a better living."

"What Rubin says makes sense," Ned Battles spoke up, "for more and more smuggling is going on right under the Mexicans' noses. This restriction on growing tobacco galls me to no end, prohibiting me—a third generation tobacco farmer, from cultivating a crop. As long as the Mexican government reserves the right to grow tobacco, an illegal trade will continue to flourish in the hands of smugglers and bandits."

The name Rubin made Emily look more closely at the elderly merchant, wondering if he might be the owner of the store she had passed earlier today, Rubin Lazro, Dealer in Hides. The sign was swinging over the group of men discussing Joshua. Perhaps this foreign sounding man, whose bushy white eyebrows framed a glassy stare, was one of those who wished Joshua captured. She listened showing little outward sign of interest as the conversation went on.

Luke Clayton laid his soup spoon aside, cast a somber gaze from man to man around the table, then stated his position.

"It's not that I don't understand the possibility of increased profits which could directly benefit each one of you if Texas were independent. What plagues me is the thought of upheaval over the land while the battle's being fought."

"Upheaval is the forerunner of change," James Morgan said, helping himself to thick slices of venison offered by Emily. "I'm one hundred percent in favor of war and will work for Texas' independence until I draw my last breath. Sam Houston's laying his plans as we speak for a defense against Santa Anna. Yes, Luke, change is coming, but I don't fear it . . . it's weighed in our favor."

"Maybe," Luke conceded, "but I still feel that efforts for a peaceful solution shouldn't be abandoned."

"There's another question besides the one of trade which would be settled by our independence," Ned Battles added. "That's the question of slavery."

Conversation was suspended as the guests waited for Ned to go on.

"Indentured servitude is a makeshift way to circumvent the laws against holding slaves in Mexico, and we're creating a volatile situation here which could result in rebellion."

"What do you mean, Ned?" Celia Morgan asked, surprising everyone with the icy tone to her voice.

"Apparently you haven't heard what happened on Jared Brown's place in Columbia last week," Ned began, stopping to sip from his full glass of wine.

"Jared and Marylou Brown from St. Louis?" Celia asked.

"Yes, the same," Ned concurred. "Seems like two of his field hands, indentured when he brought them to Texas, decided they were as free as Jared, telling him as much as they threw down their ploughs and walked off the field. They told him 'We're as free as you, we're in Mexico now. The government will protect us.' Then, they walked toward the woods. Well, Jared was dumbstruck and naturally threatened to shoot them if they went a step further. They persisted and made off into the woods, but Jared shot one of them dead in the back, the other one got away, nobody's seen him since."

"How awful," Celia exclaimed, covering her mouth with her napkin.

"One thing's for sure, no more of Jared's niggers are talking about leaving," Ned finished, laughing openly at the story.

James Morgan shook his head. "I don't go along with that, I just don't go along with shooting a man."

"Morgan!" Luke stated indignantly, "a nigger's property just like a horse, you know that! Jared was in the right, he had to stop those niggers in their place . . . set an example for the rest of the help."

Standing rigidly immobile in the background, Emily's palms ran sweat and her cheeks flushed hotly. Within the statuesque composure exhibited on the surface seethed a raging voice which longed to scream in protest to Luke's statements. He had spoken as if she weren't there, heedless to her presence. Like the stinging slap of his broad, bony hand, he had put her in her place. She was no different than the field hands he spoke of, not worthy enough to occupy space or even breathe the same air which passed through his lungs. She didn't exist. Free on paper, living outside the United States, Emily reminded herself again that she dwelled within the realm of a modified human bondage.

"At New Washington," James Morgan continued in his defense, "there are only three indentured blacks, and I hope to free them soon to let them settle on their own. All the rest of the Negroes work for wages. Living out here, trying to create a town out of timber and mud has shown me that a man's freedom is what inspires him to turn the wilderness into civilization. Those who work for wages in the colony, work harder and with more diligence than any slave I ever owned in North Carolina."

Those at the table fell silent, embarrassed and touched by Morgan's speech, but not at all ready to commit themselves to life without slave labor. Rubin Lazro wiped crumbs from his wiry mustache and directed a comment to Ned.

"I fear that someone is deliberately inciting this so-called rebellion you speak of, Ned. There's been quite a lot of talk recently about a free black, a Joshua Kinney who moves around the colonies. Not too long ago, he spent some time at Jared's place, possibly spreading his influence through the workers down there."

At the mention of Joshua's name, Emily's breathing stopped, her stomach constricted in a series of quivering spasms, and for the first time in her life, she felt she would faint.

"I know who you mean," Luke said, "he's a tall fellow, almost Indian looking, carries a big, leather bag most of the time."

"That's him," Rubin said, leaning forward as he spoke, "but I'm not so sure he's free. There's folks in Harrisburg who say he's a runaway from Tennessee, hiding out from bounty hunters."

Emily was torn between the urge to flee into the kitchen and cover her ears to keep from hearing such accusations, or to stay to learn exactly what these men planned to do about Joshua. Priscilla Battles decided it for her as she rose from the table and interrupted the men's discussion.

"Well, enough talk about war and slaves for now. Shall we have tea in the parlor? Celia, don't you think we've heard just about enough politics for one evening?"

Celia smiled in feeble agreement, but Emily noticed a hint of concern in her employer's eyes. Celia had once spoken highly of Joshua to Emily, making reference to the many times he had saved animals for her husband. From what she had said, Emily had assumed that the Morgans trusted Joshua.

"I have to apologize for not having any coffee for you gentlemen," Priscilla said, offering her arm to James Morgan, "but

Andrew Stephens says there's not a drop of coffee in Harrisburg right now."

"If I had known you needed coffee," Luke said, "I'd have brought some from my place. We've plenty, Ned."

"Oh, what I'd give for some coffee, Luke," Priscilla sighed in exaggeration.

"For you, Priscilla, I'll send a wagon with some over tomorrow afternoon."

"Why thank you, Luke. That's so nice of you to take pity on us in town," she teased. "Let's go into the parlor."

As soon as the party had left the dining table, Emily began clearing away the plates, glasses, and platters of left over food. Working silently, with little haste, she could still hear the guests talking in the next room. Dishes clattered, as unsteady hands gathered the china together, while she strained to catch the end of what Rubin Lazro was saying.

" . . . not much reason for him to bother you, Morgan. Places like Luke's is where he gathers strength. How many slaves do you have out there, Luke?"

"More than three hundred."

"As long as a meddlesome wanderer like Joshua Kinney's at large, you'd better be careful," Rubin warned.

Luke Clayton's somber, resolute voice cut through Emily with its sharpened edge, leaving her trembling at its finality.

"Any free nigger who sets foot on my place is dead before he starts talkin'."

Chapter Seven

The news that he was a hunted man came to Joshua in late December. At the busy dock in Anahuac, while sorting through the cargo of a recently arrived schooner, Joshua was surprised by a young boy who approached him. The boy said his name was Nathan and urged Joshua off to the side of the crowd.

Above the noise of travel-weary soldiers and the clanking of wagons as they pulled up for loading, Nathan strained in a whisper, through tightly clenched teeth, "I've word for you from a Miss Emily."

Puzzled by the boy's air of mystery, Joshua gave him a sidelong glance. His rough cut trousers, hitting midway between knees and ankles, were neat and clean enough. His heavy brown boots looked fairly new. But his ill-fitting jacket hanging loosely from his shoulders made him look much less fortunate than he truly was.

"Miss Emily from New Washington?" Joshua asked.

"The same," Nathan replied.

"What message could you have from her?" Joshua got keenly to the point.

Standing on tip-toe to reach Joshua's ear, Nathan whispered, "Over there, away from these men, what I have to say is important."

Guiding him urgently by the arm, Nathan led Joshua to a quiet spot behind the bustling warehouse which shadowed the two of them under low hanging eaves. Glancing nervously from side to side, Nathan stood looking up under Joshua's deep frown and quickly began his story.

"It was less than a fortnight ago . . . I drove a wagon with a load of coffee into Harrisburg. Ned Battles' place in town, that's where I was headed. And while at his place . . . in the kitchen, I was putting down the coffee, I look up and see . . . her . . . Miss Emily."

Joshua's heart beat quickened. A surge of remembrance filled the hollow of his stomach. How did this boy, who spoke so clearly, with so little trace of the common slave accent, come to know Emily on sight?

"You knew Emily before your arrival in Harrisburg?" Joshua wanted to know.

"Oh, yes, sir. I came to Texas on the same schooner with her, slept in the berth next to hers. Sometimes I think she saved me from plumb goin' crazy, all cooped up in that hole for so long. When I took leave of her at this very dock, me goin' to Luke Clayton's place outside of Harrisburg, and she to New Washington, I was sure I'd never see that sweet lady again. But there she was, standing in Ned Battles' kitchen like she lived there . . . said she had come there with the Morgans to stay a short while."

"What did Emily tell you?" Joshua urged impatiently.

"She asked me if I had ways to get around, you know, if I sometimes took Master Luke's wagon to other parts. Yes, ma'am, I told her, I'm always goin' here or there with Master Luke or their overseer. Luke Clayton's a good man to be 'dentured to, he lets his help move around."

"Go on," Joshua said, tired of the boy's rambling. "What did Emily say?"

Nathan's eyes grew wide as he delivered the warning. "There's a man named Martin looking for you. He wants you locked up."

Joshua squinted against the December sun, gazing in concentration over Nathan's head. "Why?" he asked, confused, not knowing who this man Martin was.

"There was a shootin' on Brown's farm, down around Columbia. Two field hands tried to run away. Brown stopped one dead in his tracks. The other got clean away."

"What does this have to do with me?" Joshua wanted to know. The muscles along his jawline tensed. He narrowed his eyes like slits.

"Well, this man, Martin, says you were on Jared Brown's place then, stirrin' things up."

"Stirring things up? How? What do you mean?"

"The way I heard it, those field hands was tellin' everybody they was free. They said slaves ain't allowed in Texas, and they was goin' to Mexico City where the government would protect 'em. . . let 'em live free."

"That's insane!" Joshua grabbed Nathan's arm. "I was in Columbia . . . that's true. But I never told any slave he was free."

"Miss Emily says you better leave this town 'cause Martin and some other men are out to track you down."

"Who else?"

"Rubin Lazro, the fur trader in Harrisburg for one . . . and I figure Luke Clayton, my master, favors the plot. You better go. Leave this place. You can't fight these men."

It took Joshua another fifteen minutes to get the rest of the story from Nathan. He stood rigid and angry, not wanting to believe what the young boy related. There's a panic in the air, all right, he thought as he listened. This fever of war is wrongly affecting the judgment of these men, and I have no choice but to take this warning seriously and leave.

Soon after Nathan went his way, Joshua decided to head North to the large plantation of a man named Jared Groce. His place lay far enough away from Harrisburg to give Joshua the distance he needed between Martin and those who now feared him. He could live safely at Groce's for a while.

Although Groce was an important landholder who worked his place with slave labor, Joshua genuinely liked and respected the man and felt that he could trust him. He and his frail wife were generous people, possessed of a sense of caring that over the years had kept Joshua going North to visit their plantation. Twice a year Joshua had made the trip to the rolling hill country on the Brazos River. During harvest time and planting time he had come, bringing the rich planter herbs and ointments, checking his stock and slaves for sickness or disease.

And now, as Joshua prepared to go there, he did so with deliberate speed, loading his mule for the four day trip with no time to tell Emily good-bye.

✦-✦-✦--✦-✦-✦

The trip up the Brazos River toward San Felipe de Austin was an abysmal trek through rain soaked forests carried out under the cover of darkness. The rains came both day and night, leaving the ill-defined trail a quagmire of mud which was dangerous and difficult to follow. Traveling only at night, Joshua successfully stayed clear of the throngs of ragged soldiers now flocking to San Antonio to join the forces protecting the Alamo.

Since earlier in the month, when Ben Milam and three hundred men had taken San Antonio from the Mexicans, volunteers from all over the countryside had swarmed to the old Spanish mission. But, the tragedy had come when Ben Milam was killed, early in the fighting. This turn of events had given the rest of his troops the determination to quickly force the Mexican General Cos and his fourteen hundred men to surrender and leave Texas in defeat.

Approaching San Felipe in the middle of the night, Joshua was heartened by the glimmering lights of the town. For several hours, he steered his mule in their direction, his mind not at all on the end of his journey, but cluttered with fragments of Nathan's warning, and haunted by the face of the woman who had sent it.

Emily . . . the catalyst of this tiresome journey, had sealed her place in his thoughts against his will. Her presence had seeped too deeply and clung too tightly, making Joshua uncomfortable with the feeling that now she was unshakeable—for he had been trying to forget her. In vain, he had been trying to forget the way her long silken tresses cascaded far past her waist, and he had tried to erase the nectarine taste of her lips upon his. But like the invisible spider's web one walks through without notice, Emily had left him entangled by her touch.

Joshua did not want another woman in his life, especially not a woman like Emily. Such an attachment was frightening. Threatening. And he was certain, in time, she would fade from his thoughts. The dark veils of his past overshadowed any future he could dream of with her at his side, and he closed his mind to any such thoughts. And now, he was running again . . . running away. . . always forced to flee. Would this constant flight unknowingly evolve into the pattern of his life? And if his fate were to be a fugitive forever, there was no room for a woman like Emily.

＊＊＊＊＊＊

In Jared Groce's barn, sweet smelling hay lay in bundles tied with heavy vines. Loosely heaped piles of golden straw lined a wide dirt floor where an acrid odor of animal dung caused no offense, blending naturally into the dimly lit space. Hanging from a large hook in the steeply pitched roof, a smokey lantern illuminated faces contorted in song. Blue-black and deeply furrowed, reddish-brown and creased by the sun, creamy olive and smooth as satin, the faces of the slaves on the huge plantation mingled eerily in front of Joshua. They swayed lazily from side to side to the rhythm of his song.

Joshua's own deep voice was lost to theirs as he deliberately held back, letting the slaves pour forth their familiar spiritual with all the abandon this evening allowed. They had begged Joshua to sing for them, not realizing in their insistence that what they really wanted was to be led in song. Long after the last plough had been laid aside, and the last turn of the hand crank had ginned the final bale of cotton, Joshua's presence gave them reason for gathering. The slaves ended their song in a low droning moan, rising up in a wail which spilled from the barn, across the plantation to the silent black hills in the distance.

"Sing us a new one, Joshua."

"One o' dem purdy ones we ain't heered before."

"Yeah, sing us somethin' new."

Joshua's bronze face crinkled in pleasure at the asking, and picking up his treasured banjo, he closed his eyes against the smoke filled air and sang in mellow tones.

> "There's a Yellow Rose in Texas
> That I am going to see
> No other darky knows her
> No one only me
> She cryed (sic) so when I left her
> It like to broke my heart
> And if I ever find her
> We never more will part."

He stopped for a moment, shifting in his seat while he kept his eyes closed. Emily's face loomed softly in the darkness of his vision, and he lifted his jaw slightly higher. His song continued.

> "She's the sweetest rose of color
> This darky ever knew
> Her eyes are bright as diamonds
> They sparkle like the dew
> You may talk about dearest May

And sing of Rosa Lee
But the Yellow Rose of Texas
Beats the belles of Tennessee."

Joshua's rich, mellow tones had their effect on his audience.

"De purdiest song I heered in a long time, Joshua," a thin-faced woman with sorrowful eyes murmured nearby. "My, my, dat's a purdy song."

Not raising his eyes to the voice from the crowd, disregarding the praise given the ballad, Joshua laid his banjo flat across his knees in a sign that he was finished.

"All right ya'll, let's git on wid de fiddlin'," a knarled black man, one shoulder higher than the other from a generation of fiddling, cackled to the group. The aged musician stood, one foot propped squarely on a bale of hay, the other braced rigidly to support his wispy frame. And placing his gleaming fiddle lovingly under his chin, the white-headed slave broke into a catchy, familiar tune.

Then, everyone in the barn rose to dance.

Two barrels of whiskey, gifts from Master Jared, were rolled into place. The men lined up, wide smiles splitting their dark faces, tin cups in hand. They jostled each other with elbows and shoulders to get to the free flowing liquor. The harvest was over, the crops had been laid aside, and the light work of winter lay ahead. The men were ready for a night such as this. Music swelled into the room as the celebration rose to a peak.

Two circles formed instantly, one inside the other. The men, in ragged overalls, worn thin from more than one season's washing, stood in the outer ring, slapping hands together, elbows raised. The women swirled in tattered skirts directly in front of the men, flashing gleaming smiles, and a bit of ankle, as they rotated around the barn. Lifting their arms high over their heads, the ladies teased and taunted, bent and gestured, finally pairing off with a partner. And Unca Zack's thin sweet music charged the air with rhythm.

Joshua watched the dancers through half-closed eyes, standing resolutely in the shadows, feigning disinterest in the entire celebration in an effort to keep himself distant. He did not want to encourage any woman's affections. His painful past . . . Emily . . . Lucinda . . . .was now becoming confused with the present.

But a tinge of envy stung Joshua as he intently watched a dark-skinned girl whose thick brown hair swung out from her face as she veered around her partner with ease. The stocky young man who offered her his arm looked proud beyond words to be dancing with her. And she caught Joshua's eye and winked.

"You ain't gonna dance?" a husky voice came from behind.

Joshua broke his gaze on the dark-skinned girl and looked at the one who was speaking. It was Fayetta—plump, mature, but decidedly pretty.

"I don't think so," he answered, calmly observing her sharp straight nose and fringed sloe eyes which flattered her chestnut complexion.

Fayetta, dimpled and soft, looking much younger than in fact she was, licked her well-formed lips and waited expectantly as Joshua thought back to the first time he had seen her.

He knew her to carry a deep black scar running the length of her foot. He had tended the gaping wound about a year ago, squeezing foul yellow pus from the swollen flesh as she had moaned in pain from her bed. He had marvelled that Fayetta had not lost her foot to the sharp-toothed alligator who had caught it at the edge of the swamp.

Now, he drained the whisky from his cup and set it quickly aside.

"Come on, Joshua," Fayetta urged excitedly, pulling on his arm. "Come on, Joshua, dance wid me."

He shook his head sharply, squinting at her. But she yanked at his sleeve until he stepped from the shadows of the stall where he lingered and into the light of the lanterns.

So, he danced with her. And laughed out loud, feeling awkward at first, then genuinely enjoying the movement. Fayetta tossed her skirts to the left, then to the right, directing Joshua around her as she went. He followed her teasing movements naturally, the warmed flush of whiskey making him dizzy. And when she looked up and caught his eye, he was glad she had asked him to dance.

The music stopped. Fayetta whirled away. Another woman took her place. When the fiddle started up again, Joshua found himself dancing with a series of women, both young and old, until almost all of them had had a turn with him.

They all loved Joshua so, not only because he was magnetically handsome, but also because of his charm. He had nursed many of them, or their children, or their husbands, through spells of illness in the past. And always he had treated them with gentle respect, a respect lacking in their everyday lives.

The music stopped abruptly and Joshua, flushed and warmed by the dance and drink, stood in the center of the room. His young partner kissed his cheek, giggling shyly under her hand as she broke away to find her friends. Joshua smiled to himself as he watched her disappear into the crowd.

Fayetta pushed her wide body through the dancers, carrying another tin cup of whiskey in her hand. She held it steadily in front of Joshua.

"Dis is for you," she offered breathlessly, the skin of her forehead damp with perspiration, the laces of her bodice hanging loosely from her breasts.

He took the cup and swallowed the fiery liquid in one short swig, moving closer to Fayetta, separating the two of them from the crowd.

"I see your foot has healed all right," he murmured.

"Um-hum . . . wasn't no more dan three weeks after you cured it I was back in de shed washin' clothes agin. Ain't never had no more trouble wid it," she said, her long lashes fluttering as she spoke.

"That's good," Joshua told her, suddenly aware that he was staring into her eyes . . . they were beautiful—almond shaped and heavily lashed, set perfectly in her smooth round face.

He handed back the cup.

"I'd better go."

"So soon?" Fayetta asked, disappointment in her voice. She turned his cup around in the palm of her hand.

"Yes, I must," Joshua said, pulling on his leather hat, picking up his banjo.

Unca Zack, the fiddler, had started another tune by the time Joshua reached the large slatted door. Pushing it open, a burst of cold January air rushed into the warm barn. Tying the string of his hat securely, Joshua ducked his head to go out into the cold night. He had not noticed that Fayetta had wrapped a torn shawl around her shoulders to follow him.

"Kin I walk a ways wid you?" she asked, those sloe eyes suddenly diverted from his. "You be passin' my cabin on de way."

Joshua was caught by a hesitancy in her voice. She seemed almost afraid to ask. He shrugged in response but did not answer.

She passed before him out the high door, into the cold night air.

They walked in silence for a while, the starless sky overcast and black. The chill of the evening settled over Joshua and cleared his head a little. He had really drunk too much.

Fayetta walked to Joshua's side, slightly behind him, the sound of her heavy leather shoes scraping hard ground as she took two steps to his one. She shrugged against the chill in the air and pulled her arms around her plump frame. White puffs of frosty air spilled forth as she spoke.

"How long you gonna be here?"

Joshua did not look at her but frowned darkly at the path ahead, answering as if preoccupied.

"I don't know, I've not decided . . . maybe another month, maybe until spring."

"You gonna go back to Redfish Bay when you leaves?"

At the mention of his lonely cabin where he spent very little time, a tremor slid over his heart. Going back there meant going back to Emily, and he silently cursed those awful longings for her which now began to rise.

"No," he stated flatly, "I'll be heading west."

"Gonna join in de fightin'?"

"Or tend the wounded," he finished.

They descended a hill which sloped down behind the barn and turned onto a narrow path between towering pines that led to the well hidden quarters. Small square shacks standing darkly silent, awaited the return of the revelers on the hill. The dancing would break up by midnight, Joshua knew, and the plantation overseer would ride through the quarters, checking, making sure each slave was in his place.

But now, a few stray hounds wandered aimlessly from door to door, sniffing and scratching at the rough hewn shanties.

"Shoo, now . . . shoo . . . ya'll git 'way from here," Fayetta hissed at two mottled gray hounds hovering near her cabin. They shied back at the rapid shake of her worn-out skirts, creeping off into the tangle of woods behind the cabin.

"Ain't hardly 'nuf food 'round here for me. Don't need no hongry dogs to feed," she said, placing one foot on the wide plank at her stoop. She faced Joshua squarely.

"You still sleepin' down dere wid Unca Zack?" Her shawl

dropped off her shoulders, down her back. She pulled it tautly across her hips, knotting it securely on the side.

Joshua stared at the smooth brown curve of her neck, following the graceful arch to the swell of her breasts which pressed heavily against open laces in the front of her dress.

"Yes," he answered in a husky voice, much lower than he intended.

In shameless honesty, Fayetta straightened up, locked her eyes with Joshua's.

"You kin sleep wid me. . .if you want."

She stood calmly, face inviting, that shawl twisted too tightly over her full hips. Although the light was too dim to see her clearly, Joshua sensed anticipation in her voice.

He could not say a word.

And then her round soft hand found his, pulling him closer to the musky thick smell which rose from her shoulders, wafting up from the shadows between her breasts. Her scent, like a spark of natural fire, burned urgently in his loins. As she leaned her face into his, he allowed himself to be kissed. Once. Twice. Then, finally placing both hands on the dimpled flesh of her upper arms, Joshua kissed her deeply in return.

A hungry urge, too long repressed and now without control, broke any bonds of restraint he had felt before. With one hand, he stroked the warm curve of her back. The other sought entry at the loosely tied laces across her bosom. She yielded to his search, giving forth the touch of flesh Joshua needed so desperately at this moment. When their lips parted, Joshua moaned in hushed agony, and Fayetta moaned in exquisite pleasure as she pressed her body the length of his and whispered, "Come on in. . .out o' de cold."

She pushed the door open, its rusty hinges whining thinly into the night as it gave way to a single room inside. The smell of a dirt floor wafted out. The sound of a scurrying rat faded away. Fayetta glided noiselessly to the far side of the room. She lit a small lamp, then, stopped next to a pile of rumpled cornshuck pallets and signaled Joshua over.

He stood motionless at the door, his body aching to have her. He had not been with a woman since his night with Emily and had not been tempted since then either. But now, he waited tensely at this slave woman's door, his veins near to bursting with desire.

"Over here, Joshua, shut de door." Fayetta's heavy arms made circular movements, beckoning Joshua to her squalid bed close to a gaping hearth.

The musty dark cabin smelled of rancid meat fats which had dripped too long in the ashes. And strewn all around in filthy disarray were sweat stained clothes waiting to be washed. Fayetta's big black washing pots lined the far side of the room, ready for the washerwoman to fill them up again.

Joshua strained for an image of Fayetta. The tiny flame of her lamp cast a dim yellow hue on her bulky figure.

"What's wrong wid you, Joshua? Shut de door, it's cold 'nuf in here."

There was a desperate edge to her voice. It cut through Joshua, stopping him at the door. He stepped slightly backward, appalled anew by the familiar sight and smell of the crude slave cabin. The fire in his loins quickly dimmed. This was not where he wanted to be.

Joshua found his voice and whispered, "I'm sorry, I can't come in." He could not say any more.

"What?" she asked. "Why can't you stay wid me?"

"I'm sorry Fayetta, but. . ."

"But what?" she asked, a suspicious lilt to her words. "What you mean?"

"I'd better go," Joshua mumbled, moving away.

Fayetta crossed the room quickly, skirts flying out behind her as she stopped within inches of his face. "Dis ain't de place for your kind, huh?"

"It's not that," Joshua started, "it's just. . ."

"It's jus' dat I'm still a nigger slave, livin' in nigger slave quarters an' you don't wanna stay here wid me. Dat's it," she finished her statement with a jab.

Joshua gripped the edge of the door, feeling the pain of rough wooden splinters pierce the palm of his hand. His body ran sweat beneath his woolen shirt and the room was a blur of blackened yellow.

"Well, you ain't no better'n me," she went on. "Jus' cause your mammy was an injun an' you ain't got no Massa don't make you free. I heerd how come you run 'way from Galveston Bay an' why you can't go back." With her hands on her hips and her head thrown back, Fayetta taunted Joshua with his secrets.

He stepped back, putting space between himself and Fayetta, who knew more than he wanted to hear. She did not stop.

"Been up here too long, Joshua, too long. Ain't foolin' nobody wid your secret airs. De tale already been told how you's a trouble makin' nigger, run 'way from Tennessee. Two times. Suffered de lash, an' run 'way agin. An' now you's done run 'way from one more place . . . I heered."

"You don't know anything," Joshua said angrily. She couldn't know, he had never told it.

"There are things you don't understand," he started, loosening his grip on the door.

"I know 'nuf 'bout you ta turn you in . . . iffen I should take a mind ta do it. Wouldn't be no difficulty ta me at all ta sic dem bounty hunters on your trail." Fayetta flung the words at him, punishing him for his refusal. "You's jus' a nigger like me. For all your singin' an' healin' an' fancy airs, you still ain't no better'n me."

Those dark sloe eyes which had tempted him earlier, now flamed in burning anger. And turning his back on the raging woman, Joshua hurried from the cabin, the sound of her slamming door loud in his ears. In a confused whirl of fright and anger, he cut through the quarters to Unca Zack's cabin where he sat in black silence with his knees to his chest.

Chapter Eight

The temperature had dropped during the night, falling quickly and sharply, plunging the North Texas hills into a reality of winter which caught the settlers by surprise. January, usually cold and rainy, had ended with frost on the ground, and everyone murmured in actual amazement when parts of the Brazos River had frozen.

Now, six weeks into the new year, Joshua blew warm breath against his hands, gripped his heavy ax once more and split a stubborn log. He selected another, put it in place, and swinging back with all his strength, he hit his mark precisely. Wood chips flew out, settling at his feet, the log fell in two pieces to the ground.

He had never meant to stay here so long. He should have left before now. But something nagged at Joshua, clouded his reasoning, and he couldn't take the steps to go. It was difficult to fathom exactly what was wrong, to still the foreboding which gripped him when his thoughts turned to leaving this place.

This hilly area was a dramatic change from the green level coastland stretched out near Galveston Bay. So dense with foliage, Joshua could see that everything had faded brown and dark with the season. The swollen Brazos lay to the East, a rushing snake of a river which cut its way southward through miles of forest—so tangled and wild they remained silent and unexplored. Bald cypress trees, barren of leaves, rose one hundred feet in the air, their far reaching roots spreading out from their bases, twisted and knotted in the steep river bank. And mixed among the cypress were tall live oaks with their black branches spiraling, making long dark fingers against the sky, with gray Spanish moss hanging lightly in veils, dripping parasitically from their boughs.

Joshua perspired inside his leather jacket while cold air bit his hands and face, leaving a much redder hue than he naturally carried, but Joshua didn't mind. Cutting wood in the cold winter air was invigorating. In fact, he looked forward to the chore, it kept him busy and made him feel useful. Besides, Unca Zack was now too feeble to manage the task.

The wise old fiddler, at eighty-two, welcomed Joshua's help around the place, never speaking of his failing health or complaining about the cold drafty cabin. Zack brewed strong coffee early every morning, smugly stirring his old tin pot, and no one questioned the source of this luxury which Unca Zack swore he would never do without. He could turn a deaf ear when the subject so suited him, or hear low whispers from outside his door, keeping those who came near in a state of confusion, wondering whether or not he was tuned in on them.

The old slave's uncanny ability to discern Joshua's origin so soon after their first meeting had been unsettling. The frail man had said, "Knowed your mammy was a injun de first time I laid eyes on you. So, when I sees dat Creek blood runnin' all tru your face, I says to myself . . . you's bound ta be from somewheres 'round Tennessee." He paused, narrowing his keen gaze on Joshua, then had continued on. "But you's a man what's restless . . . ain't claim dis place as home . . . not yet."

Rubbing his chapped cold hands together, Joshua took up the ax again. At this very moment, Fayetta's words still ran through his mind, forcing him to grudgingly admit that what she said was true. Yes, he had run away from Tennessee. Twice. She was right. And also vividly true were the two severe beatings, with a thin braided whip, he suffered on both returns. But what Joshua was sure Fayetta didn't know was the tragic event leading to his unsuccessful flights from the Kilgore plantation on the outskirts of Memphis. She couldn't have spoken to him like she did if she had known the truth. At least, this is what Joshua had to believe.

Swinging his ax down hard, Joshua clenched his teeth, an old anger burning fiercely in his chest. Rage, tightly under control now, slowly filtered back into his life.

"I've got to leave here," he muttered tersely, his words hanging in cold frozen air. "I can't stay here any longer."

With each firm thud of the falling ax, Joshua determined his plan of action. A small steamer, the *Yellow Stone*, was now anchored at Groce's landing. It had arrived at sundown the night before. When the gangplank fell, bridging the gap to the shore,

Joshua had watched from a distance, observing the deck, peering down the foggy hillside to the torch lit dock. The first man to emerge from the deck of the *Yellow Stone* had been John Reese, the merchant from Anahuac. As Joshua watched the tall man amble from the sloop, he frowned deeply, puzzled by Reese's arrival at the plantation. And, as he stood shadowed in darkness, he had seen the captain, a man unknown to him, with three blacks, and a soldier toting a rifle fit with a bayonet.

Joshua needed passage on the *Yellow Stone*. It did not matter where it was bound, and he felt that Reese, whom he had not seen since helping him ford the San Jacinto, was a man he could trust.

Now, the rumbling sound of moving wagons carrying cargo from the steamer's hold, echoed up from the landing where Reese was standing. With a wide black ledger braced in the crook of his arm, John Reese carefully made notations on page after page of the cargo list. Joshua watched the exacting merchant examine each barrel, crate, and sack which left the ship.

It was time to speak with him, Joshua decided. He laid aside his heavy ax. The bleak sky of morning was leaden and dreary, offering no promise of warmer hours ahead. Joshua hunched his shoulders against the growing wind, a full load of wood in his arms.

Backing through the cabin doorway, Joshua saw Unca Zack rising from his bed. Slowly, the old man pulled on his worn leather boots, measured his energy, then stood.

"Couldn't wait for me to git de wood?" he asked, knowing full well he was not able to carry it.

"No reason for you to get up so early," Joshua answered, "I've been up since dawn. They've started unloading the schooner at the landing. I think I'll go down and see what I can do."

"The *Yellow Stone's* back?" Unca Zack said, not remembering that Joshua told him it arrived last night.

"Yes, and John Reese, a merchant I knew in Anahuac, is on it. I'm gonna talk to him about leaving here."

"Be careful, Joshua. You think you kin trust him? Maybe it's best you stay close to de cabin."

"No," Joshua shot back, abruptly. "There's information I can get from him." He put down the wood, poked up the coals, and got a fire going in the hearth. "He can tell me what is going on in Harrisburg." Unca Zack was paying little attention, carefully measuring coffee into his old tin pot.

Joshua left the cabin, starting apprehensively down the brown grassy hill. I can trust Reese, he assured himself, he's the one man who's befriended me since the day I got to Texas. But the unfamiliar captain and the loud, cocky soldier on the *Yellow Stone* made Joshua uneasy.

The landing was nearly empty when Joshua arrived. Reese and a driver were examining a wagon. The side panel was loose, and they were trying to secure it when Joshua came into view.

"Seems like every time I see you, you need help with a wagon."

Reese looked up quickly, recognizing the voice before he saw the man.

"Joshua! I didn't know you were here." The merchant smiled broadly, "but I never know where you'll turn up. Don't stay in one place very long, do you? Thought you were still around Harrisburg."

"No," Joshua answered, wondering if Reese really didn't know he had been forced from town. "I left there more than two months ago . . . but not by choice," he baited.

The lean, bony merchant moved closer to the wagon as the black man fixing it began tying up the side.

"I heard rumors," was all Reese admitted.

"They were lies, Reese, lies to get me away from there."

"And so you ran," Reese said in a matter of fact tone.

"What choice did I have?"

"None, I'd imagine . . . especially when I heard who wanted you gone."

"You know who they are?"

"Every one," Reese said, looking directly at Joshua with no expression on his face. "They're men who came to Texas to make their fortunes on slave labor. I'm telling you, Joshua, they'll stop at nothing to slow the entrance of more free blacks into Texas."

"What about New Washington, and the colony there?" Joshua wanted to know. "How can land companies in the East continue encouraging free blacks to settle in Texas, when there's truly no peace for us here?"

"New Washington's doomed, mark my words, the settlement there will never prosper. Harrisburg's the town which is growing, it's becoming the center of trade. These men only need to settle the issue of war with Mexico for Harrisburg to boom . . . and they don't want somebody like you making trouble—swinging the blacks to the enemy's side."

"It's all lies, Reese. Listen." He leaned closer as he spoke. "I had nothing to do with that shooting at Columbia, nothing you hear me?"

"I believe you . . . I do," Reese sighed wearily. "But I can't convince others of that." He shoved his hands deeply into the pockets of his full broadcloth coat and walked silently away from his friend.

The wind from the river was gathering strength, blowing wet cold air across the hills, and Joshua remained silent, standing behind, unable to feel its chill. He was limp . . . tired. In his frustrated misery and overwhelming sense of helplessness, the reality of his situation became very clear: to look for any recourse other than flight was a dangerous and foolish idea. So, if Reese would take him to the mouth of the Brazos, he would sail southward to Refugio and join the Texas soldiers down there. This would put him far enough from Harrisburg, and close enough to Mexico, to allow him movement without much fear. He would fight for Texas there and prove he was not a traitor.

"Reese!" Joshua yelled at the retreating figure, his words swept away on a now fierce wind with cold rain drops falling in its path. "Reese!" he yelled again, "wait a minute, I've something to ask you."

The single dark image stopped walking, turning slowly to gaze through a gray sheet of water which suddenly fell between the two men. Reese pulled the large collar of his coat up around his face, shielding his eyes with one hand.

"What is it?" he screamed over the wind, watching Joshua run toward him, head down.

"When are you leaving?"

"Day after tomorrow."

"Take me with you," Joshua said, commanding, not asking for permission to board the merchant's ship. He wiped rain from his eyes and raised his jaw expectantly, as if daring this man to tell him no.

"How far?" Reese asked bluntly.

"To the mouth of the Brazos, where it meets the Gulf . . . then I can get a schooner to Refugio."

"Impossible," Reese said curtly, starting up the hill again, lowering his head against the blinding rain. "I'll be stopping at Fort Bend to pick up two passengers, and then at Columbia to deliver Groce's cotton. It's too dangerous, Joshua . . . for you . . . and for me."

This last statement rang too true for Joshua, setting the boundaries of Reese's involvement. With three short words he had cut to the core, why should this man risk his neck for a runaway? What would be in it for him? But Joshua refused to let it go so easily.

"It could be done, Reese," he said in a rush of words. He pulled his soaked jacket closer to his body, then walked ahead, the space between them widening as he took the path which led to the quarters.

"It could be done, you know," he yelled again. Reese made no evidence of hearing Joshua's plea. But the merchant stopped, looking darkly over at Joshua, as clear rivulets of water drained over his face. A rumble of thunder broke the silence between them before Reese yelled above the wind, "Probably so."

Joshua faced Reese squarely, calculating his position, and let the issue drop at those words. He would speak with the merchant again tomorrow and risk putting their fragile relationship to the test. Joshua was fixed on leaving San Felipe, and he had to persuade Reese to take him downstream.

Rain fell in thick sheets to the ground. It flooded the rutted path through the quarters and seeped under the sides of the shanties. Joshua passed Unca Zack's cabin, then Fayetta's, and followed the twisting trail out of the maze of shacks, up the hill to the barn.

✦·✦·✦··✦·✦·✦

It was long past dark when Joshua tired of raking and cleaning out stalls. He trudged through ankle-deep mud down the slippery hill to his cabin. He entered quietly and began to undress. The scratchy coarse cotton of his Indian robe felt good against his cold wet body. Joshua moved quietly in front of the fire, spreading his soaking wet clothing out to dry. He squeezed handfuls of water from his soft leather boots, and propped them against a chair to dry.

The winter storm had intensified to raging claps of thunder, which pierced the night with a roar, and Joshua was surprised that throughout it all, Unca Zack slept soundly in his bed. Water sloshed down the cabin roof, seeping in at the corners to create small muddy puddles and a dank humid smell.

Exhausted, Joshua fell half-asleep onto his narrow bed and tucked a fur rug around himself. He lay face down, thinking. Reese could not refuse him passage on the *Yellow Stone*, he just could not. Now that the decision had been made to leave, Joshua wanted to go as quickly as possible. Traveling by steamer would certainly be much faster than going by mule or on foot. He had one more day to convince Reese of this.

Pressing his forehead into the crook of his arm, Joshua tried to block out that nagging apprehension he had carried all day. He was going to Refugio. That was final. Either Reese would grant him passage, or he would go on alone. That was all settled, all behind him. But something else still weighed on his mind. He lay very still, staring into blackness, probing the source of this nagging. The tension in his body eased. The hint of a moan escaped his lips, and with a calm smooth release, he let his guard down. Emily's presence swept over him completely. Her face rose up exquisitely clear before him, etched by the shadows of the darkened room. His nostrils filled with the smell of her hair, that fragrant sweetness which had seemed to stay always with her. And now, for the first time since he had left New Washington, Joshua admitted to himself that he loved her. He ached to hold her in his arms once more, to crush her small body to his. But his hands were tied . . . what could he do? There was no way he could return to New Washington.

✦✦✦✦✦✦

Hard cornmeal cakes and coffee. That's all there was to eat. But in reality, it was more than enough for the two men who sat near the fire, hardly speaking, taking pleasure in their last hour together. They had both known times when there had been no coffee and hardly a piece of hardtack to sop with. Each knew hardships of the other's past and had little need to speak of them.

Unca Zack pushed himself up from his crudely built rocker and poked at the fire now blazing in the hearth. His long black fingers held a stick of wood firmly which he pointed at Joshua as he spoke.

"So, he's takin' you wid him, is he?"

"Yes, we'll be gone by daybreak."

"Don't see no reason for it, Joshua. You ain't gotta go no place. It don't make no difference ta Groce. You can stay here as long as you wants. Ain't he been protectin' you all dis time? Has you ever thought he'd turn you in? Naw, chile, naw." Unca Zack shook his head sadly from side to side. "What would be in dat for him?"

Joshua looked up from the rough surface of the table where he sat.

"It's not Groce I'm worried about. It's the men who will come here looking for me. I don't want to bring trouble to this man's place. I've pressed my luck here too far. Now that Reese will take me, I've gotta go."

"De more you runs, de more blame you takes wid you."

"I've been living in Texas a long time . . . living like I'm free . . . no trouble. Now all of a sudden, I'm forced to run again."

"Well, dere's a war a comin' an' in de minds o' dose men what fears you, you be a threat."

"I've never turned a black against a settler. Never said a word to any slave about joining with the Mexicans."

"Don't have to," Unca Zack interrupted. "De young black bucks sees you comin' an' goin' like you please. Dey hears de way you talks so proper, an' envies you your healin' trade. Deese men wants to be like you. An' dey thinks cause dey livin' outside de slave holdin' states dey can have de freedom you's got. Dey jus' don't know it can't be done." There was a vacant, faraway look on Unca Zack's face, as he too, dreamed of such freedom.

"So, the farmers blame me for the slaves who walk off their field. I've had nothing to do with it," Joshua protested.

"You's de easiest one ta blame. Dey ain't gonna take de blame demselves, now is dey?"

Joshua lowered his face into his hands, pushing tired fingers along his scalp, into his thick wavy hair.

"I'm branded as a traitor and a runaway . . . both lies." He spoke into his palms.

"But I heered you had cause ta leave your massa," Unca Zack's voice was gentle.

Joshua stood abruptly, almost knocking the frail old man to the floor. He clutched the edge of the table. "I never had a master. Never!" He shouted.

Unca Zack looked at the younger man sternly. Then, he went to his rocker, grasped the arm of the chair securely and lowered himself down. He stared into the crackling fire.

"You got free papers?" he asked Joshua.

"No," came his whispered reply.

"Well, de way I sees it, you always gonna have troubles. But, runnin' 'way every time dey comes 'round ain't no way ta set 'em aside."

Joshua sat down again at the small square table and pressed his hands together between his knees. Leaning forward in his chair, he spoke earnestly to Unca Zack.

"When the *Yellow Stone* sails, I'll be on it. And I'm not stopping until I get to Refugio. What else can I do? I'm not turning my back on Texas. I'm going to fight and help finish this matter of war. I'll come back here when this is behind us."

"More'n likely I ain't gonna be here ta see dat day."

Joshua watched the wrinkles in the old man's face soften, knowing he probably spoke the truth. By the time the war with Mexico is over, many men would have given up their places in this life.

Walking to the side of the bed, Joshua looked over what he was taking with him: a tight bedroll fitted inside his thick fur rug, his banjo tied with a leather strap on top of that, and his bag of ointments and herbs, which was never far away. He swung it all easily over his shoulder, standing awkwardly in the center of the room.

Saying good-bye was not easy. No words could come from either man which could possibly express his feelings, and the parting came down to a mumbled exchange of inadequate words and embraces.

Joshua slipped from the cabin in pre-dawn darkness, striding briskly and directly toward the river where the steamer rested veiled in fog. Glad for the added protection, he ascended the lowered gangplank quickly and crossed the aft deck's short open space in hurried, purposeful strides. Bales of ginned cotton leaned precariously against twin smoke stacks towering in black cylindrical shadows overhead. He maneuvered swiftly through a maze of coiled ropes. Waist high barrels clustered on the deck blocked his path, but feeling his way around them he soon entered a pitch black stairwell leading up to the gloomy deserted upper deck.

Splintered planks groaned and shifted underfoot. Each step creaked more shrilly than the last. And passing double sets of narrow windows lining the upper deck, Joshua crept silently sternward to a well-hidden berth.

The cubicle was dark, damp, smaller than a horse's stall. It was a musty smelling space which left no room for Joshua to stretch his long legs. He pulled the ill-fitting door toward him, leaving it slightly askew, then crouched with his back against the wall. He listened carefully, hearing nothing in the quiet of a slumbering dawn.

Finally, the light of the approaching day showed itself to him through the narrow slit between the door and the wall. Joshua watched undefined masses of shadows give way to distinct forms of crates, trunks and boxes. The sight unfolding before him now brought cast-off memories into focus. He had crouched like this before. Six years ago, while stowed away in a much larger hold than this, he had hugged his knees to his chest and counted and analyzed freight around him in order to keep himself calm.

For thirty days, in the bowels of the *Celeste*, he had stayed cramped in a corner, soaked with perspiration wrought by fear. And the guessing game he had played with the cargo, as the schooner had made its way from Memphis, to New Orleans, to Galveston Bay, had kept him quiet, kept him sane, and in the end, had saved his life.

He thought of Lucinda . . . the slim, fragile young slave girl who had kept Joshua alive while he had hidden in the damp hold of the *Celeste*. Lucinda had been traveling with her master and his wife on the same ship, also headed for Texas. When she had boarded at Vicksburg, Joshua had spied her as she walked past his hiding place. He had been struck by the pretty young girl's appearance and manner. And later that same day, when the opportunity had come for him to catch her eye, he had brazenly beckoned to Lucinda, motioning for her to slip away from the ship's rail, to come to him. Lucinda had not even flinched as she looked at the handsome young stowaway squeezed into that small dank hole under the bridge. At Joshua's motion, Lucinda had silently moved away, only to return with a tin cup of water and a piece of bread.

No words were spoken on that first meeting, and as Joshua had sipped the water and chewed the hard bread, he had instinctively known that this pretty young girl understood his plight and would not betray him. And as the days slipped by, the two of them found themselves meeting for a few moments each day. They began to whisper short messages to each other and to speak of their different but similar plights. Lucinda brought Joshua food and drink every evening, late, after her mistress had fallen asleep. And no one noticed her quick departures and returns. No one seemed to pay any attention to Lucinda's secret mission.

Lucinda was bright, almost joyful. She never complained . . . greeting Joshua with a smile. The slim slave girl seemed genuinely happy to be able to help Joshua, although she surely knew the severity of her punishment if she were caught. But fear was not something she had talked about. Joshua cautioned her daily to be very careful, to perhaps vary the time of evening when she came to him. But the young Lucinda brushed his fears aside, reassuring him that no one was watching her, that her mistress trusted her and often let her go her own way. Joshua was deeply concerned, but in reality, he did little to discourage her visits. He looked forward to her pretty face and recently had found himself thinking of her long after she had departed. And so, Lucinda protected the handsome stowaway, nourished him and helped him pass those long dark nights and days with a cherished bit of human contact, which had made the trip less painful.

Five days into the voyage, Joshua began to notice distinct changes in the way Lucinda treated him. She looked at him with adoration in her eyes. She took any opportunity to brush her hand over his. And she would stay at his side so late into the night, that Joshua would have to urge her to leave. He had not wanted this girl to fall in love with him. These kinds of emotions had no place in the type of lives they had to live. He could not return to Lucinda the same type of feelings she had for him. Finally, Joshua had confronted her, trying to dissuade her girlish impressions of love, to convince her that although he was extremely grateful for all she had done for him, there was no reason for her to believe that his feelings ran deeper than gratitude.

Ten days into the voyage, Joshua's instinctive fears had turned into a nightmare of reality which haunted him to this very day. Lucinda was caught stealing. She had taken a large piece of dried beef from the mistress' food storage trunk. The beating which she suffered had been so severe that Joshua had been able to hear the crack of the leather strap as it was brought down across Lucinda's back over and over again. He had listened from his hiding place under the bridge to her high thin screams, and had winced in his own pain at the sound of each blow. After the beating, Lucinda had been left in a pool of her own blood with hands bound, for two days.

The young slave girl did not come again to Joshua's hiding place. She never arrived to give him comfort and drink, for she had died in her master's cabin, never regaining consciousness, and her body had been tossed overboard.

Since that harrowing time six years ago, Joshua had been trying to make some sense of Lucinda's death. But the memories of this naive, caring young girl, who had not lived to make it to Texas, caused him great shame to this day. Joshua had been helpless to stop Lucinda's fate. Perhaps he had not done enough to keep her from coming to him. But one thing he knew, when he had left the *Celeste*, he carried a permanent wound in his heart. Lucinda's misguided love and his own inability to give her anything in return, had left him with a hollow feeling he knew he would live with for the rest of his life.

✦-✦-✦--✦-✦-✦

For Joshua, then approaching nineteen, running away had been a final act of desperation. Leaving his mother, Sepulpa, crying softly into her woven blanket as she had chanted a stream of prayers in a tongue still foreign to him, had nearly broken his heart. Her round dark eyes had glistened with fright, but she had said nothing as she kissed him good-bye. She knew her son's chances of successfully escaping the plantation were slim. And knowing this, she had preferred that Joshua run away than grow old in the bondage of an unjust slavery thrust upon the two of them when Doctor Eli Kilgore had died.

Shifting his weight on the hard plank flooring, folding his legs tightly together, Joshua allowed himself to recall those days of growing up in the doctor's huge pillared house and his escape to Texas.

Joshua's mother had been Doctor Eli's cook. As a free Indian woman earning her keep, she had passed her days at the doctor's wide-bricked hearth, stirring pots in the fire for hours on end. She had even been given two slave girls to help her. And the three of them ground corn, dried herbs, and gathered baskets of vegetables from the rich sunny garden which lay at the back of the house.

Sepulpa's lean bronze son had the run of the place. He had grown up knowing the privilege of freedom, childishly ignorant of his tenuous stature and happy to roam the streets of Memphis, recognized as the boy who lived with the doctor. No one ever spoke of the boy's father, not even his mother. And Joshua never thought to, or dared to bring up the subject. He had contented himself with playing among the thick blooming wisteria bordering the three story mansion. He had chased rabbits and squirrels across the wide lawns, routing them from sculpted hedges which banked against the spiked iron fence. But what Joshua remembered more vividly than anything about those days, was the odd smelling room where Doctor Eli Kilgore had treated his patients.

The room had been dark with polished mahogany and richly patterned oriental rugs. At one end, the doctor's huge desk was positioned directly in front of ceiling high glass cases which were bursting with leather bound books. And it was under a low hanging shelf that Joshua had sat on many occasions, watching the doctor treat his patients.

Eli Kilgore had never complained about the young boy's presence. He had let him come and go as he wished, occasionally even asking Joshua to hand him an instrument or a book from his desk. And as the doctor's eyesight had begun to fail, he had turned to young Joshua with more frequency. It was not long before Joshua had become the old man's eyes, mixing and measuring vials of potions, grinding powders, and crushing herbs. By the time Joshua was sixteen, he had been able to apply a poultice, set a broken limb, deliver a baby, or revive the unconscious. And Sepulpa had stood by in proud silence. She had seen her son's intense curiosity and quickness to learn come to fruition under Doctor Kilgore's guidance.

The protective shelter of the doctor's home had more than fulfilled Sepulpa's search for a secure place for herself and her son. Both had begun to believe that their way of life was unchallenged.

But this calm secure haven, this fount of learning had crumbled overnight when Eli Kilgore had died. And in a very short time,

Joshua and his mother had become the chattel of Livingston Kilgore.

Within a week, the doctor's son sold the house in Memphis. Within two weeks, Joshua and Sepulpa were carted away to a tobacco farm where extra hands were needed. Joshua protested fiercely. He foolishly insisted he and his mother were free. But more than once, Livingston Kilgore had beaten him into silence, and Joshua had stopped talking altogether. But his anger seethed like coals under ashes, a burning reminder of this injustice.

Sepulpa understood her son's rage, a rage so violent it bordered on madness. It had kept him planning and plotting some means of escape, a way to leave their filthy hovel. She understood this rage well enough to tell him after his second aborted escape, that she had been secretly hoping the patrollers would bring back his body if they had to bring him back at all.

But, they had brought him back alive, tied him to a maple tree in the very center of the quarters, and whipped him three times in one day. The other slaves, Sepulpa included, had been forced to witness, standing in the sun from morning to dusk, no food, no water, only Joshua to watch.

And when the sinewy overseer finally cut the young man down, everyone felt sure he had learned his lesson and would certainly stay put. They were wrong. For as soon as the gashes on his back healed, Joshua left for the third time, taking refuge on the *Celeste*, successfully entering the Gulf of Mexico.

Now, Joshua huddled in darkness. Loud footsteps crossed the deck below. He tensed in the narrow berth as the captain barked orders to the crew.

"Stow those barrels on the aft deck, there's no more room over here," a curt New England accent clipped his words. "Move it. Move it further on back."

The thunderous rumbling of rolling barrels vibrated the ship and Joshua leaned back, curving into his hole, hoping no one was coming up. He cradled his head against raised knees. He closed his eyes and waited until a gentle rocking and the hissing of steam told him they were at last underway.

A pale sun was breaking through sheets of gray clouds. More light bathed the upper deck. Joshua could see through the crack there were two wooden crates stacked very near the door. They were constructed of freshly hewn slats, crudely nailed together. Uneven letters in smeared black paint read, Colonel James Morgan, New Washington, Galveston Bay.

Supplies for the colony. A hollow ache pulled at his insides. Cargo for New Washington . . . perhaps something Emily would use in the colonel's house. Emily. He swallowed hard. His yellow rose . . . he wished he could see her just one more time, if only to tell her good-bye. Desolate and lonely, hunted and despised, he wanted the touch of her warm flesh against his. He wanted the strength he knew she could give. But, in sad acceptance of the danger he was in, he knew Emily was lost to him forever. There was no future for them.

The grinding thud of boots in the stairwell echoed louder with each step that brought the intruder closer. Joshua held his breath. He leaned forward, cautiously peering through the crack in the door. Searching the hazy space, he focused on the spot where the stairs opened onto the upper deck. From his cramped hiding place, he stared. First, the jagged silhouette of a tilted hat emerged, followed by broad shoulders hung with ammunition. Joshua recoiled sharply as the gleam of a bayonet caught the light.

Chapter Nine

Fever raged on Galveston Bay. Some virulent force crept un-
expected and uninvited into the settlers' homes. Blistering the
tongues of frontier children, it suffocated them as they slept, and
viciously racked the bodies of the elders, leaving them like
skeletons in their beds. And no one knew what to do to stop it. No
one had a cure for this deadly plague now thrust on New
Washington in the midst of preparing for war.

A calm dread prevailed at Orange Grove. Celia Morgan lay
spent and feverish in her gleaming four poster bed. Her breathing
came in laborious gasps. Her hair lay witch-like about the pillow,
and the youthful strength, which had shone from her face, had
drained away in the last five days.

Emily smoothed white cotton sheets neatly over Celia's thin
shoulders, then laid her hand against the sleeping woman's
forehead. It was still very hot. Taking her hand away, Emily
frowned, weary and puzzled that Celia's condition remained
unchanged. Dipping a wad of cloth into a basin of cool water,
Emily gently wiped her mistress' temples, cheeks and forehead.
Moving in slow motion, not fully aware of her actions, Emily
ministered to Celia's needs, in an effort to make her more
comfortable. She could do no more.

A dull ache in the small of her back inched its way into her
shoulders and neck, pressing her body with its strength-sapping
presence. Her eyes watered thinly from lack of sleep, as the fifth
day of this gruesome vigil began to take its toll.

Emily shifted slightly in her chair, pulling it closer to the side of
the bed. She leaned forward over Celia Morgan and listened to her
breathing. It continued to come in rasping gasps as if it would stop
at any moment. Emily sighed deeply as she lifted the cloth from the

sleeping woman's face to wet it again in the basin. Absently, she squeezed it tightly and drops of water splashed in dark stains across the front of her blue wool dress. Paying little attention, Emily pulled her frayed shawl more securely around her arms. The room was cold. No fire burned in the small sleeping area which was raised above the living quarters. Its eastward window was open, catching the sun. Now the room was fully lit, shining with winter light, the distant sounds of the waking plantation came in muted tones through the window.

Emily walked over to look out. She stretched to relieve the ache in her back, and pushed aside white lace curtains which filtered uneven light. She could see out over the land, beyond the ring of oaks bordering the main house. There were soldiers camped all over the grounds. Smoldering fires dotted grassy areas. Men huddled in groups, talking, smoking, cleaning their rifles. Her gaze went on, past the quarters where no one lingered, on to the barns and stables, where she could see Sam trying to harness an ox.

The huge ornery animal refused to stand still as Sam tugged and yanked at leather straps, making sure the fittings were secure. Emily could tell he was cursing the silent gray beast under his breath. When he finally had the animal hitched to the wagon, Emily saw James Morgan approach abruptly, gesturing to Sam.

Emily could not hear what the two men said, but from their expressions and movements, she guessed they talked of a journey. It appeared that Morgan wanted Sam to take the wagon someplace.

"Miss Celia any better?" Hanna's loud whisper came to Emily from the doorway. She turned.

"No, no change," she answered, turning to take a pile of fresh linen from Hanna. "She's still hot . . . hasn't opened her eyes since late yesterday."

Hanna shook her head and came closer to the bed. "She's jus' wastin' away, lyin' dere like dat. Massa Morgan's powerful worried 'bout her."

"I know," Emily said, placing the clean cloths on a low oak chest. "I saw Sam hitching the wagon. Is he going to Harrisburg?"

"Naw, not Harrisburg. I heered dem talkin' in de yard. Dere's a sloop tied up at Fort Bend. Got some cotton an' some sugar brought down from up de Brazos. Massa Morgan sendin' Sam out to pick it up."

"Oh," Emily feigned interest. She masked the disappointment in her voice. She had been hoping Sam was going to Harrisburg and might get some news about Joshua.

The nervous anxiety she felt for Joshua had faded to a desperate longing to see him once more. If not see him, then at least to hear of his safety . . . to know what had become of him. This was all she hoped for as the days slipped by. She needed to know he was still alive. Emily found strength in the thought that if Joshua were alive, he would return to her.

Did he get Nathan's warning, she wondered. Had he left New Washington for good? These questions came to her during the day and throughout the night, making life without knowing very difficult. She thought of Joshua constantly, reliving their last tender moments together, remembering the gentle way he had touched her. She convinced herself that his passion was equal to hers. There was no time for doubt. She shoved it aside, holding fast to her belief that he would return.

Life in the colonies was harsh and primitive. The Morgans treated Emily fairly enough, but living in the Texas frontier was lonely and dangerous. Joshua's presence in her life had made it more tolerable, but now, he was gone. It upset her that she knew nothing of his decision to leave. He had sent no word or message to her. This life without him was no life at all, but she contented herself with waiting.

Hanna took her place at Celia Morgan's side. With a light touch, she carefully arranged ashen strands of hair about Celia's drawn face. Hanna's small brown hands worked nimbly, smoothing dry tresses into place.

"Iffen dis fever spreads to de soldiers, us gonna need a heap o' cloth to tend dem an' more food dan us got on de place right now." She continued to stroke the sleeping woman's hair. "Don't know how Massa Morgan thinks us can keep on fixin' for deese soldiers widhout no help. An' now wid de missus sick near to dyin', ain't nobody to do all dis work 'cept us. I don't mind doin' for de missus an' de folks what lives here, but deese nasty soldiers, come here from all 'round . . . now dey don't know how to act." Hanna looked directly into Emily's face and pursed her lips. She was angry. "I knows I's tired o' pushin' 'em out o' my kitchen, an' Sam says iffen one more o' dem comes grabbin' at me . . . well, he gonna go right crazy an' kill him."

"They'll move on," Emily said. "Just do like I do and stay out of their way." She wiped her brow with her fingertips, easing the creases brought on by so little sleep. She understood exactly what Hanna meant. The last two months had brought such large numbers of soldiers to Orange Grove that it was becoming more and more difficult to keep enough food prepared to feed all of them.

"You stay with the misses for a while, Hanna. I'll get some fresh water."

"I'd rather be up here, 'way from all dose noisy soldiers. Don't hurry yourself none to git back. I's fine right here. 'Sides, you needs to git some rest. Go on now, git some rest. I's jus' gonna sit here by Miss Celia, poor lady, lookin' so tired an' wasted out." Hanna peered at the still figure on the bed and shook her head slowly.

"I can't rest now," Emily said, pausing at the doorway. "There's too much to do."

"Suit yourself," Hanna replied, "I's content to sit right here." She squeezed water from a fresh cloth and started bathing Celia Morgan's pale, lined face.

It was difficult backing down the narrow ladder, Emily pushed tired stiff legs awkwardly beneath her. She headed through the empty lower rooms to the wide door separating the house from the kitchen area. She stopped, looking out cautiously. A roguish group of soldiers gathered between the buildings. They were standing around in coon skin caps and deer skin jackets, their whiskered faces haggard and thin. They were trading tales of skirmishes with Indians and Mexicans. They argued, cursed, and drew on their pipes.

These were the men of the Texas Navy, summoned by Colonel James Morgan to gather at Orange Grove to prepare a plan of defense before moving on to Galveston Island. Newcomers to the territory, some from as far away as Georgia and Kentucky, listened to the long time settlers speak of Santa Anna and his advancing forces. With six thousand men in three huge columns, the Mexican general's troops outnumbered the Texans many times over. Nonetheless, all those waiting at Orange Grove were spoiling for the fight.

Emily thought about all there was to be done. There was a pile of jackets, pants, and blankets to be washed and mended, waiting for her in the shed. There was meat to be dried, soap to be made, and grain to be ground into flour. And, in the middle of all this preparation for war, she had to care for Miss Celia.

Lowering her lids to form half-closed eyes, Emily bit the inside of her lip. She dreaded walking through this tangle of men, but there was no other way to cross to the kitchen. Pressing the shallow basin of dirty water against her ribs, she stepped outside and the pungent odor of burning wood immediately filled her head.

The air was cold and damp. Blankets spread to dry in the pale winter sun lay like torn bits of cloth on the grass. Mounds of scrap metal were piled all around, ready to be melted into bullets. The slaves who tended their master's horses were busy pouring feed into troughs and shoeing the animals. Emily walked straight ahead, without looking up, and passed into the throng of soldiers.

"Hey, gal, were you goin'?"

Emily shifted her lowered eyes sharply, taking in a young man squatting at her feet. She stopped, made no response, then continued on as the hem of her dress brushed the soldier's shoulder. He reclined on one arm, stretching out in her path and demanded once more, "I asked you where you was headed, gal." His voice was taunting, carrying the suggestion of laughter.

Still, Emily kept her eyes lowered. She stared right through the man as if he were gone, and pressed her lips tautly into silence. One hand gripped the rim of the water basin, the other formed a fist at her side, and she stood there rigidly, waiting and watching. She was determined to say nothing to provoke him.

The man ran his tongue across full, coarse lips and stretched more fully to block her way. Emily waited, ramrod straight, while other men turned their attention on her. She just stood there, frozen in anger and fright, never lifting her eyes an inch. She could tell from the shadows which moved on the ground that others came forward to watch.

"You insolent nigger bitch," the soldier growled, his tone more accusing than angry. "You could be branded for not answerin' me . . . or lashed with my whip. You know that?" His voice rose, he leaned up in her path. His eyes were cold, vacant glints of blue. Emily saw he was testing her, pushing her silence to the limit. She pulled her full lower lip between her teeth and stood as if mute, looking down at him.

Suddenly, the soldier reached toward her. She felt his hand close painfully tight around her ankle. Without even thinking, she yanked it free, never taking her gaze from his face. His eyes soon lost their sultry taunt, flaming wild and open in surprise. He lunged like a panther seizing its prey, catching the calf of her leg.

Emily braced herself as he caressed her leg. His cold dry hand rose up past her knee to touch the soft flesh of her thigh. She was hollow, drained, sickened at his touch, and she wanted to spit into his upturned face. Then, with a twist of her wrist, the only movement she made, Emily drained the water basin into those eyes which gleamed up at her.

"Damn you, bitch!" He let go of her leg. "Damn you!" he yelled again, wiping water from his eyes. As soon as she was free, Emily ran the short distance into the kitchen. She could hear, as if through a tunnel, the roaring laughter of men who had been watching. She bolted the heavy door behind her.

A wave of nausea choked her, gagged her, crowded her throat as if to stop her breathing. She sagged against the rough pine door, eyes closed, heart racing so fiercely it trembled the front of her dress. The men outside continued their laughing, scoffing teasing in loud raucous peals.

"That one shore 'nuf got away, Robbie."

The soldier said nothing.

"Quicker'n a jackrabbit," another added.

"A pretty little thing," a low voice injected.

The soldier, Robbie, now spoke, as if the whole matter were a joke. "Don't mean nothin'," he said, "ain't worth the trouble o' chasin'."

Emily moved from the door to stand near the fire. She warmed her shaking body before the flames. Fair game, that's what I am, she thought. Like a squirrel or a rabbit, I can be captured, taken.

Frontier life had shown Emily its cruelest side since her arrival, testing her strength to survive over and over. She had found herself pitted against forces of nature and actions of men which were outside any previous experiences she had ever known in New York. Certainly, the city had its dangers, but none had been as immediately threatening as those which existed in Texas. She lived now in a constant state of uneasiness, never sure what dangers waited within the fragile security she struggled to maintain at Orange Grove.

Realizing she still clutched the water basin against her side, she loosened her grip and placed the shallow tin pan on the table. So much needed to be done. She moved to the storage room to take out corn which had to be ground. As she bent to fit the large iron key into the lock, a rattling sound at the bolted door stopped her. She turned quickly. The sound was coming from the outside door. It rattled again. Then, there was pounding and finally a voice came through it.

"Emily, you in dere? It's Sam, open de door."

She listened carefully. It was Sam all right. She rushed to push back the bolt.

"What's wrong wid you? Why de door all bolted up?" he asked. "De massa sent me to talk wid you," he told her, entering the room.

Respectfully, Sam removed his torn cloth cap from his wooly head and wiped his face on his sleeve. He looked around behind him.

"Now, where'd she go?" he said, turning back to the door, looking out from side to side. "Dere you are. Git on in here." He gestured rapidly as he spoke. And a thin young girl, not older than five, stepped shyly through the door. She was dirty, barely clothed. Her mud streaked legs stuck thinly out of a tow sack shift, and there were layers of rags bound around each foot, taking the place of shoes. The child's face was thin and peaked, not sad, just gauntly small, and her round black eyes were like pieces of jet glinting darkly up at Emily.

"Dis here be Ria," Sam said. He touched the girl's shoulder. "She be de chile o' Lucindy Timons, who died from de fever jus' yestiday."

Emily said nothing. She let her breath drain out slowly and looked closer at the child.

"Lucindy was a free woman," Sam went on, "an' dis chile here be free, too. An' Massa Morgan wants her sent down to Columbia where she got some kinfolk to care for her."

"What do you want me to do?" Emily asked.

"Well, Morgan says to me, 'Sam, get Emily to clean her up a bit, den, de two o' you take de wagon an' carry dis gal out to Fort Bend. Dere's a steamer tied up dere now, an' dey kin carry Ria to Columbia.' So, I's leavin' her here wid you. She ain't got no more'n what's on her back. De wagon be leavin' by noon. I be waitin' for ya'll down by de stables when you's ready to move out."

Sam looked at the girl once more, then awkwardly slipped out the door. Emily and Ria stood together, watching each other curiously.

✦·✦·✦··✦·✦·✦

The wagon was large with a long flat bed enclosed with high boarded sides. The wheels stood taller than Emily herself, dwarfing Ria in their shadow. Emily helped the child into the back, handing her a soft bundle of extra clothing and a little food. Ria crawled eagerly to the back of the wagon, squirming childishly into a pile of hay and carefully examined her new clothing again. She touched the red cotton dress she was wearing. Then, she smiled over at Emily as she ran a small finger over the hard surface of her new leather shoes. They were brogans, shapeless and ill-fitting, but the first pair she had ever had. To Ria, they were wonderful. She sat with her legs stretched out directly in front, toes pointed up.

Emily latched the back panel of the wagon in place. Then, she climbed up in front beside Sam. He quickly slapped the reins against the oxen and started the wagon rolling. It rattled and groaned over the uneven trail as Sam clucked loudly to keep the slow moving animals plodding along. Soon, they left the busy plantation behind and entered the wild grassy plains.

The road to Fort Bend was well traveled, distinct and open, though broken occasionally by small groves of trees. The faint winter sun which had shown itself that morning now disappeared behind an overcast sky. Emily sat quietly in thought, glad that no wind stirred the cold damp air.

She had never been this far from the Bay and was anxious to see what lay beyond it. James Morgan had given Sam explicit instructions: "Deliver the girl to the captain of the sloop, take on what cargo was on board for the colony, and return the next day to New Washington." Sam carried two letters of passage, one for himself and Emily, the other for Ria to travel downstream.

They rolled through acres of prairie grass, knowing they could not reach the Brazos before dark, but wanting to go as far as possible while the light of day still held. Timber lining the wagon path stood mottled gray and green. The evergreens, lush and colorful, contrasted with barren branches of willow and oak. A profusion of brambles and twisted vines lay flush with the trail, and the sound of scurrying forest animals could be heard over the grind of the wagon. At a narrow point, after rounding a curve, Sam brought the wagon to an abrupt halt. A herd of more than twenty deer bounded across the trail. Ria stood in the back of the wagon, her dark eyes level with its high sides. She watched the deer silently, her curious eyes round and shining.

Hours passed, and as the dim gray light of evening faded into darkness, Sam walked ahead of the wagon shining a lantern while Emily took the reins. A death-like stillness surrounded the travelers. They pressed on in the blackness, cautiously entering the still darker path ahead.

Ria had wearied of watching the monotonous landscape and had fallen asleep in the hay. Emily thought about the tiny girl, curled tightly under a scrap of blanket, her soft bundle under her head. She seemed to be so brave, considering all she had been through. Or, maybe it was her innocent acceptance of Emily as her protector.

Without any resistance, Ria had allowed Emily to bathe her in a wide tin tub. Emily had scrubbed the girl, washed her hair and then, plaited it neatly in several rows. A flash of surprise had sparked Ria's expression when Emily had pulled a red cotton dress over her freshly done hair. Ria had wiped a small hand down the skirt of the dress, murmuring one of the few words Emily had heard her speak.

"Purdy. Real purdy," she had said, fingering the material gently. And then Emily had motioned the girl to sit down and let her tie on her new shoes. Ria had not liked them at first. She had walked back and forth in Emily's cabin, testing and flexing the stiff, heavy shoes. Soon it was time to leave, and Emily had gathered a few things together, tied them in a bundle, and had joined Sam at the wagon.

Now, the oxen stopped on their own. Sam walked back to the side of the wagon. His lantern shone like a pinpoint of light in the darkness of the prairie. He stood looking up, a yellow glow encircling his face as he spoke. "We'd best stop here."

"Why here, Sam?"

"We's pretty near de river. I kin smell it. Can't git too close whilst it's dark. It's best we sleep right here in de wagon an' go up to de sloop in de mornin'."

Emily understood. It was far too dangerous for three blacks, traveling alone to approach a strange ship in the dark. So, Emily slid over and let Sam climb up to maneuver the oxen off the path.

They settled easily into a small stand of trees, protected from the trail and the shore. Emily got in the back with Ria, though Sam insisted on staying with the oxen.

"I don't need much sleep," he protested. "I kin do widout. I'd rather sit out here wid de animals an' jus' wait for de mornin' light. Now, you go on an' git you some rest," he told Emily.

His words reminded her of Hanna's advice. Was it only this morning she had said the same thing? The day had been long, exhausting. Emily felt the full weight of it all as she lay her head down next to Ria's. Her eyes followed the intricate patterns of shadows playing over the clouds, and a wolf, not far in the distance, sent a mournful cry to the sky.

Chapter Ten

The glint of reflected steel flashed menacingly at Joshua, and shrinking into protected shadows, he waited, observing the intruder. With echoing thuds of finality, the soldier's boots hit the steps, and eerie vibrations like the thunder of cannon spread shock-like throughout the ship.

A profile emerged in the gloomy half light to reveal the scraggly silhouette of a bearded man whose cowhide hat was perched at a rakish tilt. Moving with the taut, calculated steps of a hunter, the soldier came out of the pitch black stairwell. He stood in the dimly cast haze of dawn peering around, searching.

Now coming fully onto the upper deck, the soldier paced heavily forward, then turned around. His ghostly image materialized in Joshua's line of vision. Then, throwing up his hairy chin, he roared in a voice which cut through the haze and stung Joshua right in the face, "Kinney . . . I know you're up here . . . show yourself to me."

Joshua remained silent, watching the stout, muscular soldier advance. The shimmering bayonet at the end of his rifle was lowered and pointed, leading the way.

"Show yourself," the soldier roared again. "I ain't got no patience for huntin' you out."

Joshua's breath came in shallow gasps. The inevitable confrontation had come. And with a stealthy step, as if stalking the soldier, Joshua slid from the darkness, creeping in feline movements, into the light from the narrow windows. He straightened slowly to the full length of his height.

The two men stood facing each other, the hunter and the hunted, glaring through distrustful silence broken only by the swishing of the Brazos River fanning out behind the steamer. The vessel rocked forward on the rushing water as the captain barked orders down below.

With a halo of lightening shadows behind his pallid face, the soldier appeared wildly driven, determined to hunt Joshua down. Breaking out in a sneering narrow grin, his lips curved away from uneven teeth and he began to advance more rapidly toward Joshua. The steel blue blade at the end of his rifle came closer and closer, finally resting sharply in the middle of Joshua's chest. The soldier pressed it, twisting and digging to rip away the coarse brown cloth of Joshua's loose fitting shirt. And then with a painful jagged sweep, the knife drew blood the length of Joshua's smooth bronze chest.

Joshua leaned sharply back as the blade pulled away. A deadly cold grimace was etched across his face, and as he pressed his lips together, his hands clawed deeply into his own thighs.

"I ain't got no use for runaways," the soldier stated, his voice low and hoarse. Moving the bayonet up, he gouged it deeply under Joshua's chin. "If I had my way, I'd run this knife clean through your black throat and sell your hide for the bounty."

Joshua stood firm. Perspiring, but not moving a muscle. Not even blinking his eyes. With his chin pushed upward by the press of the blade, he had to lower his eyes narrowly to see this soldier. And in his fright, he slowly began to calculate this man's position among those who commanded this ship . . . he weighed the power of the soldier's threat.

"Reese is a fool," the soldier went on, putting more weight on the blade so that it nearly cut off Joshua's breathing. "He's a weak, foolish man with abolitionist ideas . . . ain't no place for him out here in Texas. Ain't no place for your kind neither."

The soldier leaned on Joshua with all his weight, forcing him backwards until Joshua fell down with the knife still pressed sharply into his flesh. He lay there glaring pure hatred at the soldier who boldly continued his threat.

"I ain't got no say 'bout who the captain carries, but as soon as we touch shore . . . you're mine. Don't git no crazy ideas 'bout jumping ship, 'cause I'll shoot you before you can ever reach land, then I'll make sure I run this blade right through your black heart."

The soldier grunted, then roughly swinging his rifle away, anchored it securely over his shoulder. Giving Joshua one last piercing scowl, he turned to descend the damp wooden stairs.

In the narrow space where he had fallen, Joshua arched his back, taking deep gasping breaths, blowing in and out, slower and slower, struggling to gain control of his anger. The scream of protest held captive within churned convulsively with no manner of escape, as tears of humiliation slid from his eyes. Slumping down hard against the clammy rough boards, he felt a sticky wetness stream down his chest onto the waist of his breeches.

It was suddenly very hot in that place, smothering, still, as if in a tomb. His lungs pulled deeply but no air rushed in, his mouth opened to cry but no sound came forth. Then, wrenching himself from that cavernous hole, he crossed the deck in three deep strides and stopped at a tall open window. Cool damp air bathed his angered flesh, sweeping over him like a healing balm. It lessened the frustration which now made him tremble . . . calming him, soothing him, quieting his fury.

Joshua leaned into the mist, not really seeing anything, his face raised to the sky as if praying for whatever strength would be needed to survive this journey down the Brazos. For he had no intentions of quitting this voyage. He would make it, somehow, to the Gulf of Mexico. He would conquer this danger, he assured himself; he had been in worse situations than this.

Danger . . . a sulking dark shadow which lengthened and shortened, never retreated far from Joshua's life. Though sometimes, it created the false illusion of disappearing into his past. And, at times like those, when he felt at ease, Joshua basked in that peaceful space without worry, remaining on guard, but much less suspicious of every man who crossed his path.

Joshua thought back to six months ago when he had been earning and keeping the settlers' respect, working side by side in the colonies with them. And until that uprising in Columbia last fall, he had been welcome wherever he had gone. But now, to them, he was a threat—a treasonous, dangerous man, capable of inspiring a feared slave revolt. Though their fears had no basis at all, the men, women, and even the children, spoke in horrified whispers that such a thing could happen in Texas. But the fact remained, they had convinced themselves of this danger.

Joshua passed the next two days in a blurry shift from semi-dark to blackness. He ate hard dry bread and pieces of salted beef which he pulled sparingly from his bedroll. Reese had brought him a tin pot of water, never speaking of the incident with the soldier. No one entered the deck again as Joshua waited for the *Yellow Stone* to arrive at the landing at Fort Bend.

On the morning of the third day of travel, the steamer slowed and the engines died. The shallow draft vessel cut easily through the muddy water as the captain rushed around below. He bellowed commands to the deck hands to safely maneuver his ship to the landing. Joshua crept to a window and looked out.

A light rain had begun to fall, as if the fog which rose from the river now returned in a drizzle to the land. The shoreline, banked with thick lush foliage, quivered with the noisy chirping of hundreds of sparrows and joined with the loud croak of bullfrogs. Carved out of this thicket, like a dusty brown scallop, was a cleared semicircle flush against the shore.

In this area, two smartly dressed women wearing wide striped skirts and deep broad bonnets stood waiting amid trunks and satchels. A short fat gentleman, smoking a very long cigar, hailed to the captain of the *Yellow Stone*. The man's blue frock coat was vivid in the rain as he paced back and forth along the shore. His knee high boots were splashed with mud, spotting their shiny black surface.

As the steamer came closer, the women drew closer to one another, finally embracing in relief and excitement that the vessel had arrived at last. Their gentleman companion climbed down the muddy bank and caught a rope thrown ashore by the captain.

Within minutes, the gangplank, a crudely built footbridge of slatted wood, stretched the short distance from the ship to land. The women descended the slippery bank first, their hems dragging through mud despite attempts to lift the heavy fabric aloft as they stepped carefully toward the steamer. Each carried a large cloth satchel draped with paisley scarves and fringed shawls. They shook their bonneted heads in dismay. Traveling through frontier Texas was a discomforting challenge at best.

Joshua leaned into the shadows at the window's edge, afraid the women might spot him. He watched them cautiously board the *Yellow Stone*, then turn and wave good-bye to the gentleman who stayed behind on shore. As Joshua watched the balding man step back from the landing, three tiny figures emerged from the thicket. A man, a woman, and a thin small child. He strained to see better.

The woman's face caught his eye, drew him in with a riveting pull that took all breath from his body.

It was Emily, his fragile, his lovely Emily.

A warm flush came over him and his eyes flicked closed for a moment. Joshua laid his head back against the wall, away from the window. Why was she here? Why with Sam? And who was that little girl? His breath drained out in long slow streams, then he turned to look down at the gangplank again.

The little girl walked in front of Emily. Her bony shoulders were loosely covered with a ragged square of blue wool. She thumped her heavy boots against the footbridge, delighting in the sounds she could make. Emily trailed directly behind, one hand placed lightly on the child's shoulder, the other lifting her skirt from the dirt. She carried herself stiffly, almost regally, her jaw thrust forward. Her long hair was pulled loosely away from her pale smooth face. Joshua watched her delicate slim frame, which belied the strength within, pass onto the *Yellow Stone* and out of his view. Sam followed them, hat in his hand, a nervous set to his face.

"What business do you have here?" The captain's loud voice rose in the stairwell. Joshua dropped to his knees and crept to the opening.

"We's got dis chile here . . . " Sam started.

"I'll speak to him, Sam," Emily interrupted. Her clear oval tones washed over Joshua like warm soft waves of water. He clenched his fists in anxiety.

"I have papers here from James Morgan at Orange Grove," Emily continued. "This girl was recently orphaned. The fever took her mother. She's free . . . here are her papers . . . and has relatives at the Varner plantation near Columbia. My employer, James Morgan, asks that you take her downstream and see she's delivered to the Varner place."

"Let me see those papers," the captain said.

John Reese's voice now entered the conversation. "Didn't I take you out to the Morgan place last fall?" he asked Emily.

She looked around to see the man who had brought her to Orange Grove and was grateful for a familiar face, remembering John Reese to be a kind man.

"Yes," she answered him. "It was September, last year."

"It's all right, Roberts," John Reese told the captain. "This girl is from Morgan's place, she's a house nigger over there."

The captain did not answer.

"Let's take the child and get moving," Reese said, "no reason to doubt those papers."

"Put her on the upper deck," the captain finally spoke in clipped annoyed tones. "Tell her to stay put . . . outta my way. I don't need no pickyninnies underfoot." Captain Roberts walked away and Joshua heard Emily caution Ria.

"Go on up, Ria. Don't go wandering around . . . stay put until you get to Columbia. Don't worry, you'll be all right. Go on now."

There was silence. Then, the sound of Ria's footsteps on the stairs. Joshua quietly slid back into shadows, flattening himself against the wall. Ria came up, turned away from him and quickly skipped to the opposite end of the deck where she could look out over the water.

Joshua sat in agony, knowing Emily was so close, knowing there was no way for him to speak to her. His heart was so heavy it seemed not to beat. Soon she would be gone.

He moved to the window, anxious to get a glimpse of her as she returned to shore. Seeing her now was more than he had ever hoped for, and these last glimpses of her would have to last him for a long time . . . maybe forever.

"What's Morgan's high and mighty free niggers doin' board this ship?" In a nasty sting, the soldier's voice came up the stairwell to Joshua.

Emily turned. It was Clabe. Her eyes grew dark with anger. She turned to leave the ship.

"Don't be in such a hurry, Missy," Clabe said, catching hold of Emily's arm. "Might jus' take you down river with me." He laughed and squeezed her flesh until Emily winced.

He laughed.

"Let me go," Emily said firmly. He had no right to detain her.

He twisted his hand around her skin more tightly.

"You still walkin' around like you're better'n any other nigger wench in these parts. Well, I aim to show you you're not."

"Let me go," Emily yelled now, trying to break away. She pulled from Clabe, but he only placed a second hand on her other arm. He spit on the deck. "I'll let you go when I'm good an' ready." He yanked her toward him until her breasts crushed against his jacket.

Sam moved protectively forward but made no motion to interfere. He watched Clabe with angry eyes.

Clabe put a hand under Emily's chin and tilted her head away from his face. Then, he slid his hairy mouth along the curve of her neck into the swell of her bosom.

Emily pushed against him. He buried his face deeper in the front of her dress.

"That's enough," John Reese spat out. He came closer to the soldier. "Let her go, Clabe."

Clabe lifted his eyes to Reese, not loosening his grip on Emily. "Who the hell are you to tell me what to do? You nigger lovin' Yankee. Stay outta this."

"Get off my ship," Captain Roberts shouted now. "Both o' you niggers get off this ship. Clabe, let the wench go. I want both the niggers off. I got a ship to get movin'. . . ain't got no time for this." He strode toward Emily and Sam. "Go on, now, get ashore so's I can get movin'."

Clabe thrust Emily from him with such force she fell to the deck. Her head cracked against the wooden railing. Sam glanced nervously around, then reached down to help Emily. She held onto his arm, letting him lift her to her feet, letting him mold his body as a shield over hers as he moved from the deck toward the gangplank. "Come on, let's git 'way from here," Sam said lowly in Emily's ear. "Dis man is mean. I knows dis man . . . come on now, let's git on shore."

And under the protection of Sam's anxious urgings, Emily fled the *Yellow Stone*, angry, frustrated, head throbbing with pain. Moving closely together as if molded to one another, Sam and Emily started down the slatted footbridge.

The sound of gunfire split the air.

Emily tensed, expecting to feel the crack of a lead bullet crash into her skull.

"Oh my God, Sam. They're going to kill us," she screamed.

"Jus' keep runnin'," Sam said over her head. "Don't look 'round. Jus' keep runnin'," his voice was tight with fear.

The sound of her own small boots scraping hurriedly against the gangplank was quickly lost to another volley of rifle fire from behind. Sam jumped ahead of her, landing on the muddy bank and scrambled up to lean back and help Emily onto shore.

"Come on, Emily. Come on."

Sam dragged her breathless body toward him, setting her on trembling legs to follow. She felt disoriented. She struggled against some invisible weight which widened the distance between them. Sweat poured from her temples, down her neck, into her tight fitting bodice. Heavy skirts tangled around her ankles threatening to pull her to the ground. She stumbled. The wild lush thicket blurred into a rush of green and brown, as Sam pulled her into the cover of a dense juniper bush. Small branches tore at Emily's face and neck, prickly thorns punctured her skin.

"Hold your fire, Clabe," John Reese's voice shot angrily over the water.

"Not on your life," Clabe shouted back.

Gunfire ripped the air again. Emily clutched Sam tightly.

"Look," Sam whispered to Emily. He pointed through the bush. Emily lifted her head from the ground, squinted in the direction he indicated, then widened her eyes in surprise.

"Over dere," Sam said. His voice rushed out in a loud rasp. "He be shootin' at de water, not us."

Emily slowly turned her head to the right, her eyes taking in the figure of Clabe leaning far over the ship's railing, aiming directly into the water.

Clabe fired again.

"It's Joshua!" Emily said, disbelieving what she saw.

Her breathing became labored, forced. Her stomach tightened as she watched Joshua swim toward shore, then climb up the bank. His leather jacket and breeches were heavy with water. He struggled clumsily up the bank, slipped down, and fell back toward the murky water.

A final shot from the *Yellow Stone* exploded, stopping the fugitive where he lay. Blood spurted from his heaving shoulders in a quick burst of deep red, settling in large vivid droplets on the black earth beneath him.

"Oh, Joshua!" Emily screamed. "Sam, he's shot!" She stood up, against Sam's protests, pressing her hand to her lips. Sam pulled her back down into the bushes.

"It be Joshua all right." Sam's tone was reverent, astonished. "But you stay put . . . outta sight," he cautioned Emily. She lay back, feeling a weakness come over her, draining all her energy. She pressed her hand so hard across her mouth to keep from yelling out that she didn't feel the cutting edge of her own teeth against her flesh. Tears spilled from her eyes as she choked back her sobs. She watched her lover lie bleeding on the ground twenty feet from where she hid.

Joshua lay in a crumpled heap, his blood staining his shirt a darker brown, spreading across his shoulder, down his arm. Emily grew weaker as Joshua's blood seeped into the sticky black riverbank.

"Ah ha! I got the nigger," Clabe's triumphant yell reverberated against the tangle of vines and trees along the shore.

"Joshua!" Emily screamed, trying to stand again, pushing Sam's restraining hands away.

"You stay back," Sam hissed, yanking her forcefully down into the cover of foliage. "Dat soldier jus' as soon shoot you, too."

Emily went limp, burying her head against raised knees as she huddled in the bush with Sam. A flaming lump raised painfully in her throat.

A rapid exchange of heated words was taking place on board the *Yellow Stone*.

"Ain't no matter concerning me," Captain Roberts' New England brogue was clear. "T'was you who wanted ta carry the nigger downstream, Reese. Makes me no difference what happens now. I've got cargo an' passengers ta worry about."

Reese was silent, staring stone-faced at the twisted, bleeding form on shore.

"So . . . let it be," Reese finally spoke, moving abruptly away from the aft deck. He shoved both hands deeply into the pockets of his black broadcloth coat, turned his back on those who remained gaping at the railing, and headed toward the stairwell.

"Let's move on," he mumbled to no one in particular, walking slowly up the stairs. His eyes were sunken deeply into his skull, and his head was bowed stiffly as he masked his face with no expression. Reese disappeared onto the upper deck.

Emily and Sam crouched in the brambles until the top heavy vessel had steamed out of sight, around a bend in the river. Then, pushing aside the protective growth of the juniper, they scrambled out into the open, running quickly to Joshua's side.

Chapter Eleven

It was nightfall when they arrived at Orange Grove, the wagon rattling too loudly as Sam drove the oxen close up to Emily's cabin. Under shifting patterns of moonlit shadows they carried Joshua, still unconscious, into the dark musty cabin. He slept as though dead, an ashen pallor dulled his golden bronze flesh and a moist film clung all over his body. His breathing was shallow, fragile.

"Take the wagon around to the stables. Act like nothing has happened." Emily quickly took charge. "Then bring me fresh water and any clean cloth you can find." She held the door open for Sam, her hair wild and flowing about her face, her dress stained crimson with blood.

"Put fresh straw in the wagon, and bury the bloody straw. Hurry, Sam, hurry. I'll need you to help me here."

The nervous man slipped off, melting into darkness, and Emily pushed an iron bolt securely across the door. Turning, she looked down at Joshua.

"Dear God, spare him," she spoke lowly, haltingly. "Please don't take him from me now."

The taste of her own salty tears on her lips went unnoticed as she carefully peeled away blood soaked rags which bound Joshua's gaping shoulder wounds.

He had been struck high on his left shoulder, directly below the collar bone. The lead bullet had ripped through his body, tearing away flesh on either side of the wound. Two angry red holes, swollen and bleeding drained his life from him.

Emily leaned her face down close to Joshua's. The odors of blood, earth, and near-death did not reach her. Pressing her moist cheek against his, she let her tears wet the feverish surface of his skin. She whispered as if speaking a promise,

"I love you, Joshua, I love you."

A light scratching sound came to her. It reminded Emily of the constant grating of rats scurrying through the walls of her wretched rooms in New York. It was a sound not easily forgotten. It had frightened her as a child; it annoyed her as an adult. But now it brought her up sharply, and she raised her head in the semi-dark cabin to listen again. It came from the base of her door.

Emily tossed her tangled tresses back from her face and wiped her swollen eyes with the hem of her bloody dress. She crept cautiously to the door and stood there listening.

"Sam, is that you?" her soft whisper rasped, strained with fatigue.

"Naw, Miss Emily . . . it's me . . . Hanna," the childish voice whined through the door.

Emily pushed back the heavy bolt, opening the door just wide enough to let Hanna slip through.

"Sam tol' me what happened, but he's scared to come back up here. Say's it might look suspicious for him to be hanging 'round your cabin. He sent deese," Hanna finished, giving Emily a bundle of rags and a pail of water. Then she went and stood at the foot of the bed, stretching her neck forward to see Joshua's bloody wounds.

"He gonna die?" the girl asked.

Emily hugged the bundle of cloth to her chest, "I pray not," she said, moving to stand at the head of the bed. "He's lost so much blood . . . I'm afraid, he may not . . . " her voice cracked. She could not go on. Emily dropped to her knees at Joshua's side and lay her forehead against his arm. "He just can't die, Hanna. He just can't."

Emily's shoulders heaved with sobs she tried to keep within, but her misery was evident to Hanna.

"He's gonna make it," Hanna said, her voice stronger, more in control. "Don't you worry. I's gonna stay right here wid you till he come 'round." The slight nervousness Hanna had carried with her into the room vanished, and she walked up behind Emily, placing both hands on the kneeling woman's shoulders.

"What you need me to do? Huh? Tell me what you wants me to do so's we kin git on wid healin' dis man."

Emily raised her tear stained face to Hanna's. She was right, there was much they could do to keep Joshua from dying. Emily rose from her knees.

"Tear these cloths into strips for bandages. We've got to stop his bleeding."

✦✦✦✦✦✦

The sun was pouring through the single cabin window when Emily and Hanna realized that Joshua's wounds had ceased their constant seepage, and that perhaps they had stemmed the bloody flow for good. Weary, surrounded with blood soaked rags, the two women smiled faintly at one another in unspoken agreement that the battle had been won. Joshua still had not regained consciousness, but the slightest flush of color had returned to his face, and sweat no longer poured from his brow.

Emily poked up the coals in the hearth and tossed soiled rags into the yellow flames. She stared at the curling twisting pieces of cloth reddened with Joshua's blood as they changed from red to black, and finally, into ashes. As blackened smoke rose up the chimney, she felt the weight of her sadness depart with it. Joshua would live, she was certain. But whether or not he was free of danger, the danger from men like Clabe, closed in around her heart, sapping her sense of relief. How long before he would run again? Be trapped again? Fall under the torture of men who hated him again? There must be a way to end this madness, Emily thought. He cannot run forever. And as if reading her thoughts, Hanna broke the silence with a question.

"You think dat soldier what shot Joshua gonna come here lookin' for him?"

Emily shook her head from side to side, not raising her eyes from the golden flames which warmed the chilly cabin.

"No, I don't think he'll come here," she answered. "I'm sure he thinks Joshua is dead."

"Dat's good," Hanna sighed, leaning back in her straight backed chair.

"But others will come." Emily went on as if Hanna hadn't spoken. She let her words slip out on the edge of a sigh.

"Others will come here looking for him . . . that is, if he stays around here." She kept her back to Hanna, head lowered deeply, face flush to the warming flames. "You see, there's a plot against Joshua. A wicked plot. One so vicious he'll never escape it."

"What kinda plot? What you mean?"

"A plot to stop a slave revolt . . . a revolt which never happened."

Hanna let the words sink in, turned Emily's statements around in her head, then put it all together.

"You talkin' 'bout dat uprisin' down 'round Columbia last fall? Dat's de onliest revolt I ever heered 'bout in deese parts."

Now Emily turned to face the young girl, her eyes like brown sunken pools of velvet. There was a sadness at the corners, a softening which slightly aged her. And she laid the back of her hand against her warm cheek as she answered, speaking words which seemed to come from a distance.

"He's blamed for that you know." Her tone was gentle, matter-of-fact, not angry or bitter as Hanna had expected. "He was in Columbia right before that happened. The incident was blamed on him."

Hanna scoffed. "Dat was jus' a few crazy niggers what thought dey had freedom. Wasn't no real uprisin' down here. Wasn't nothin' like what Nat Turner did when he tried ta lead dem 'chillen o' Egypt' out o' Virginny. Now dat was a revolution."

Emily paced the length of the bed, hardly listening to Hanna's description of how the news of Turner's rebellion five years ago had reached her plantation in North Carolina.

"When Joshua's well enough to be moved, we'll hide him," she said, stopping directly in front of the seated girl. She looked down intently. "At least until this war is over . . . things will settle down then."

Hanna lifted round innocent eyes to Emily. "Where?" was all she asked.

Emily continued pacing, her lips tucked between her teeth. "What about Sam? Does he know where someone could hide safely . . . for a long time?"

Hanna stood quickly. Her small mouth opened as if to protest. "I don't know 'bout gittin' Sam caught up in dis no more. He's been . . . ," she stopped in mid-sentence, suddenly confused.

Emily stared at the anxious servant who looked to be on the verge of tears.

"I's sorry," Hanna started, twisting a piece of her ragged skirt into a tiny knot. "I can't speak for Sam . . . he kin do what he wants . . . it's best you ask him direct. But I reckon ain't nobody 'round here knows more 'bout where ta find or hide a body dan Sam . . . lessen it be Joshua Kinney."

✦✦✦✦✦✦

Long hours alone at Joshua's bedside folded softly into daylight, then turned dark again before Emily ever felt the strain of her vigil. When a burning pain behind her lids drew them closed against her will, she acquiesced by curling into the space at the foot of the bed. Relief came like splashes of cool water on a steamy summer day, the aches and stabbing pains in her shoulders gently ebbed.

A late winter wind brushed tree limbs against the cabin roof, limbs knocked and tapped but did not frighten her. Emily listened to the swift wind as it whistled through her chimney, drafting out the barren hearth, across her rough wooden floor. She should get up and light a fire, keep the cabin warm, but her tired exhausted body lay stiff and unmoving. In a minute, she thought, in just a few minutes, I'll get up and stoke the fire again. But those minutes never came, at least not to Emily's knowledge, for she immediately fell into a deep black slumber that carried her dreamless throughout the night.

A dreamless night was rare for Emily. She could easily count, without thinking twice, the number of nights without visions. The scenes which played before her sleeping eyes were always different. They changed nightly. But always they were there. Dreams of flight and running, being chased by dogs, or sometimes being chased by men. Dreams of standing unnoticed in crowded places where others rushed around in a frenzy also came in various forms. But always she was alone. Never did she have a companion or an approachable stranger to turn to for comfort within these ceaseless visions. The dreams did not frighten Emily. They only left her with an uneasy awareness of the strange, lonely life she was living.

Day to day living frightened her more than her dreams. Texas shocked her with its raw swampy vastness, its lack of settlement unnerved her. Accustomed to the crowded streets of a city, Emily often felt lost and disoriented by the flat coastal plains spreading out to the Gulf. And then there was the Gulf itself, yawning far beyond the Bay in an empty sheet of lapping waves which carried very few vessels to port. It was a lonely expanse of water and land. It gave her the feeling of being at the very ends of the earth . . . if such a place existed.

But Joshua had been the one bright spot in Emily's otherwise lonely existence. His arrival into her life had sparked the first true feelings of belonging she had ever known. He had seemed to know exactly the source of her loneliness, and without ever speaking of it, she had sensed the same in him. Perhaps they had been meant to soothe each other, to bring a calm relief and order to one another's lives. The loving moments they spent together had been fulfilling beyond expression, the end of a clouded search.

And now, as the wind crept into the dark cabin corners, Emily shivered slightly in her dreamless sleep. The tapping limbs on the roof overhead lulled her further into a weightless slumber.

❖·❖·❖··❖·❖·❖

His shifting body awakened her. There was only a slight movement of his leg, but it immediately caused Emily to sit up. She pushed her heavy tangled hair from her eyes, nervously gathering it with both hands to knot it slightly at the back of her head. She kept her eyes on Joshua's face. He had not yet awakened, though he moved his head from side to side, a low murmur escaping his lips.

Emily eased off the bed and shook out her skirts. The cabin was terribly cold. She leaned down closer to search Joshua's face, inspected his padded wound, then went to the chimney to start a fire. She scraped out cold ashes, placed several logs in the hearth, banked it with kindling, and struck a large sulphur match to it all. Within seconds the dry wood crackled and flamed.

She had water to boil, and luckily, a few tea leaves to brew. She set about brewing a strong cup for herself. She would have to go up to the big house today, there was no way she could stay away any longer.

Hanna had covered for her yesterday, telling James Morgan Emily was ill, possibly coming down with the fever, and how he surely didn't want Emily up to the house, now did he? No one had come for her. No one had tapped on her door for two days, but if for no other reason than to get some food, she had better go up to the house today. Emily was afraid to leave Joshua alone and she had no one to trust except Sam or Hanna.

Emily put a pinch of tea leaves into her tin pot of boiling water, covered it and sat down on a small stool near the fire to wait. She laid her soft, flushed cheeks in the palms of her hands and stared into thin yellow flames. Her mind was blank, empty from waiting. How much longer would he sleep, she wondered? The anxious tremors which had left her during the night now eased their way into her stomach.

She moved to the table and poured dark steaming tea into a metal cup. It burned her fingers, but she did not put it down. Lifting the hot liquid to her lips, she rested her gaze on Joshua once more.

He lay looking up at her, observing her with his soft honey-colored eyes. She caught her breath when their eyes met.

"Joshua," Emily let his name drop with hushed relief, watching his smile come to her through glittering flecks of gold in his stare.

Quickly, Emily set her hot mug on the table, closing the space between them in an instant. She pressed warm fingertips to the side of Joshua's face. His hands moved up to cover hers. And gathering her skirts to one side, Emily sat lightly on the edge of the bed.

Joshua's gaze was intense, and he seemed pleased to see her, though a shadow of sorrow remained. He licked parched lips and tried to lean forward. Emily placed a restraining hand against the coverlet.

"Don't try to move," she cautioned. She took a ladle of fresh cool water and held it to his lips. He swallowed eagerly.

"How long have I been here?" Joshua asked.

"Three days now."

Joshua's lids fluttered shut as an almost imperceptible sigh came forth. He winced as he struggled to turn. He faced Emily, but again she pushed him gently back.

"Lie still or the bleeding may start all over." Emily peeled away soiled cloth from his shoulder and carefully examined his wounds.

"Where were you going?" She asked.

"Refugio."

"To stay?" She felt his body tense under her palms.

"No, not for good," Joshua whispered after a moment's silence. Leaning upward, placing one hand on the back of Emily's neck, he pulled her tenderly closer. Emily's lips stopped within an inch of his. He murmured, "I was coming back for you."

Then, he kissed her softly, genuinely, as if confirming his promise, declaring his love for her in a way he had not done before.

Emily's hair fell in a veil around Joshua's face. Its long dark tendrils caressed his bronze skin, and she kissed him back with a rush of relief. He had stated his feelings for her. It was a heady moment, the verity of his presence was almost too much to accept, the warmth of his lips upon hers made it real, made this moment hang suspended like a jewel in her mind, to be treasured and polished with time.

He loves me, she thought, and I'll never be without him again. I'll find a way to keep us together, and smoothing the crest of his dark wavy hair, she resolved to stake her future on Joshua.

* * * *

The mistress of Orange Grove sent for her much sooner than she had expected. As Emily removed her white cotton apron, Hanna stopped measuring rice from a waist high barrel and made her feelings known.

"What you think de Missus kin do? Wid de Massa Morgan now gone off to de Island, ain't nothin' she kin do."

Emily listened, calmly folding her apron into a neat flat square to lay on the table. Her face was a mask of non-feeling, though a slight lift of her jaw gave traces of unwavering determination. She turned away from Hanna and looked out the window.

The first warm breezes of March now rippled the leafy oaks. She scrutinized the trees in amazement. The limbs were covered thickly in green. Had they ever been bare, she wondered? Had their lush emerald shades ever faded? Spring had arrived so quickly.

"Even if Miss Celia kin help protect Joshua, den what?" Hanna continued in disapproving tones. "What kinda life kin you have wid a hunted man? He's mighty handsome, all right, but you best forgit 'bout dat runaway an' let him go on 'bout his business. You's jus' askin' for trouble, hookin' up wid Joshua Kinney."

Emily gripped the window ledge in frustration. She did not want to hear words which rang too true, but it was hopeless to think of turning her back on Joshua now.

After two weeks of carefully nursing Joshua, making him strong enough to travel, she and Sam had taken him to Redfish Bay.

Leaving him there alone, in an old abandoned cabin with very little food, had been the most painful thing Emily had ever done.

Joshua was safe. His wounds would heal, but Emily worried about the lack of certainty in his future. She was still fearful of the dangerous rumors plaguing him. She wished he could be free of them, but until the war with Mexico was ended, he would have to stay away from Galveston Bay.

During the time spent together, in those quiet evenings before her fire, Emily finally learned the story of Joshua's past. Reluctantly he told her of his life in Tennessee, and of Lucinda. Emily shared his anger as he spoke; she had burned with the same sense of wrong done to him, and then had vowed to help him prove his freedom. He was not a runaway slave. Joshua had been born as free as she. He deserved a chance to state his case, and Emily hoped that speaking to Celia Morgan would help resolve the long standing rumors about Joshua's past.

Ignoring Hanna's biting comments, Emily took up a flickering oil lamp to ward off the rapidly approaching dusk. She crossed the breezeway between the kitchen and the main house, went through the empty living quarters and climbed up to the dim sleeping area where Celia Morgan lay resting. Still weak and not fully recovered from the fever, Celia had developed the habit of rising early to tend to most of her chores, then resting in the middle of the day, to rise again near dusk to close down the kitchens and plan the work for the next day.

Today she had not left her bed at all. The mistress sat propped up with feather pillows, dim yellow lamps illuminating her pale, drawn face. Her eyes had little sparkle left, and she motioned Emily into the room with slow, calculated movements.

"Sit down, Emily," Celia's voice quivered. "What is it you wanted to see me about?"

Emily could not speak right away. She looked down at her own folded hands, suddenly realizing the brazeness of her intended request. She felt uncomfortable now, hesitant to speak.

Celia Morgan broke the silence. Her unsteady voice began to grow stronger as she spoke.

"These are difficult times, Emily. Everyone is frightened. We all wonder what direction the Mexicans will take." She gazed vacantly up to the ceiling. "To think that the Alamo has fallen . . . Travis, Bowie, Crockett and all their men are dead. Ah, it's a gruesome reality, this war." Celia closed her eyes and let her head fall back on the turned spindle headboard.

Emily sat silently, letting her mistress express what was on her mind.

"Can you imagine what it must have looked like?" Celia drifted on in her quivering voice. "One hundred eighty-two men, stacked and burning? Heathens . . . only savage heathens could have done such a thing."

Emily nodded, though Celia never looked her way. She shuddered, visualizing the burning of those who had lost the battle at the Alamo. And now, the wives and children of those same men were stranded, helplessly alone throughout the colonies. Panic vibrated the land, and settlers, infused with a great sense of doom, were fleeing eastward in droves. They were abandoning their homes, their livestock, and treasured possessions, in an attempt to escape the advancing army of General Santa Anna. And in this wake, the colonists left blazing towns which quickly reduced to ashes, all the progress at settlement which had been made.

"But, you've not come to me to speak of this war, have you?" Celia looked at Emily.

"Not directly," Emily answered, rushing on with her request. "It's Joshua . . . Joshua Kinney I'd like to speak to you about." Emily tensed, watching Celia's face closely.

"Joshua Kinney . . . yes . . . Joshua. You've been caring for him in your cabin, haven't you? I heard he was shot at Fort Bend." She said this evenly, carefully, calculating her words. Emily could detect neither approval nor reproach. She drew in a breath.

"You knew he has been here?"

"Not much happens at Orange Grove that misses me. He's gone?"

"Yes," was all that Emily admitted.

Celia leaned further back into her pillows and lifted her chin.

"I've known Joshua since I first came to Texas. He was here, living on this very land, alone. In those early days, trying to get this settlement started, I doubt Mr. Morgan and I could have done without his help." She coughed into a crumpled handkerchief, then wiped her eyes before going on. "I've heard the rumors about him . . . that he's a runaway . . . that he's dangerous. I don't know about all that. Maybe it's true, maybe not . . . anyway, he's been helpful to us here at Orange Grove." Now, Celia looked at Emily with tired eyes. "What did you want to ask me?"

Emily twisted her hands together nervously, then started.

"Joshua told me some things while he was healing in my cabin. I believe what he said . . . I think he told me the truth." She paused and took a deep breath. "Joshua was born free. He's not a runaway slave. He was forced to work as a slave on a tobacco farm in Tennessee . . . but he was never sold. There are no papers on him." She pressed damp palms together and continued. "The freedom papers on him and his mother were destroyed when they were both put on the tobacco farm."

"What do you want from me?" Celia was frowning.

"How can Joshua get freedom papers again? How can he prove he's not a runaway?"

Celia smoothed the coverlet across her stomach, seeming to concentrate on a distant thought. She fingered the stitching which ran in a pattern of leaves and roses along the border of her blanket. "It's probably impossible," she said.

Emily plunged ahead. "Isn't there some way you or Mr. Morgan could help?"

Celia's rough, red hand closed in a fist. "That would take a lot of checking . . . letters to write . . . correspondence. I doubt James would get involved. Why should he?"

Emily was dauntless. "I was wondering . . . well, since most of the Negroes here are free, if Joshua could be listed as belonging to this colony, wouldn't that just about be the same thing as freedom papers? He helped build up this colony."

Celia pressed her lips into a firm line. The wrinkles on her forehead deepened. "That would be up to James, Emily."

"Would you speak to him when he returns?"

Celia Morgan unexpectedly laid her hand on the fold of Emily's skirt. "I'll do what I can. You have been a blessing to me, working so hard, running the house while I've been laid up here in bed. I'll do what I can . . . but, as I said before, these are very difficult times, and James has matters of war on his mind."

Chapter Twelve

The end of March brought news so distressing and shocking that, at first, the settlers on Galveston Bay refused to believe it. General Santa Anna's vow to eradicate Texans from the territory had evidenced itself in a horrendous way. Three hundred ninety Texas soldiers, falsely believing their surrender would be treated in humane terms, had been rounded up and massacred in cold blood at the tiny town of Goliad. Even their commander, Colonel James Fannin, after being assured he would not be shot in the head and would be properly buried, was cruelly murdered by a bullet through his brain, then he was stripped naked to be tossed on a pile of human corpses to rot. This was an outrage the colonists could not tolerate.

Settlers continued to flee in advance of the savage Mexican troops, while General Sam Houston marched his ragged volunteer forces just slightly ahead of Santa Anna's professional columns of soldiers. In the appearance of a retreat, Sam Houston continued moving toward Harrisburg, though the president of the Texas Republic, David Burnet, was growing impatient with General Houston's delays. It was well known in the colonies that President Burnet had sent a curt message to the commander of the Texas forces which read:

> Sir: The enemy are laughing you to scorn.
> You must fight.

But, Sam Houston, a quiet man who carried his plans in his head, paid no attention to this message and continued marching eastward.

Emily listened to all this talk of war, knowing she was directly in the path of the approaching forces. The battles had always seemed so far away, taking place in towns she knew nothing about. Her ignorance of the geography of the land kept her unsure of the proximity of the fighting, but such an outcry had arisen after the Goliad Massacre, that she began to sense imminent danger.

So far, the people living at Orange Grove had not started to flee, though James Morgan was now permanently stationed on Galveston Island, maintaining coastal protection against an attack by sea.

There were very few men left in the settlements now. They had taken up their muskets, cartridges, flints, and rifles fixed with bayonets, to head eastward to join Sam Houston. Those without proper arms carried clubs, heavy pieces of iron, and pouches of shrapnel to be used in the cannons. Enraged, burning for revenge, these untrained troops thronged through Orange Grove from distant cities in the United States. Victory or death. Independence for Texas. These words echoed over the plantation as men packed their gear to march off to join the fighting.

Emily spent her days cooking large quantities of food, washing and mending blankets for the troops, and listening for news of the war's progress. Everything she heard was discouraging. Despite the enthusiasm of the soldiers, everyone knew that the Texans lacked sufficient men and money to wage a successful defense. The United States continued to maintain a hands-off attitude in this struggle which flamed along its border.

And, in the midst of all this turmoil, a strange occurrence took place at Orange Grove. It left Emily both frightened and relieved.

On a late afternoon in early April, two men rode onto the plantation. Bearded, dirty, saddle-weary, they looked no different from all the other soldiers who had drifted through Orange Grove in the last few months. With their horses laden with bulging sacks and bundles of supplies, it was evident they had been traveling for some time. There was a grim set to their faces though, a definite facade of men with a mission. They carried an air of determination which caught Emily's attention at once. She stopped stirring the large boiling pot of grease and lye, now bubbling over the open fire, and let her soap making wait. She laid aside her large wooden paddle and watched as the riders approached.

"Who's the owner of this place?" a red faced man spoke. His protruding belly settled softly into his saddle. With a printed handkerchief, he wiped sweat from his flushed neck, then wound the dirty scrap of cotton around his throat.

"James Morgan," Emily answered. She waited, expecting them to ask for a place to rest, or water and feed for their horses.

"Go fetch him," the large man ordered.

"He's not here . . . he's on Galveston Island with the Navy men."

"The Texas Navy, huh?" He turned to his partner who sat behind, picking his teeth. "This here's the place of the colonel who commands the Texas Navy. We got the right place this time," he scowled down at Emily. "Well, who's in charge here?"

"The missus."

"Go get her."

"I'm sorry, sir," Emily hesitated, "she's taken to her bed . . . down with the fever."

"Take us to her, then," the stranger ordered, already urging his mount toward the house.

Emily ran in front of them and waited at the breezeway until they dismounted. She then led them through the house to Celia Morgan's room.

"Wait here . . . I'll see if she's awake." Emily left the men standing outside the room and quietly approached Celia's still, straight form. She was not sleeping, only lying listlessly on her pillows, staring out the small open window.

"Excuse me, ma'am," Emily started. "There're two men who want to talk to you. They asked for Mr. Morgan and when I told them he wasn't here, they said they'd talk to you."

"Oh . . . send them on to the island, Emily. Probably some more military men . . . they need to speak with James. I know nothing about what's going on with this war." She lifted a blue-veined hand as if dismissing the subject, too tired and sick to think of it.

"I don't think they're military. They don't have uniforms. Seems like they just want to talk with you."

"All right. I'll see what they want."

Emily stepped out and motioned to the men. They went brusquely past her and Emily slipped out of their way. As she returned to making soap at her boiling pot on the smoldering fire, she wondered about the mission of these two strangers.

✦·✦·✦··✦·✦·✦

It didn't take Emily long to find out. In the kitchen the very next morning, Hanna brought information garnered from the reliable black grapevine.

"Henry Gasper's boy came down from Harrisburg last night," Hanna moved closer to Emily, speaking in a whisper as she went on. "He tol' Sam dat dose men is bounty hunters from Tennessee. Dey was askin' questions 'bout de whereabouts o' Joshua. Seems dey got some paper ta bring him back ta Tennessee."

Emily swung around and grabbed Hanna's arms with both hands. Her face paled as a hollow, draining sensation washed through her body.

"What did the Missus tell them?" she asked.

"Well, from what I got from Sam . . . seems like de Missus acted like she ain't never heered o' no one called Joshua Kinney. Even tol' dem bounty men dat more'n likely he be down 'round Columbia, cause dat's where a mighty lot o' free niggers be livin' now." Hanna sucked in the sides of her puffy cheeks, pursed her lips and watched Emily carefully. Finally, she crossed her thin arms across her flat chest and asked, "Now, why you reckon Miss Celia done tol' a lie like dat?"

✦✦✦✦✦✦

Emily had never ridden a mule before. And now, the unfamiliar press of the sturdy animal's body under hers was becoming almost comfortable. As she guided the sure-footed mule along the edge of Galveston Bay, her apprehension about starting this journey dissolved like the shifting sands which drained in rivulets back out to sea. The blazing globe of a setting sun lay one dimensional over the water. Its reflection rippled forward, lapping at the shore, shimmering to brighten her path.

After more than an hour's travel, she wanted to stop and rest, but in order to reach Joshua before dark, she knew she had better press on. Both Sam and Hanna had warned her that unless she rode steadily, without stopping, there was no way she could get to Joshua's cabin before nightfall. She had made up her mind to get to him as soon as she could, to let him know that he could come back to New Washington. The bounty hunters had left the area. Celia Morgan was on his side. Weren't these reasons enough to quit this exile and come back to her? She hoped to convince him of this.

The chill of dusk was descending, seeping through her thick woolen skirt, finding its way to the flesh of her thighs. She curved her fingers into small fists, then pressed them warmly under her shawl; a draping, tattered piece of cloth flung quickly over her shoulders. In this position, she plodded toward a high cane brake, which marked the point where Redfish Bay cut deeply into the land.

Seagulls circled and dipped over the towering mass of dry cane poles which stood dark and sinister just ahead. The birds made an eerie silhouette against the streaked purple sky. Fields of swamp cane like this were foreign to Emily, but common along the coast, and there was no way to reach Redfish Bay without cutting directly through this one.

She nervously dug her heels into the mule's sides. The agile animal twitched its long, pointed ears, lowered its elongated head and picked its way through the boggy marshland. Emily hoped to pass through while the little sun that remained could guide her to the end of the brake.

Like a gathering of outstretched arms springing uniformly from the ground, the tall cane poles soared arrow-straight into the air above her. As she entered, the cane arched and met, rustling and chafing overhead. The twisting cavernous tunnel swallowed her. A dank smell of rotting vegetation arose. It seemed as if this powerful, decaying odor sought to harm her and erode her very flesh with its pungent humid presence.

She had crossed this brake once before, huddled miserably in the back of a cart with Joshua lying nearby. Sam had cautiously maneuvered the blackened corridor to come out onto the grassy prairie where an abandoned shack stood partially hidden. They had left Joshua there quickly, so they would not be missed at Orange Grove. Emily had wept openly, inconsolably, at first refusing to leave. Joshua had held her tightly, pressing his face into the warm hollow of her throat, and had spoken in rough commanding tones.

"You cannot stay with me. I won't let you." His torment undercut each word, and Emily cringed with each one. "It's dangerous and foolish to even think of staying here. Go back to Orange Grove with Sam, hurry, before you're missed."

Joshua pushed her from him, and she saw the dull sadness clouding his honey-colored eyes, and knew he had spoken out of love. She had brushed her lips across his brow, his eyes, his angular jaw, then, left him. Since that night, there had been a void in her soul, a gnawing pit of emptiness which nothing could assuage. Only vivid recollections of those few weeks spent together in her cabin could blunt the sting of this loneliness.

Those precious days alone. How she remembered them!

Joshua at first was too weak and semi-conscious to even notice Emily hovering constantly at his bedside. Then, they experienced the warm circle of their embraces as they sought and gave comfort they both needed. Gentle, surprising moments of happiness occurred, which had seemed to spring from a source beyond them both, culminating in a keen awareness of the depth of their commitment.

These were the memories Emily treasured.

When Joshua had spoken to her of his life in Tennessee, Emily came to understand the source of his pain. She now understood why his future had no shape. No form. No plans could come together that he could rely on, and therefore, he had been forced to turn away from promises to her. It was a painful reality for Emily, but, at least, she understood.

Over those days together, Joshua prompted her to speak of things of her past. She shared her memories of New York with him, describing the rundown, thin-walled rooms where she had grown up. He had listened silently to her as she told him of the crowded Negro sections of the city where free blacks fought in the streets over discarded scraps of food, and men lay idle in foul, wet gutters. She had disillusioned Joshua, verifying, that for many, life in a free state really meant no more than the chance to be master of one's own slow starvation.

Real freedom did not exist in New York, nor in any Northern state. The free Negro was held in such contempt and disregard that legislators had created numerous laws and regulations to keep him out. Such flagrant hatred and oppression had forced Emily to leave the North and come to Texas.

Joshua understood Emily's confusion about leaving New York. He had felt the painful sense of loss and aloneness hanging peripherally to her life. His life was not so different from hers. When he had held her closely, as the only promise he could give, they had talked, touched, and dreamed, passing a short time in a world of their control.

Emily was nearing the end of the rustling tunnel. She pressed against the mule, but he did not go any faster. He stepped along at an even pace, steadily drawing her out of the brake. Arriving at the wide opening at the end, where the reeds fanned out in varying heights to permit more light to enter, she saw a figure standing, as if waiting for her, under the limbs of a low hanging oak.

Emily sucked in a short breath. Her throat closed in anticipation, and the rush of blood which went to her head made her slightly dizzy. Joshua, she thought, he's safe and well. She pulled the reins more tightly, leaning forward over the mule's long neck. She bit her lips, surprised, happy . . . straining to see him clearly in the violet shadows of dusk. Emily trembled as she approached, vainly running a shaking hand over her streaming, tangled hair.

He looked at her but made no move to meet her.

He stood as if waiting, but his stance was nonchalant.

She called out, "Joshua!" He made no reply, and then suddenly, everything seemed odd and strange.

Like a blackened curtain of evil slowly descending between them, Emily saw that it was not Joshua at all. The realization came in slow motion. Like bits and pieces of a shattered vision, she fought to keep it from forming. Her mouth went dry. She stifled a scream. It was Clabe who was waiting for her.

Clabe now turned his face toward her, fastening a purposeful gaze on Emily. In deep resolute strides, he crossed the swampy land, coming nearer, staring with a fixed, evil scowl. Emily pulled the reins up taut with a jerk, stopping the mule abruptly. She looked around anxiously. There was nothing, no one at all to help her. It was black, black, black. The sun had left her so quickly. When had the purple sky turned its back? Where was that cabin where Joshua waited? And why should this soldier be here on Redfish Bay?

Emily jumped from her mule and started back toward the brake which now appeared like a darker shade of black rising in a wild shaggy clump from the swamp. Her boots sank deeply into the wet soil. Scrambling forward, Emily tore at reeds in her path to enter the humid cavern again.

But she did not enter very deeply.

Clabe caught her by the length of her hair and pulled her painfully backwards. Emily screamed with such fright and pain that her throat burned raw as her cries fell mutely into the darkness. The spikes of cane, which raked her skin as Clabe shoved her brutally to the ground, caught her skirts and ripped them open. She struggled against the crush of his body, clawing blindly at his face and neck. The firm solid weight of his barrel shaped chest pressed her into the cool damp earth.

There was a grunting, panting sound above her. It seemed to fill the tunnel, then echo back, bouncing off the living walls. It never grew louder, only stronger and more rapid, as Clabe clamped Emily's hips between his thighs.

Emily screamed again, forcing her anguish to the heavens with every ounce of strength she had. It was useless. There was no one on the Bay to help her.

Clabe threw her skirts up over her face. Then, he pressed a large hand down on the fabric, muffling her cries. The other hand tore at the soft flesh of her inner thighs, and just as Emily's fingernails cut into Clabe's pulsing hot neck, a flash of pain ripped through her body as he descended on her with an initial thrust.

Her cry, so bereft of anger and full of pain, rose in a wail in the tunnel. She pushed against him. He pressed down harder, both of his hands now over her face. She was trapped.

With a forced detachment, Emily suffered the torture of his painful assault. She endured the attack, floating in and out of consciousness as he forced himself on her again and again. Emily concentrated on the cool, damp earth under her neck in order to block out the pain.

Until, finally, he was spent.

He thrust her from him to the side of the trail and spoke for the very first time.

"I told you I'd finish with you. You lousy nigger whore. You ain't no better'n the rest o' the darkies 'round here . . . an don't go forgettin' that either."

＊-＊-＊--＊-＊-＊

Consciousness brought excruciating pain. How long she had lain in the swampy cane brake, she did not know. It was still dark, and a moon, which showed itself from time to time as black clouds left its surface, intermittently illuminated the prairie. Emily could see her mule standing small and straight under the boughs of an oak. He stood as if waiting for her to come and mount once more to continue their journey.

But, as she tried to stand she fell weakly to her knees. Sobbing in disgust and pain, Emily crawled on hands and knees out of the reeds. Her hair was matted with soil and leaves. Her ripped skirts dragged heavily through the mud. And the burning surges of pain which coursed her body made her cry out with each movement.

Emily inched her way to the wide base of the spreading oak tree and slumped against its bumpy surface. There was no way she could do more than give herself over to the draining exhaustion which pulled her rapidly into darkness.

--*--*-*-*

It was Joshua. Really Joshua. Leaning so closely over her face. Running his warm fingers the length of her chilled arms. He was real . . . and there were tears in his eyes. Tears lay gathered there, not yet spilling over, but glazing his look with a sad, crystal shine. He only stared. Emily knew if he should blink, the pools of water would flow down his cheeks. She looked away from him.

It was light . . . but it was misty light. It filtered through a heavy fog which crowded in from the bay. It shut out all except Joshua's presence, surrounding them both with a wet, white chill. The mist seemed to cut them off from the rest of the world, and if it had not been for the continual press of Joshua's warming hands on her skin, Emily would have thought this was one of her dreams.

"Don't say anything," Joshua cautioned. He put those same warm fingers to the side of her lips. Emily winced in pain. Joshua touched the torn, bruised flesh at the corner of her mouth. Then he picked her up and held her to him, carrying her easily into the fog.

He climbed onto her waiting mule and placed her gently in front of him. They started off, his arms wound protectively across Emily's shoulders. She let her weight fall fully against him. They rode for what seemed to be a very long time. Then out of the fog a cabin appeared, a tiny one room shack on the edge of a thick stand of pines. Filmy drifts of vapor separated in front of them as they cut their way to the door.

Inside, Joshua placed Emily gently on his crude straw pallet. She lay silently looking around as he knelt to start a fire.

The rough hewn timber of this weathered shack was draped with silvery spider webs. They filled the corners and hung down from the rafters. The dust and grit of several seasons lay thick in spaces between the planks. There was little, save the pallet she lay on, to indicate that someone had actually lived there. Joshua had stacked a small amount of wood near the crumbling mud-stick chimney, and a rusty pail sat half full of water. Joshua left the fire struggling in the hearth and came to sit beside Emily.

"I know who did this to you," he started, reaching to take Emily's hand in his.

"How could you?" Emily asked. Her face was like a mask.

"Yesterday, I left the cabin early," Joshua told her. "I went far along the bay, looking for oysters. When I returned, I saw that soldier from the *Yellow Stone* standing outside the cabin. He acted like he was looking for someone. He was waiting around." Joshua stood and went to the door. "I hid in the woods, watching until pretty late in the afternoon. It was almost dark when he finally moved on toward Galveston Bay." Now, Joshua turned and looked down at Emily. "He was the only man I've seen since I came here. He did this to you . . . didn't he?"

Emily did not want to answer, but when she saw the twisted frown on Joshua's face, she nodded in agreement. The flood of tears he had been holding back, now poured forth at this admission. He sat down beside her, pulling her head onto his shoulder. Emily felt the wide expanse of his warm hand which almost covered her head entirely.

"You're staying with me," he promised. His voice was soothing, calming. "I'll never let you leave me again." There was conviction in his tone, a firmness that Emily believed. Joshua rocked Emily tenderly in his arms, stroking her silky hair as he murmured, "We'll be together . . . from now on. You'll never be away from me again."

He covered the two of them with his fringed leather jacket, and she slept in his arms, torn, crumpled, and dirty as she was. But, Joshua never slept, he only lay there beside her and vowed in silence to protect Emily forever.

Chapter Thirteen

It rained for the next ten days. Water fell in torrential gusts, not only along the bay, but throughout the territory from the Colorado River to Harrisburg on Buffalo Bayou. All the rivers and creeks surged out of their banks. The prairie became a quagmire of mud, a treacherous swamp threatening to swallow the thousands of settlers now abandoning their homes to escape the approaching Mexican Army. Trails disappeared under quivering sheets of water and travel was nearly impossible.

Emily watched Joshua deftly work supple deerskin into a set of oval saddlebags. As if guided by ancestral instinct, his slender fingers wove a string of leather in and out of tiny holes, pulling it tautly as he went. He worked intently, head down, almost oblivious to Emily's presence. She moved closer, crouching on the dirt floor in front of the empty hearth. Her large dark eyes followed every movement Joshua made. They sat that way in silence until Joshua tied a final knot and laid the bags aside.

He covered Emily's hand with his. "If the rain lets up in the morning, we'll start out early . . . daybreak."

Emily leaned back, away from Joshua and let out a sigh. She pulled her hand from his and made a fist in her lap.

"Joshua," she hesitated. "We'd better go back to Orange Grove. It's safer there . . . safer than Mexico." She straightened her shoulders, waiting for his reply.

Joshua stood, rising in a slow easy movement. "It's a trap. Colonel Morgan will never list me in the free colony. Just because Celia Morgan didn't turn me in . . . doesn't mean a thing. Don't fool yourself, I can't go back to New Washington." He pressed angry fingers through his wavy hair. "We're heading west, to Refugio. The Mexicans won't bother us, you'll see."

"But, Joshua," Emily protested. "You haven't heard what I have heard at Orange Grove. People coming there say the Mexicans burn and slaughter anyone, black or white. You know what happened at Goliad . . . San Felipe. There's not a family safe west of the Brazos."

"San Felipe? What about it?" Joshua frowned, thinking of Unca Zack and his own promise to return.

"It's gone, that's what," Emily said. "Burned to the ground. A pile of ashes . . . no one is left there, Joshua, no one. We can't get through the Mexican lines."

"I'm not going back to New Washington." Joshua was firm. "We're going to Refugio. There, we can make connections to get to Mexico. After that, no one will know or care about where we are." He turned from Emily, walking to stand at the open doorway. He spoke with his back to her. "All I want is to be safe with you . . . and that cannot happen here."

Emily rose and went up behind Joshua, slipping her arms around his waist, resting her cheek in the warm curve between his broad shoulders. The soft suede of his jacket filled her head with an acrid sweet smell.

"I want the same," she said. "But I want it here . . . in Texas. Maybe you're wrong about Colonel Morgan. He can help you, Joshua. Go back to Orange Grove. Talk to him. It's a chance and it's better than running away again. We'd never make it to Refugio."

Joshua turned slowly in the circle of Emily's arms, faced her and gathered her to him.

"Are you saying you won't come with me?" His voice cracked, his grip tightened. There was a shadow of frightened doubt which passed quickly over his face.

Emily pressed her cheek to his chest, silent for a few moments. Joshua placed a gentle hand under her chin and lifted her lips to his. Emily leaned back and looked deeply into Joshua's eyes.

"I'll go with you," she decided, "wherever you want to go. There's no life for me here without you."

+-+-+--+-+-+

The cabin door stood open onto a vibrant green forest of pines. Slanted shafts of yellow sunlight cut through the slender trees, disappearing into the ground. Emily had felt those warm rays of sunshine on her lids before she had even opened her eyes. Now, lying still, half asleep on her pallet, she lingered in the warmth of this hazy April sun.

She looked around. Joshua was not in the cabin, nor in the clearing just outside the door. Emily turned to lie fully on her back, putting her hands beneath her head. Staring at the crudely patched roof, lazily tracing patterns of split logs, she let memories of the night before come back to her. A smile tugged at her lips when the beauty of those moments were remembered.

At first, Joshua had been reluctant to approach her, sensitive to the terrible ordeal she had just endured. But, when Emily had reached for him, rejoicing in the smooth touch of his naked skin, he had gently responded by guiding them to the crest of their passion, reaching the pinnacle of their union. He had stroked her and caressed her, bringing her desires flaming to the surface. She had clung to him, not in desperation, not in possession, but in a powerful magnetic fusion which had made them one.

And now her body, perhaps even her very soul, seemed illuminated by the glow of their love. Emily felt as if an aura of intensely brilliant light hovered all around her, telling the world that she was a lucky woman. For she had captured Joshua's heart at last, and they would stay together forever.

+·+·+··+·+·+

Joshua led the mule right up to the cabin door. It was loaded with a bedroll, his soft tan saddle bags, and a bundle of wild onions, yams, and other roots just dug from the forest. Securing his canteen over his shoulder, he entered the cabin.

"I see you're awake," he stood smiling with the sunshine filling the doorway behind him. Joshua held himself erect although his injured shoulder seemed slightly lower than the other.

"Are we leaving now?" Emily sat up quickly and pulled his Indian robe over her breasts.

"Yes," Joshua answered. "The mule's all packed. The sun is full up, and we'd better get moving while the weather is holding."

Emily slipped her dress over her head, rolled her pallet into a bundle, and handed it to Joshua. Kissing him lightly on the lips, she said, "I won't be long." Then, she slipped out the cabin door.

The forest's grassy carpet pressed damp and cool under her bare feet. Emily cut through towering pines, passing in and out of sunny patches, soon arriving at a clear rushing stream. Bending, splashing handfuls of the icy water on her face, Emily drank deeply, lingering over the stream to look around. The woods were lovely . . . green, fresh and raw under filmy drifts of morning fog which hung in scattered clouds among the pines. Huge stands of ferns sprang from the bases of tall straight trees. Leafy vines climbed up their trunks, entering low hanging branches to intertwine with spongy boughs of Spanish moss. Balancing on her knees, Emily bent and drank again.

Through the forest, reverberating across the stream, a strange grinding sound came to Emily. It grated on her ears, echoing between the pines. She lifted her head to listen to the intense creaking in the woods. As the sound grew louder, Emily moved cautiously, crouching low to the ground to back away from the water. The creaking noise came closer, Emily's heart beat faster, and with frightened eyes, she turned to run, just as an eerie voice shot out of the fog.

"Please, can you help us? Ohooh . . . Miss . . . can you help us?"

Emily continued to creep backwards, watching the spot from where the voice came. The grinding sound intensified, an awful whining which pulled her stomach into a frozen knot.

"Oooh, Miss . . . please don't run." The voice now begged. Emily halted, peering across the stream to see a form partially hidden in the mist on the opposite bank. It had enough shape for Emily to discern it was a woman. A white woman. Gaunt and death-like, the lone figure stared over at Emily. She was a vision of sickness and horror. Her thin narrow face lay chalky white against the dark fabric of a ragged black scarf tied around her head, and the shredded remains of a muddy dress stuck tightly against her legs. The stranger stood wavering, trembling, moving from side to side as if the air were stirred by a gusting wind, and when her lips moved in another desperate appeal, her cry was drowned out by that frightful creaking noise.

Then, out of the forest behind this figure, a companion emerged. The shock of white nappy hair springing from a loose bandana was the only clue to the black woman's age. Her ample, sturdy frame came forward in firm strong strides, and she pulled a crude truck-cart along behind her. It creaked and groaned to a halt at the edge of the rushing stream.

The aged slave woman towed a wagon of the simplest kind—a cart fit with wheels made of rounds sawed off a large tree, fastened to a wooden axle with wooden pegs. A tattered sheet hung over it all, creating the appearance of a tent.

Now, Emily moved closer. She yelled over the water, "Where did you come from?" Stepping into the water, she waded toward the two women as the figure in black answered.

"Up the San Bernard River."

Emily felt the sandy creek bottom shift under her bare feet. Lifting her skirts, she pushed through the current, coming closer to the shore. Voices floated through the mist.

"Now, Miss Cora, you gits on in de truck wid de chillen," the aging Negress ordered her mistress.

"I told you . . . I'll walk, Lydia . . . I'm fine," the frail apparition protested.

"Naw, Miss Cora. Ain gwan let you step off inta dis wader, ain no way you kin go one step more."

Emily reached the opposite bank as Cora stepped into the water. She extended her hand to the tired traveler.

"You have children with you?" Emily asked.

"Shore do," Lydia answered, plunging forward, wagon in tow. "Two babies. Miss Chrissy ain but two year ol', and de baby . . . Lawd . . . de baby ain seen two weeks yet. Miss Cora no more'n jus' delibered dat chile 'fore us had ta take ta de road. Poor ting . . . ain got no business truckin' tru mud like dis."

"How long have you been traveling?"

The exhausted woman, pressing heavily on Emily's side, spoke up.

"Ten days. Ten horrible days. The Mexicans burned us out." She was breathless, strained. Emily could see pulsing veins in Cora's neck. "They took everything we owned, then set the whole town on fire. We were lucky to get away alive."

"There were no men to help you?" Emily asked this question in fearful realization that the enemy was not far behind. There was no help for anyone on the roads.

"Not a one left in de settlement," Lydia said, spitting the words in disgust. "If dey wasn't killed at Goliad, dey's off a marchin' wid

Gen'ral Houston. Dat's where Massa Tom be right now . . . marchin' wid de Gen'ral. Us aims ta catch up wid Massa Tom in Harrisburg. Dat's where us is headed."

Emily helped Cora onto shore, settling her on the grassy bank before turning back to give Lydia a hand with the wagon. Grasping the rough splintered tongue of the cart, she pulled with all the force she could muster. The wagon resisted, tilting dangerously low to the water. A baby wailed loudly from beneath the tattered sheet, and when Emily rushed to the side of the wagon, she was startled by the sight of a tiny squirming bundle, and the round frightened eyes of a little blonde girl. The children rolled around in the lopsided cart, scraping painfully against its rough hewn planks. With Lydia's powerful urgings, the wagon was finally guided up the shallow, sandy bank.

With bruised and trembling hands Emily took up the small blonde girl, while Lydia comforted the howling newborn.

"Dis lil man be hongry. Reckon you's got de strength ta feed him, Miss Cora?" She rocked the screaming infant in the crook of her fat black arms.

"Give him to me," Cora said, unbuttoning the front of her mud caked dress. "I've got milk enough. It's all right." She took the child from the huge old woman and easily put him to suckle at her breast. With a reddened shaking hand, she brushed the baby's fine sandy hair from his forehead. Cora looked up at Emily.

"We lost our ox at Cedar Bayou. When we tried to cross, we got bogged down. The water moved so fast, and it was so high . . . we couldn't get him out. Ah, it was a pitiful sight, really pitiful." She shook her head. "We pulled him, beat him, but the poor animal just didn't have the strength to get free. The cart was starting to fill up. We feared loosing it, so we cut the ox free . . . left him in the middle of the bayou, drowning. Oh, God, it was awful."

"Shore was," Lydia agreed. "When last I looked at him, wasn't nothin' I could do . . . jus' turn my back an' keep on walkin'. I hopes ta God I ain neber gonna have ta go tru nothin' like dat agin in my life. Neber." Lydia began bathing the girl's small feet in the stream as she spoke, her ample frame bent double at the waist. Crooning reassurances, the slave splashed cool water on Chrissy's thin dirty legs.

"Do you have any news of Harrisburg?" Cora wanted to know.

"Only that General Houston's on his way," Emily told her, then added, "and the President's set up the government there, but I heard this more than ten days ago. I don't know what's happening now."

Cora gently removed the baby from her breast and laid his sleeping form across her knees. Lifeless blonde hair fell in stringy shadows over her face as she watched the tiny infant slumber.

Emily shifted her gaze from Cora to Lydia. So, these were the people she had been hearing about, the homeless settlers scraping over the prairie, running from the burning, looting Mexican Army. She stretched out her hand to Cora.

"Come with me. There's a cabin not too far."

And quietly, without speaking again, Emily led the stranded settlers to the clearing where Joshua waited.

✦-✦-✦⋯✦-✦-✦

"We've had nothing but hard bread and water for the last six days," Cora said, rolling a small piece of dried fish into a ball, slipping it into Chrissy's mouth. "The little food we were able to take with us ran out very quickly. We were afraid to leave the trail and hunt roots."

"Dat's de truf for shore," Lydia said. "I sees many a place where I thinks . . . now more'n likely dere's young tubers in de ground, good eatin' tubers . . . but we's too scared ta stop so's I kin dig em up. Lawd, we's been hongry so long." Lydia cracked open another oyster and slid it over her thick pink tongue. She winked at Joshua. "Deese is de best oysters I eber ate. Been a spell since somethin' dis good pass 'tween deese teeth." Her hearty laugh filled the small cabin and lightened the mood for a moment.

"No one can go West," Cora started up. "The Mexicans have columns of men stretching from San Felipe de Austin, south to the Gulf."

Joshua paced in silence as the frail woman spoke.

"Every town is burned," she went on, "there's no one left at San Felipe . . . no one. I just hope we can get to Harrisburg."

Emily looked up and caught Joshua's eye, narrowing her stare in concern. Cora's words settled over them both. There was more danger to the West than either of them had believed. Joshua pulled his eyes from hers, and in an abrupt movement, he walked out the cabin door and headed toward the bay.

"Why don't you try to sleep for a while?" Emily suggested as she rose to spread her straw pallet near the small fire struggling in the hearth. "All of you should rest. You can't go on as you are."

"You's right," Lydia said, taking the sleeping infant from Cora. "Miss Cora, you lay on back, now. I kin take care o' dis chile. You needs rest ta get your strength back. Go on, now, lay back." Lydia helped her mistress settle down on the pallet, then scooted back into a darkened corner, rocking the baby back and forth.

Emily left the women alone and went to sit on the stoop of the cabin door. She watched Joshua's tall lone figure walk solemnly along the bay. With his hands firmly clasped behind his back and his head lowered, Emily could tell he was worried. Would he have to go on west without her? she wondered. Would he leave the women alone to fend for themselves? She turned Cora's words over and over in her mind as the afternoon sun rose higher in the sky and the forest turned steamy and wet.

When Joshua finally turned toward Emily, she could see, even from a distance, that there was a calmness in his expression. As if he had somehow purged himself of his many fears and doubts which had been plaguing him since she had known him, he now stared at her with a serene look. He took long steps in her direction, not stopping until he towered closely nearby.

"We'll hitch your mule to their wagon and start out for Orange Grove." The decision was made. "Let's start as soon as possible."

✦-✦-✦--✦-✦-✦

Near dusk, as wispy shadows at the end of the day began to fade the countryside gray, Joshua slapped a stinging switch against the mule's hindquarters and pressed him faster toward the plantation. The animal doubled his steps, lurching unevenly over sticky black soil which sucked at his hooves and threatened to bring the wagon to a halt.

Rain drizzled down from ragged purple clouds filling the travelers with a dreaded anticipation that heavier rains were coming. As they walked, their stony faces displayed a controlled urgency. None could speak. Reaching the protective haven of Orange Grove was all that mattered.

Emily and Lydia walked behind the creaking truck cart, while Cora and her children rode inside. The white haired Negress carried a pail of water to douse the grinding wheels from time to time to keep them from catching on fire. She would toss the water with strong heaving thrusts, then utter oaths against "de enemy what be hot on our heels like hounds set on a coon." Then, she would run wet hands over her shiny black face and start to curse the heat.

For April, it was intolerably hot, and the fading sun brought no relief, it only set the stage for the emergence of twice as many mosquitos as had pestered them in daylight. The baby lay swathed completely in Cora's dirty black scarf, but Chrissy slapped and hit at the stinging insects which left a scattering of red welts on her tender young flesh. The little girl did not complain. She did not cry. She sat huddled under her mother's arms, with listless, vacant eyes focused on nothing in particular.

It was not long before Emily began to see others like her companions. The refugees of the flatlands, were trekking to safety with all their possessions heaped haphazardly onto carts. Whimpering children sat atop bursting feather mattresses, or were carried awkwardly in the arms of frightened slaves. Horses, pigs, cattle, and dogs mingled with the throngs of people, who ran like terrified fugitives away from the pursuing enemy.

More than fifty families now jammed the muddy roads leading toward New Washington. When the Morgan's sprawling plantation finally came into view, Emily's breath caught in her throat and her stomach twisted fiercely into a hard knot. Orange Grove looked like a battlefield.

A scarred plain of blazing fires and sunken ruts lay before her. Flatbed wagons, shallow carts, and sleighs of all types were strewn from the edge of the forest right up to the back door of the main house. Gaunt, faceless men and women wandered in confusion and panic among the loose cattle that had been driven into the camp. From this tangled pool of frightened settlers rose the moans and wails of sick children.

Emily lifted her skirts and ran forward toward the large house, leaving Joshua and the women behind. Such chaos! Such suffering! In the short time since she had left Orange Grove, it had become a gathering point for stranded, homeless Texans. She took wider steps, paying no attention to the muddy earth which tried to slow her down. The wind off the bay gathered strength, pressing warm salty air against her skin. Emily held her hair back from her face with one hand, turning quickly to cup the other around her lips in an effort to direct her voice over gusting winds toward Joshua.

"Take Cora and the children to my cabin," she yelled, her words swept away into the deepening dusk. "I'll go on to the house." Warm drizzling rain settled on her cheeks, soaked into her dress, and crept into the tops of her worn leather boots. As the wind now whipped her billowing skirts around her, Emily headed to the house to see what she could do.

Windows in the main house blazed with oil lamps, the chimneys belched black clouds of smoke, and a throng of slave children huddled in frightened clumps at the back door. Emily rushed past them and entered.

"So, you's back," Hanna shot at her as soon as Emily closed the heavy door to the kitchen. Standing on a high stool, dropping foodstuffs into a tall curved barrel, Hanna stopped with her hand in mid air. "High an' mighty 'bout time you showed your face 'round here." The girl's displeasure at Emily's absence was evident. "De massa done come back from de island . . . powerful mad you ain' here tendin' ta Miss Celia. Powerful mad wid you, he is."

Emily moved quickly out of the way as two slaves rolled a large barrel out the door. Other field hands came in with another empty one for Hanna to fill.

"Why are you packing up all the food?" Emily asked.

"Cause dey's leavin'," Hanna said.

"Who's leaving?"

"Massa Morgan, Miss Celia, an' some more white folks what got nuf sense dan ta stay 'round here an' wait for de Mexicans ta come an' kill em. Ain' nobody gonna be here when de enemy come but sick white folks an' niggers." Hanna got back to her packing, looking away from Emily as if she had been dismissed.

"How is she? Miss Celia?" Emily wanted to know.

"Worse'n when you was here. Don' know how she even gonna make de boat trip ta de island. Ain' got no strength at all." Hanna never lifted an eye toward Emily.

Emily spun around on her heels and fled through the house, brushing through the crowd of strangers milling there, crossing the living quarters to the narrow step ladder leading to Celia Morgan's room.

She stopped in the doorway to find James Morgan leaning over his wife, trying to get her on her feet. Celia's eyes fluttered open, and she caught sight of Emily.

"Emily . . . the house . . . my furniture . . . watch out for it all." Her voice was trembling with fear and sickness. "Stay here, don't you run away again and leave all my things to thieving Mexicans." She was frantic. "James says I must leave. Emily, promise me you'll watch over the house. Don't let anyone take my . . . "

"All right, Celia," James Morgan interrupted his wife's rambling. "She'll stay with the rest of the darkies. Don't worry. Now, come and try to stand, Dear. We've got to leave." He looked over his frail wife's head at Emily. "Give me a hand, here."

Emily hurried to the bedside as Celia Morgan swayed heavily against her husband, then sat down again on the edge of the bed.

"I'm too weak, James," she said. Tears streamed down the sides of her face, and she pressed pale hands to her chest in confusion. "Leave me, James. I can't go with you."

"Yes, you can make it, Miss Celia," Emily reassured the frightened woman. "Just let me help you up." Emily put both hands around her mistress' waist and lifted her to her feet. With James Morgan's aid, she managed to get Celia down the stairs and through the house to the edge of the open breezeway. There, James Morgan turned to Emily.

"Stay with her. I need to make sure the boat's ready." He wiped perspiration from his dripping brow and looked around in concern. In the crush of frantic people, he seemed to be a stranger on his own land. "I've got to find someone to help me load it. Looks like all the darkies have either run off or are too scared to be any help to me."

The dark wet night cloaked much of the chaos, settling over the ragged tangle of men and women like a black misty veil. The rain had stopped and fires illuminated circles of land, and the smell of smoldering pine was so thick Emily could taste it. She calculated her words as she watched James Morgan lower Celia to the damp plank flooring. When he straightened up and stepped off the porch, headed toward the bay, she took a deep breath and told him, "Joshua Kinney is here." Morgan turned to look at Emily.

Her large dark eyes held his for a moment too long. She steeled herself for whatever reaction might come, for she had no assurance at all that James Morgan would welcome Joshua's presence at

Orange Grove. In the bedlam which prevailed at this moment, she took the risk of finding out where James Morgan stood on this issue.

He broke his gaze on her with a jerk of his head, and Emily recognized a slight softening to his face.

"Good," the master of Orange Grove finally said. "I can use a man like Joshua right now." He strode away from the two women, letting the heavy night air close in behind him, but called back from a distance where he could not be seen, "Where can I find him? I need him right now."

"In the stables," Emily shouted after him, knowing that was where Joshua would have waited for her. She pressed her lips together in worry, hoping that Joshua would trust James Morgan enough to show himself. With a sigh, Emily dropped to her knees beside her mistress. She cradled the sick woman's head against her shoulder, knowing that this could very well be the last time she would see Celia Morgan alive.

Chapter Fourteen

In shrill bellows across the prairie, the cry "Mexicans" passed in warning. Whipped into a state of panic, settlers pushed eastward, determined to cross the Trinity River and find safety in the United States. Escape took precedence over safeguarding possessions. Furniture, trunks of family treasures, and valuable handmade tools were discarded all over the countryside. Empty houses, so quickly deserted, stood open and skeletal with meals still on tables and pots boiling in hearths. Cattle wandered aimlessly along the roads, following the pathetic confused Texans who struggled toward an unknown salvation thought to be somewhere in the east.

Emily knew it was useless to think of leaving Orange Grove. No one knew exactly where the Texas Army camped or what Sam Houston's plan of action was. Talk of American intervention in support of the flagging Texas Army circulated on everyone's lips, but hopes for victory faded each day as Houston retreated further and further toward the Trinity River, appearing to flee from Santa Anna. Help from the United States seemed the only answer.

With the main house abandoned and no one really in charge, Emily found herself taking over in the absence of the mistress of Orange Grove. She was a house servant, no more than that, and in the opinion of many, a lot less. But for now, she had to take control.

Emily moved through the four main rooms of Colonel Morgan's split log house making sure windows were boarded over, valuable furniture removed, and Celia Morgan's silver candlesticks were buried in the woods. Black and white, free and slave, all women who were able pitched in to help Emily secure the plantation.

A barricade of logs, barrels and scrap iron sprang up around the newly created fortress. A small arsenal of rifles and shotguns lay positioned, ready for use. It was war, and the reality of it brought a deathly calm to the handful of men left behind to defend the colonel's sprawling home.

Starting her days before sun-up, often after sleeping right in the kitchen next to the hearth, Emily was totally exhausted. Hauling water, boiling clothes, gathering and preparing food, taxed her endurance to the limit. Hanna, Lydia, and several other slave women helped as much as possible, but the burden of managing the house now fell fully on Emily's shoulders. Driven by her promise to Celia Morgan, she did not stop to consider that she was in danger.

Out on the plantation, Joshua helped Sam herd livestock into pens built hastily in the woods. They continued to load arriving flatboats with provisions to be ferried over to Galveston Island. There was no shortage of food.

Evening's approach caught Emily stirring a large pot of boiling beef. Heat radiated up from the fire, closing in around her face in scorching waves. The humid night air pressed in off the bay, so wet and hot that Emily could scarcely breathe.

"Put them in now," Emily said to Hanna. "Put them all in . . . it doesn't matter if some aren't peeled." She was so tired and hot she felt she might faint, and her mind was not on this pot of potatoes and beef simmering in front of her right now. Food had to be prepared and people fed, although some of them were too sick and weak to even feed themselves.

"You reckon dem Mexicans really gonna come dis way?" Hanna was scared. She had been crying off and on for the last two days. "Dey gonna round us all up an' shoot us . . . jus' like dey did at Goliad. I knows it . . . I knows it comin'."

"Stop it, Hanna." Emily was losing patience with the girl. Her constant babble kept everyone on the place upset. "Maybe they'll come, maybe not. Don't think about it. We've got enough to do to keep our minds off that. Anyway, there's no place to go . . . except into the woods."

"I thinks I's jus' 'bout as scared o' de woods at night as I be o' dem Mexicans. Ain' much choice fo' me."

"The Texas Army has probably already caught up with Santa Anna. I'll bet Sam Houston's whipped the Mexicans soundly." Emily tried to sound convincing.

"Don't know 'bout dat," Hanna was skeptical. "From what I heered, dem white folks ain' rightly shore but what Gen'ral

Houston done already crossed over inta de United States. Dey seems mighty disgusted wid him."

"That's just talk, Hanna, crazy talk."

"Maybe," Hanna said, dropping onions, one at a time, into the boiling liquid. "But de onliest news what eber come on dis place was what de Mexicans done did ta us. I's yet ta hear a word 'bout some fightin' we done won.".

Emily knew Hanna spoke the truth. Sam Houston had yet to lead his first attack, and there were rumors that his men had threatened to desert. If General Houston would not advance on his enemy, his men stood ready to mutiny.

Emily changed the subject as she ladled half of the hot stew into a wooden bucket. "Feed those at the house, Hanna. I'll take what's left down to the quarters. Those who can, should move off the place tonight, hide in the woods." She stopped mixing the stew with her wide ladle and looked directly at Hanna.

"Lawd. Lawd. I's so scared," Hanna's words came out in a husky sob which gave way to open tears. "I wisht I was still in Carolina . . . ain' been nothin' but a bad time eber since I come here. Dis is de awfulest mess I eber been in." The young girl smeared tears across her cheeks with a dirty hand. "What we gonna do?"

"We're going to get the rest of the women and children into the main house, that's what," Emily said testily, taking hold of Hanna's shoulder. "You've got to help me, Hanna. Get a hold of yourself and stop that crying. Now, take this food up and feed the men at the house. I'm going down to the quarters and see about Cora and the others there. Hurry, we don't have much time."

Emily thrust the heavy wooden bucket into Hanna's shaking hand, picked up her pail of the same boiling stew, and hurried down the grassy slope behind the house. Cutting through the maze of snorting, pawing horses and men bent over low fires talking, she wondered if there was any hope that the people trapped at Orange Grove would really be able to protect themselves.

Skirting the edge of an uncontrolled campfire, Emily yanked her hem away from creeping flames and beat at the scorched fabric with her free hand. Straightening up, she caught sight of a writhing, snake-like figure in black moving steadily among the cabins. The woman was pointing and poking with a thin black cane as she went from cabin to cabin. It was Wilena, the body wrapper. She shuffled along in a dogged fashion, directed by some ancient instinct that carried her precisely to the hut where a body lay. And when a corpse was located, Wilena staked her cane at the shanty entrance and hobbled into the dark interior. Emily watched Wilena go off to do her deathly chore, remembering how this toothless, wrinkled woman had performed her ritual on Diana.

I never thought I'd see so much death at Orange Grove, Emily thought, taking a deep breath to still the quaking tremors tugging at her chest. Then, she cautiously entered her cabin.

Stepping over sleeping forms, she made her way to a far corner where Cora sat huddled with her two children.

"How are you feeling?" Emily asked.

"Much stronger," Cora answered, pushing herself up to a sitting position. "I'd like to help you . . . I can pour lead, help with the cooking." She started to rise, but Emily placed a gentle hand on the woman's shoulder.

"No," she cautioned. "Stay here with your children. You're not strong enough to do more. Having Lydia to help with the cooking and feeding has been a blessing. You rest . . . you'll be needing all your strength for the days ahead."

Emily glanced around the crowded room. There was one other white woman there, sitting against the wall, cradling a little boy on her lap. The boy's leg was bandaged with stained cloth and Emily knew he was feverish with pain and infection.

The woman's eyes caught Emily's. "Is there any water? He's so hot."

Emily stepped nearer, bending to place the back of her hand on the child's brow. It was dry and hot.

"I'll get you some," she told the worried mother. "Here, I've brought a pot of stew. Try to get him to eat." Turning back to Cora, she added. "You and Chrissy should eat also. This may be the last food we'll be able to prepare today. We don't know what to expect." Emily placed the food down and left the cabin, hurrying up the hill toward the dimly lit kitchen.

Another night of waiting and watching was upon them, and Emily had an ominous premonition that their luck was running out. If the Mexican Army were really headed toward New Washington, it would not be long before Orange Grove would be invaded.

As she climbed onto the open breezeway and entered the smokey kitchen, Lydia's voice greeted her.

"... an' dat's de way it was. No more'n fifteen minutes ... dat's all de time it took for dem Mexicans ta make a pile o' ashes outta de town. Miss Cora, de chillen an' I slipped out de back o' de house an' hid in de brake, waitin' til de Mexicans moved on. Den, we loads up de truck-cart wid a little food an' took ta de road. Wasn't nobody much left dere anyways, wasn't no reason ta stay dere. Leastwise, here, you's got 'nuf men ta put up a good fight ... "

"Gonna need a heap more hands dan what's on dis place ta turn 'em back," Sam cautioned Lydia. "We ain' eben got 'nuf bullets made ta use de guns we's got."

Emily walked to the far side of the hot, stuffy kitchen, taking in what Sam had said.

"You don't think we can defend the place?" she asked.

"Naw, not fer long," Sam answered. "De way I hears it, dere's more'n a thousand soldiers marchin' wid Santa Anna. Don't sound too good ta me." He nailed a circular piece of wood into the top of a barrel, then scratched a crooked *X* on the side. "We's gonna hide as much as we can tote into de woods. Ain' no use in feedin' de Devil." He pushed the barrel onto its side and started rolling it out of the kitchen. Hanna and Lydia immediately began lowering sacks of corn and sugar into another cavernous container. A single lantern gave off a hazy yellow glow, casting flickering shadows on the laboring women.

"How Miss Cora doin'?" Lydia inquired about her mistress, not interrupting her rhythmic swing as she lowered a sack of flour into the barrel.

"She seems stronger," Emily answered. "But I'm worried about that little boy with the infected leg. He's burning up with fever."

"Poor chile," Lydia said, "most likely he gonna lose dat leg. I ain' neber seen nothin' so bad off, eben on a grown man."

Emily searched around for a full bucket of water.

"No more water up here?" she asked.

"Naw," Hanna answered, "but I kin run down ta de well an' fetch some."

"No, I'll go," Emily said, reaching with tired arms to take a shallow basin off the wall. She wiped her hands on the front of her apron, then used the tip of the stained cloth to mop perspiration from her brow. With urgent steps, she left the kitchen and headed toward the well.

Fatigue had made her light-headed, dizzy, and other than a piece of salted beef this morning, she had had nothing to eat. Still, wet air off the bay closed in, sapping her energy, leaving a vacant emptiness inside.

A crown of twinkling stars hung over the land. Bright glistening points spread in patches on a solid black sky. Emily lifted her thick long hair off her neck, but no breeze cooled the surface of her skin. She looked out over the horizon where a fire roared, rising straight up from the ground in leaping twisting flames. Flashing white-hot with intensity, the luminous combustion lit up Orange Grove. Emily could see men gathered around it, patiently turning pieces of iron into hot, molten liquid. Throughout the night they would work, creating bullets and knives. She searched the night for Joshua, then saw him pass the blazing pyre, kneeling to pour a ladle of molten lead into a cast.

She had hardly spoken to him at all in the last three days. As they both had taken up the task of fortifying Orange Grove, there had been no time for them.

Emily filled with pride as she watched Joshua from a distance. She was proud that he had not run away to Mexico, proud he had taken his chances in Texas. This was where he belonged, he was instinctively tied to this land, and Emily felt he wanted to call it home. In the midst of the confusion of preparing for war, no one had questioned Joshua's loyalty.

Tonight, no sounds from the quarters disturbed the night air. No spirituals drifted up in rhythmic magic and no childish voices taunted in play. As if abandoned, the deserted log shanties faced one another mutely over a river of mud which had once been a road. Silence weighed upon the quarters, but Emily knew behind each door a family huddled in fear.

Turning away from the blazing light on the horizon, Emily cut down past the cabins to the isolated well. Under the lacy cover of a huge willow tree, she lowered a staved wooden bucket into the hollow watering hole. It floated, then sank and filled. Steadying herself to lift the heavy bucket, Emily took a deep breath, reached for the curved handle of the iron crank and put her full weight to the task.

The sound of footsteps approaching from behind stopped her.

Emily glanced over her shoulder. "Sam?" She waited for a moment. No one answered. Strange, Emily thought. Someone is there, just beyond the willow boughs. "Sam? Is that you," she called again. Surely, it's Sam, she assured herself, who else would be wandering out of the woods?

And as she calmed herself, believing it must be Sam, the realization that the Mexican soldiers were not far away shot through her like a driving pain. A chill ran over her arms. Suppose it was one of them? Them! Here! Now! Emily pressed her lips together, not breathing at all. She listened again.

The muffled sound of boots on grass made Emily's legs go weak. She clutched the edge of the well.

"Who's there?" she yelled, anger now rising in her voice. "Show yourself!" Once more, there was no reply.

Emily turned back to the well, frantically grinding the hand crank in a circular motion. She hauled the bucket of icy water to the edge and held it up in front of her with shaking, slippery hands. Peering into the cavernous darkness before her, Emily waited, breathing in deep labored gulps as she pressed herself against the moss-covered well for support.

The shadows of the willow tree parted. A man came forward, approaching quietly, no rush to his steps. The moon took advantage of the opening he provided and washed over the intruder's face.

"You! It's you!" Emily screamed. "Stay away from me!" She heaved the full bucket in a wild forceful thrust, and water sloshed out in a frenzied spray directly into Clabe's bearded face.

Backing away, Emily screamed, "Leave me alone . . . stay away from me!" Now, angry tears ran from her eyes and her shrieks were hoarse and raw.

Clabe set his long black rifle on the ground, ripped off his cowhide hat and tossed it into the shadows. As Emily scrambled further into the woods, he advanced in an unsteady gait toward her.

"Ain't nobody comin' to help you," the words were low and threatening. "Ain't you learned by now, I get what I want, an' ain't no need for you to go shoutin'?"

"Don't come near me," Emily growled, feeling cornered, trapped by this relentless stalker. Hatred, fear, and anger all welled up in her chest. "Please, leave me alone."

"So, now the nigger wench is begging, is she? Well, I ain't got no plans to leave you alone." Clabe lurched forward. Emily stumbled backward, circling around the well again. She jammed herself against the eerie willow tree, cringing under its dripping fronds. Wispy branches left stringy shadows on the bearded soldier's face, and Emily placed her hands behind her back, touching the tree trunk, feeling for something to throw. There was nothing.

Out of the humid blackness, Clabe's large white hand shot forth. Pawing and tearing, he closed in on her waist.

"No, no . . . get away from me." Emily pushed at him as the rancid smell of whiskey pressed down on her. Wretched contractions jolted her, but she managed to get one arm between his body and hers. She pushed back with all her strength and spun out of his drunken grasp.

"Jus' like some lil ol' rabbit," Clabe's words were thick and slurred. "All soft an' quick to jump." He laughed and stumbled forward, throwing himself at Emily. Together, they crashed to the ground, his body's dead weight on top of her. Emily lay trapped, suffocating.

A tree limb snapped above them. Clabe looked up, leaning away from Emily. Squinting with bleary, drunken eyes, he peered around. Emily pushed herself out from under Clabe in time to see Joshua emerge in the moonlight.

Silver light bathed his copper face, giving him the appearance of a man carved of wood . . . highly polished and immobile. He clutched a thick tree limb with both hands, raised overhead, poised to strike. Swiftly, in a flash of movement, Joshua delivered a blow of hatred and anger, crushing the side of Clabe's bearded face.

There were only two sounds in the forest: bone splitting from soft torn flesh, and the thud of Clabe's body as it rolled to the ground.

Emily never screamed.

On her knees, she scurried back, away from the body, crouching low to the damp earth with her hands pressed over her mouth. Blood raced to her head, perspiration ran from her temples, and paralyzed with fear, she stared at Joshua.

Splattered with blood, he stood clutching a stout limb with an iron grip.

"Oh, my God . . . Joshua . . . he's dead." She gaped at the man's head which was split open from his hairline to his jaw. "Joshua! You've killed him!"

"Yes," Joshua agreed in a flat leaden tone. "I've killed him. It's done." He threw aside the blood stained log, hurling it deeply into the woods. Leaning down to slip his hands under Emily's quivering arms, he pulled her to him, almost roughly, pressing her head to his shoulder with the expanse of one large hand. Emily buried her face in his jacket, sobbing.

Joshua said nothing, only gripped her with an intensity which seemed to fuse the two of them together. Firmly rooted where he stood, Joshua remained rigid and unmoving as Emily's sobs continued.

She lifted her head slowly, daring to look once more at Clabe's bleeding fatal wound.

"You've killed him . . . Joshua, what will we do?"

Joshua gently pushed her away, holding her shoulders as he spoke. "We have to leave here . . . now."

"Leave New Washington? Where could we go?"

"North. If we can get to the Trinity River, we can make it north into the United States."

"It's impossible to get . . . " Emily halted. She leaned back against Joshua quickly. "Listen. Someone's coming!"

The damp earth beneath them trembled with advancing footsteps.

"Shush," Joshua hissed lowly, putting a hand on Emily's mouth. They stood in silence waiting.

"Clabe? You down there?" Words boomed loudly through the trees. Another soldier was coming. "Clabe?" he called again, nearing the well.

Joshua shoved Emily in front of him, forcing her to walk out of the shadows, into the moonlight. A stumpy little man walked up to them, dwarfed by the elongated shadows from the overhanging boughs.

"You darkies ain't got nothing better to do than hang around out here?" The man's face twisted into a sneering grin. "I'm looking for Clabe Ledbeder, seen him?"

"No, sir," Joshua hurried to answer. "Ain't seen a soul. Somethin' you need?"

"Water. The men at the house need more water. Clabe was coming to get some . . . wonder where the drunken bastard is."

"I'll bring some water right up," Joshua offered. "Right away, two big buckets . . . I'll be comin' right up." He held his breath hoping the soldier would not try to pass him, hoping the moon would not betray him, hoping Emily could keep control.

The runt of a man rubbed a bristly chin, shifted his eyes from Emily to Joshua, then said, "All right, but hurry it up, boy. I'm not gonna wait while you fool around with this gal."

"No, sir, I'm bringin' it right up."

With one last suspicious look at the two of them, the soldier turned on his heel and left. Emily began to shake uncontrollably.

"What are we going to do? He'll be back."

Joshua leveled his eyes with hers, holding firmly to her shoulders as he spoke in slow, clear tones. "You take the water up to the house. I'll get rid of the body."

Emily was horrified. "Where? Where are you going to put it?"

"In the swamp behind the cabins." Joshua leaned down and grabbed Clabe's lifeless body by the arms, dragging him toward the swamp.

"Go on, now. Take that water to the house," he urged Emily.

And she did as he ordered, walking on trembling legs to the front of the house toting two large buckets of water. About a dozen ragged men lounged behind their crude barricade, smoking, drinking, and waiting.

" 'Bout time you got here," the same runt of a soldier yelled out when Emily appeared. "Bring that bucket over here."

Praying that she could control herself, Emily struggled under the weight of the water, making her way to where the soldier sat.

"Put it down, here," he commanded, pointing to a spot very near an open barrel of whiskey. Moonlight bathed the men in an eerie silvery light, and Emily could tell that they were very drunk.

"You sure you didn't see Clabe Ledbeder down there at the well?" the soldier persisted, rising on his knees in inquiry.

She looked down. "No, sir. I didn't see nobody there."

"Hump . . . drunken bastard . . . probably gone off in the woods with some fresh nigger wench." He leaned back on his heels, squatting in Emily's path. Eyes clouded by whiskey raked Emily from head to toe. "I want you to stay here," he decided, "might be needin' some more water, or food . . . anyway, it's gonna be a long night waitin' for these damn Mexicans to show. Might need a little entertainin'," he laughed deeply.

Emily froze. She had to get away.

"Why don't I jus' run to the kitchen an' bring up some stew that's ready and hot. The men might like that," she eased closer to the seated man, letting her skirts brush his knee. "Then I'll be happy to stay and serve ya'll," she humored him, forcing a sweetened tone into her voice.

"You do that," he agreed, leaning up toward her waist. "Go get the stew, then come keep me company." He roared in laughter.

"Yes, sir," she said, slightly bowing as she backed away. "Won't be more'n a minute. Be right back."

Backing out of the light of their campfire, Emily fled to the edge of the house, then broke into a frantic run, rushing breathlessly down the hill and straight into Joshua's arms.

"You've got to go on without me. We cannot leave together."

Joshua kissed her tear streaked cheeks, lips, eyes, holding her with a vice-like grip around her waist. "I won't go without you," he spoke into the tangle of her long raven hair. He was angry that she would ask him to go. "You're coming with me, Emily . . . I will not leave you again. If I leave, you go with me."

Emily pressed both hands to the back of Joshua's neck, forcing his face closer to hers. She whispered in a frenzy, "You must. You must go without me . . . it's too dangerous to try to leave together. Those soldiers . . . they want me there . . . at the house. If I don't come back, they'll come looking for me." Emily was crying as she talked, writhing as if to get free of Joshua's grip.

"Emily, come with me. Now! Damn those soldiers. Damn this war. I will not leave Texas without you." The anger and rage in his voice frightened Emily. She ran her fingers along the side of Joshua's face, tracing the curve of his jaw, the swell of his lips. She looked at him knowing that what she wanted more than life itself was to go with him now . . . to stay with Joshua forever . . . but it was impossible.

"Joshua, that soldier is suspicious. If we leave Orange Grove together, we're in trouble. How far do you think we could get before they'd find us? Bring us back? Or shoot us on sight? I'd be missed . . . not you. Go on, leave this place, you have to get away." These last words were spoken in a rush of frantic urgings.

Joshua shook his head, denying her advice, not wanting to hear more. "I'd rather stay here and be taken, than go on without you."

Emily ran her fingers through his dark, wavy hair, then pressed his head to her breast. "I love you, I love you so very much."

Joshua lifted his face to hers, and she saw tears wetting the surface of his skin. There was agony harbored behind those honey-colored eyes. He could not leave her again.

"All right," he started, "I'll go as far as Anahuac. I'll wait there. Three days. Come to me there . . . I'll wait for you."

"Yes . . . yes . . . " Emily agreed, anxious for him to be on his way, afraid the soldier would come looking for her. "Go to Anahuac, wait for me there three days. I'll get away somehow."

"Promise me. Promise me, Emily . . . you'll come? I cannot leave you here like this unless I know I'll see you in Anahuac."

"I'll be there . . . three days from now. Don't worry, my love. Nothing will stop me. Nothing."

Joshua crushed her to him, kissed her deeply, then he let her go. As the black humid night closed in behind him, Emily knew she had kissed Joshua for the very last time. This war had wrenched her lover out of her arms. It had destroyed their future together.

Chapter Fifteen

General Don Antonio Lopez de Santa Anna de Lebron, President of Mexico and Commander in Chief of the Mexican Army, raised his crystal goblet of tepid champagne and toasted his bride, Melchora. Beaming with pride as he looked into the young woman's dark almond eyes, the handsome dictator struck a pose of self assured arrogance.

His three cornered hat and medal laden breast coat lent credence to the rumor that Santa Anna openly referred to himself as the Napoleon of the West. At forty-two, with an impressive history of military victories, the charismatic general basked in a glorious opulence he felt was his due. Tall, broad shouldered and narrow waisted, he emerged as a curiously striking figure crossing the vast Texas flatlands in pursuit of Sam Houston.

As the gigantic spoked wheels of his low riding coach ground slowly over the soft black soil, a rhythmic cadence of metal clanking on wood echoed vacantly over the prairie. Hooves thudded dully on either side of the carriage, giving Santa Anna an immediate sense of protection afforded by armed dragoons.

Melchora Barrera demurely refused the general's offer of more wine by lowering her jet black lashes and turning her head aside. Long straight hair brushed softly across her shoulders, resting darkly on the cream colored satin of her traveling dress. With a jeweled hand, she pushed her heavy tresses back and away from her face.

"You don't care to join me in a toast to our future?" Santa Anna asked in a slightly thickened tone.

"No more wine for me, *Señor*," Melchora said, now lifting her eyes to meet the general's. "I'm beginning to feel a little dizzy. This heat, *Señor* . . . it's unbearable." She pulled a square of cotton lace from the folds of her skirt and dabbed at her brow, then, rested her hand over her nose. Momentarily blocking out the rancid odor of sweating horse flesh sifting into the darkened compartment, she asked, "Is there never a breeze to stir the air in this part of Texas, *Señor?*"

Santa Anna made no reply, letting the snorting of restless animals fill a short silence. He busied himself with uncorking another dark green bottle of French champagne which he pulled from a crate at his feet. "So, I drink alone on my honeymoon," he muttered querulously, more to himself than to his bride.

Now it was Melchora's turn to remain silent, having already learned that her new husband had a low tolerance for alcohol. After no more than two glasses of wine, he spoke crossly to all in his presence. She had no desire to start an argument with her husband of less than two months . . . for Melchora Barrera, a girl of seventeen, still naively believed that her marriage to the President of Mexico was valid.

The authenticity of the general's marriage to this youthful beauty from San Antonio was never openly questioned. But behind intricate lace curtains adorning the windows of the best homes in the city, the matter of Mrs. Barrera's only daughter's marriage to the President of Mexico was a popular topic of discussion.

Melchora's mother, a sultry widow of substance and influence, remained tight lipped on the subject. And, while making her social rounds in the provincial town where the Alamo had fallen, the aging beauty astutely insisted that Santa Anna had begged for her daughter's hand. According to her, the matter had been agreed upon. The President himself had personally arranged the ceremony. So, if Mrs. Barrera had, in fact, known that the priest performing the ritual was really a soldier from Santa Anna's ranks, she had wisely kept this information from her ecstatic daughter. By maintaining a facade of innocence to the community, the widow Barrera had cast a deepening shadow of doubt on the vicious gossip surrounding Melchora's wedding.

Santa Anna managed to pour himself half a glass of wine before his coach lurched to a grinding halt. He quickly drained the sparkling liquid with one forceful swallow.

"*¿Por qué nos paramos?*" the dictator yelled to the coachman, sticking his entire head and shoulders out the velvet curtained window of his elegant carriage. Receiving no response to his inquiry about why the coach had stopped, he angrily tossed his heavy glass to the ground. "Why are we stopping again? Why?" Santa Anna bellowed in disgust. He fumbled at the gold plated door handle as he tried to get out. "Can we make no progress in this uncivilized marshland? I am tired . . . sick and tired of all these delays." His voice grew thinner and more highly pitched with each word, and a purple flush crept up from the high stiff collar of his dark blue uniform.

"*Cálmate, Señor,*" Melchora murmured in an effort to calm the enraged dictator. "*Cálmate, por favor, Señor.*"

Santa Anna paid no attention to his bride's request, brushing her small pale hand from his arm. He stepped from the coach with one long stride and sloshed through mud to the head of his expedition.

Surrounded by a crowd of festively uniformed dragoons, Santa Anna waited, arms crossed on his broad chest for someone to explain this irritating holdup.

Colonel Juan Almonte, the President's aide, rode up on a large feisty bay and stopped at a distance from his leader. "Your Excellency," he started, pulling himself regally erect in his saddle, "the river is much too high and dangerous for you to cross. The carriage cannot be ferried, I'm afraid."

"What do you mean? I cannot cross? It is imperative that I reach General Sesma as soon as possible. You know he waits our reinforcements at San Felipe de Austin."

"This is true, Your Excellency," Almonte agreed, lifting a bearded chin in a haughty gesture of confidence. "However, I am sure it will take at least two days to ferry the wagons, artillery, and provisions to the other side. The coach, Your Excellency, will have to be returned to Mexico." The overweight aide sucked in his puffy cheeks and fixed Santa Anna with a nervous stare, as if daring the general to refute his decision.

Santa Anna turned his back on Almonte, childishly clenching his fists in anger as a black scowl set on his face. He seriously scrutinized his traveling headquarters.

The low slung carriage, adorned with gilded scrolls and leather fittings, pulled by six white mules, stood mud-splattered in the afternoon sun. Behind it waited a smaller carriage for his commanding officers, the bulging wagon of camping gear, and a string of at least two hundred pack mules. Camp followers, mounted and on foot, joined the entourage. A bevy of beautiful women were included in this category.

Santa Anna waded through mud back to the velvet draped window and leaned toward Melchora.

"It appears that the carriage cannot be ferried across this God-awful river which separates me from the rest of my army." His annoyance was evident.

"And what does this mean?" asked Melchora. "Will we turn back?" She tilted her delicately pointed chin toward the general, waiting his reply.

"I will not turn back," Santa Anna said tersely. "But, here is where you and I must part."

"But, *Señor*," Melchora protested, "the carriage can be returned without me. I prefer to go on with the campaign. Please, do not make me leave you now."

Santa Anna covered her tiny hand with his in a surprising gesture of tenderness. "And who would I trust to guard my silver, save you?" His voice was convincing, persuasive. "You will agree to make the trip?" His question was a decisive statement.

Melchora leaned back against the soft leather cushions and pulled her brown velvet cape together with both hands. She shifted slightly, adjusting her position to see Santa Anna more clearly. Reclining in the dark shadows of the stuffy compartment, she concealed her angry pout from her husband. "If this is what you wish, Señor," she finally answered.

"Good. Good," Santa Anna was relieved there would be no argument, no ugly scene in front of the dragoons who stood watching. "I will send a trunk full of silver to the city with you, and you shall be installed in my apartment at the palace." He turned back to Almonte, who had remained at the head of the train. "Almonte, transfer all the silver and coin to this carriage. I want an escort to accompany my bride back to Mexico City. Quickly, now, quickly, we cannot lose another moment."

After a hasty farewell on the banks of the Guadelupe River, Melchora, sitting among silver goblets, candlesticks and coins, was pointed toward Mexico City under the protection of four heavily armed guards. Santa Anna barked orders to the leader of the train.

"I charge you with the responsibility of depositing all silver and gold coin to my accounts at the palace. And, I expect you to guarantee safe arrival of my beautiful wife at the palace within a fortnight."

"Do not fear," the young captain in charge answered. "The trip will be hastily and uneventfully made. This I guarantee."

Santa Anna dismissed the entourage with a wave of his hand and turned back to consult with Juan Almonte. Full attention could now be devoted to crossing the swollen river in order to continue tracking Sam Houston and the ragged troops, who had eluded him too long.

In Napoleonic style, Santa Anna sat atop one of his cages of prized fighting cocks and allowed himself to be ferried over the swift water on a crudely fashioned log raft. Then, reclining on the opposite side of the river, he ate a large piece of opium while observing the rest of the crossing. Suddenly bored with the Texas expedition, he called for another bottle of warm champagne and a curvaceous young girl to drink with him.

✦·✦·✦··✦·✦·✦

By April 7, 1836, Santa Anna arrived at San Felipe de Austin on the Brazos River and picked up seven hundred fifty of General Sesma's reinforcements. The Mexican leader's intention to hurriedly cross the Brazos was dashed when he saw that not only had Sam Houston recently burned the tiny town to ashes, but had also removed all serviceable boats. Santa Anna immediately set his men to building two flatboats. After completing the log rafts, he was surprised by gunfire from the banks on the opposite side of the river. A scouting party of Texans were entrenched there, firing wildly to keep him from crossing. Santa Anna was furious.

In the first open conflict between Santanistas and Sam Houston's troops, Santa Anna positioned his twin brass cannons on the shore of the river and started shelling his enemy. This exchange was so intense that after four days, the general decided to move further downstream and attempt a crossing at Fort Bend. He left behind a squadron of Mexicans under Sesma's command and proceeded on his way south.

At this time, Santa Anna was not really sure where Sam Houston had established his camp. Scouting patrols out in the field had last reported the Texans near Groce's plantation, twenty miles upstream. As the Mexican Army headed further south, the commanding officers wondered about their leader's plan but did not openly question it. They had all learned that Santa Anna's unpredictable temper and irrational behavior, constantly modified by large doses of opium, played havoc with the strategy of the Mexican campaign.

✦-✦-✦--✦-✦-✦

Inside the pitch-black compartment of his swaying carriage Santa Anna slumbered in a drug-induced state as his clanking train of wagons and pack mules wound southward along the dark Brazos River. Lying motionless under a finely woven blanket of Peruvian wool, a red satin pillow beneath his bare head, the dictator slipped deeper into his opium fantasy, oblivious to the raging norther whipping prairie grass flat to the ground. With knee-high boots to protect his feet and legs from the unusually cold April winds, the dozing general left strategic decisions to those who were second in command.

By midnight on April 10, the huge expedition ground to a clanking halt at an impressive log structure set back from the river. Its sloped roof, supported by three knotty posts, extended sharply down and out toward the road. The new, two-story building loomed tall and straight in the moonlight and was cloaked in the smell of freshly hewn pine. Still pale and oozing gum, it cast out the glow of low burning oil lamps, inviting the strangers to enter. It was a tavern . . . Mrs. Elizabeth Powell's tavern, the only resting place on the Brazos River between Columbia and San Felipe de Austin.

Juan Almonte shifted in his saddle and looked around to see that the entire train had stopped. He dismounted, grumbling and cursing the cold north wind as he slid from his horse.

"You wait here," he told another aide, "I'll go and see the owner of this place." He straightened his coat, tightened his belt and pulled on a pair of white kid gloves. Walking with the air of authority he rightly commanded, Almonte quickly disappeared inside the isolated tavern. He stayed inside only a few moments.

With the negotiations completed, the general's second in command emerged and approached Santa Anna's coach. Opening the stiff leather padded door, Almonte spoke to his leader in firm, clear tones.

"Your Excellency . . . Your Excellency," Almonte repeated until Santa Anna opened his eyes and focused on the dim lamp his aide was holding. "We have arrived at a resting place for the night." Juan Almonte ventured closer to Santa Anna, placing a large hand on his shoulder.

"What do you want?" Santa Anna muttered crossly, shrugging the officer's hand away.

"We've come across a tavern, I believe that's what it is. Perhaps you care to pass the night inside, Your Excellency." Almonte backed up slightly as the general sat up, groggily blinking his eyes.

"A tavern? Where?" Santa Anna spoke in a hoarse rush of words. "Where is this place?"

"Just a few paces ahead," Almonte answered. "I've spoken with the proprietor, an English woman . . . a Mrs. Powell, suggesting she offer this shelter to us. I informed her that food enough for fifty officers would also be most welcome." There was a boasting undertone to his words.

"And?" Santa Anna asked, now throwing aside his blanket, moving to the open door.

"And, how could she dare refuse my request? Of course, the tavern is yours if you wish, Your Excellency."

"But of course, Almonte. But, of course." Santa Anna was suddenly wide awake, smiling, looking forward to the luxury of an evening in decent quarters. "Take me to this woman." He fussed with his ruffled shirt and picked up his plumed hat. "I must express my appreciation to her for this generous offer."

Santa Anna stepped briskly from the carriage, pulled his three-cornered hat down firmly, and followed Almonte up a muddy narrow walkway. Smoke bellowed from a tall black chimney, and in a large low window, the silhouette of a woman was etched sharply against dim yellow light. The tavern offered vacant rooms on this deserted strip of land facing the Brazos River.

Almonte entered first, turning back to hold the slatted pine door open for Santa Anna. Pressing winds off the river gusted into the room, rattling fat oil lamps swinging from low flat beams. At the huge blazing hearth, a stone-faced woman stood, arms crossed firmly across her narrow chest. Her bonneted head was thrown back with a haughty stare and her lips were compressed into a thin red line. She fixed the two men with a look of disgust and waited in front of the fire as Almonte approached.

"Mrs. Powell," Almonte started, hurrying to the woman's side. "This is General Don Antonio Lopez de Santa Anna, President of Mexico." He bowed slightly and stepped back, giving Elizabeth Powell full view of the general. Santa Anna walked up to the thin angry woman.

"On behalf of my dedicated officers, I thank you for your generous hospitality." Santa Anna nodded, not removing his Napoleonic headgear.

Mrs. Powell said nothing. She did not move an inch nor blink an eye. Her expression conveyed her lack of respect for the foreigners arriving at her tavern.

Santa Anna appeared not to notice. "Almonte," he ordered, "a table by the fire." He quickly strode to the opposite side of the room to wait as Almonte shoved a long heavy table across the floor. "I'm freezing," Santa Anna complained. "Hurry, get me a chair."

Another aide positioned a high-backed chair at the end of the table and motioned for his leader to sit down.

Setting his ornate hat to one side, the Mexican general turned and snapped his fingers. "Some champagne . . . a crate, Almonte. Yes, bring in a crate of champagne and my medicine chest, too. I'm not feeling well this evening." He ran a small hand over his cheeks and lips, nervously watching as Almonte and an officer left the tavern.

"Come, men. Sit," he motioned to those still standing near the door. "Join me. We have plans to make." The dictator broke into a wide smile as his commanding officers gathered around, ready to hear their leader's strategy.

The parchment scroll spread out under wavering light contained a network of black lines inked on its brittle surface. Bold twisted markings represented the major rivers emptying into the Gulf: the Guadalupe, the Colorado, the Brazos, and the Trinity. Scattered between were circles of various sizes representing towns of substantial population. Those which had fallen into Mexican hands were crossed over with large red stars: San Antonio, Gonzales, Goliad.

"Harrisburg," Almonte said in a decisive tone while handing Santa Anna his chest of medicines, "according to our scouts, Carlos and Rogelio, this is where President Burnet and the government of Texas are now located."

"When did the patrols return?" Santa Anna asked, snatching his square mahogany chest from his aide.

"Only hours ago."

"Why didn't you tell me of this development?" Santa Anna's voice was full of anger. He flipped open the gold-cornered box and removed a small piece of opium.

"I felt it best not to disturb you, Your Excellency." Almonte shifted his eyes at fellow officers, imploring support.

"That is no excuse!" Santa Anna bellowed, pushing a lump of the dark opiate into the corner of his jowl. The general stood, leaning over the table. Placing his face nearer Almonte's, he shouted, "Information as valuable as that should be conveyed to me immediately. You stupid bastard! Is this the caliber of command I have at the head of my troops? A man who withholds crucial reports brought back by scouting patrols?" His rage was complete. He paced in front of the fire, waving his hands, yelling at the ceiling, totally out of control.

The soldiers at the table sat silently, eyes averted, heads lowered, knowing this outburst would pass as suddenly as it had appeared. For each one had suffered, at one time or another, a similar verbal lashing for not following orders . . . orders often given on the spur of the moment and usually without contemplation.

"We cannot let them escape!" Santa Anna roared, spinning around quickly to stare at Almonte. "Who exactly is at Harrisburg?"

"President Burnet and his cabinet . . . about twenty men," Almonte answered, controlling an undertone of disgust in his voice. "They are negotiating with a German captain to take over the command of his schooner. It is thought they plan to use it to escape to Galveston Island."

"How far away is this place, Harrisburg?" Santa Anna rushed to the table, peering down at his map, frantically searching for the town.

Almonte lowered a pudgy finger to the brittle parchment, tracing the distance from their position on the Brazos River to an area on Buffalo Bayou, near the twisting San Jacinto. "About thirty miles, Your Excellency . . . thirty miles northeast."

Thirty miles . . . thirty miles," Santa Anna calculated. "That's three days travel, wouldn't you say?" His eyes lit up and flashed brightly at his side.

"Yes, General," Almonte agreed, an even tone to his voice. "I think we could make the trip in three days, easily, I believe."

"The government of Texas is mine!" Santa Anna shouted, circling the long wooden table as he preached to his men. "If Sam Houston will not turn his forces and make a stand . . . we will capture the president of this rebel republic and be finished with this wretched campaign." The agitated dictator then sat down abruptly and began picking his teeth with a splinter of wood.

On the edge of this military exchange, beyond the vision of the Mexican soldiers, a small tow-headed boy crouched near the fire testing his ability to understand the foreign tongue now spoken in his mother's tavern. Joseph Powell had lived most of his thirteen years in the wild Mexican subprovince and had, with little effort, managed to pick up the native language. He sat quietly, listening to this exchange of information between Santa Anna and his aide.

"At daybreak we leave," Santa Anna continued. "Cross the Brazos at Fort Bend and turn the troops toward Harrisburg. We will surprise this arrogant Mr. Burnet . . . stop this game of hide and seek . . . and with the President in our hands, the campaign is over." He raised his arms high in a gesture of surrender and roared in laughter at the thought of his victory. His commanding officers cheered this statement, pounding fists on the table to emphasize their pleasure. The end of this war was in sight.

Elizabeth Powell settled in a wing-backed rocker far from the fire, sat ramrod straight, staring hostilely at the soldiers who spoke in a rapid chatter she did not understand. The strong-willed widow despised the Mexican government and refused to even try to master their language, but secretly she was proud of her quick-witted son and his amazing ability to speak in Spanish. Now, angry at having to feed and house these crude, loud foreigners, she slipped her hand into the pocket of her blue checkered dress and felt for the cold steel of her small hand revolver. They'll not harm me nor me child, she thought, before I do harm ta them first. She looked over at Joseph sitting cross legged at her feet. His ruddy face fell slack and somber, his round blue eyes were fixed in amazement on the animated soldiers. He did not seem to fear them, but sat in awe at the fact that Santa Anna was actually there.

The British widow folded her slender fingers around the barrel of her gun, gripping it loosely, but taking confidence in its weight. She thought back over her decision to stay at the tavern, a choice she had made despite much criticism.

Everyone had fled the area except the widow Powell and her son. She had helped pack her neighbor's wagons, telling them in her haughty English accent, "I've naught ta gain by runnin' away from all Mr. Powell worked so hard ta provide me. He's gone now, and this is me home. I'll be damned if I'll give it over ta anyone without a fight."

And that is exactly what she had meant. Elizabeth Powell stood firm, intent on protecting her property singlehandedly.

Reaching to shake Joseph by the shoulder, she said, "Get ye ta bed, son. Ya'll not be sittin' up through the night watchin' the likes o' these men." She leaned forward in her rocker and ran a warm hand over Joseph's back. "Get on with ye, now, it's late."

The young boy eased himself up, not taking his eyes off the group of men at the table and headed to a rope ladder which led up to the loft. Quietly, as if he feared disturbing the rowdy troops, he climbed into the drafty space where his feather quilt was spread.

He placed his ear flush to the floor and continued to listen to the soldier's discussion. Joseph tried to understand what they were planning. It became a kind of game; identifying familiar words, guessing at those he was not sure of, repeating phrases in his head. After a time, he began to realize that he was privy to important information. Santa Anna was plotting the capture of the Texas government! Right here in his very own house!

As the night wore on, Joseph could not sleep. The voices rising up kept him straining to learn more. By dawn, he had made his decision. He would warn Sam Houston of this plot. He would find the Texans' camp, and he had to get there quickly.

As light started to filter into the tavern, drunken Mexican soldiers began stumbling out of the warm lower room, into the cool morning air. While they struggled to assemble themselves for their long march eastward, Joseph Powell slipped down the rope ladder, out a back window, and saddled his dark brown mare.

Chapter Sixteen

Like smoke drifting over land, the clouds surged and rushed across a pale gray sky. In rapid swirls, the frothy vapor shrouded a full moon that continued to hang in the heavens, though dawn had long since broken. The air was cold, too cold for mid-April, and incessant north winds created chilling damp gusts which blew through the forest in sheets of wet mist.

Joshua stopped near the knarled trunk of an enormous black oak, pulled a crumpled bandana from inside his stiff jacket and wiped water from his face. Easing off his leather hat, letting it hang by a string from his neck, he ran a shaky hand through his hair. Hungry and tired, after more than twelve hours on the run, Joshua ached to rest. Leaning one shoulder against the damp tree, he looked beyond its shimmering branches past veils of Spanish moss, into a clearing just ahead. He squinted, took a long step closer, then parted a bristly mass of juniper blocking his view, and as the morning fog moved and shifted, he strained to focus on a large campsite at the edge of the forest. Joshua sucked in his breath. This was the Texas Army!

From his protected position within the thick foliage, Joshua could see the camp very well. Nestled in an open space surrounded by tangles of dense undergrowth, smoldering mounds of charred wood sent curls of gray smoke to the sky. Scattered pits, like deep scars on the ground, provided islands of warmth for ragged soldiers shivering under muddy saddle blankets and rain soaked capes. As the drizzling mists of dawn laid a moist film over Sam Houston's troops, the north wind eased its fury, leaving an uneasy silence in its wake.

Softly, Joshua crept forward. Making his way over water-logged soil, he neared the men. A crowd of flatbed wagons was stationed along one side of the clearing. A sentry stood nearby, one muddy boot propped firmly against a tall spoked wheel as he gazed over the campsite. The lone watchman leaned over, placing the weight of his rifle the length of his raised leg. The dark wet fur of his coonskin cap dripped water down his back, leaving black stains on the smooth brown suede of his thickly fringed coat. The soldier threw back his head in a wide yawn, then moved closer to the wagonside as if to ward off the wet chilling rain.

From where Joshua stood, he could see the entire layout of the Texans' camp. Shifting his gaze from the tired sentry, he watched as men slowly started to rise and move around. Most were dressed in rags of patched leather breeches, ill-fitting waistcoats, crushed wool shirts, and stiff cowhide hats. There was no sense of order or uniformity about them. They were simply independent men united to fight Mexicans under the direction of General Sam Houston.

To the left of where Joshua stood, gathered around a flaming campfire, a group of black men warmed their hands and feet as they passed a chunk of dried beef. Drinking from a gourd dipper, they mumbled lowly among themselves. Joshua watched for a moment, then deciding to approach them, he dropped to his knees and slid between narrow spaces where the undergrowth was not so thick.

The wet earth was cool and slick under his palms. Joshua could feel water seeping into the front of his jacket. Staying close to the ground, he pulled himself around the curve of the clearing to come up directly behind the black soldiers. Halting in the shadow of a lush fern, Joshua made a low whistling sound, a warble he knew the men would recognize. He waited, whistled again softly, his heartbeat quickening as one man turned his head in surprise upon hearing the familiar signal of the black grapevine.

Joshua shrank back. One black soldier rose, tugged at the damp collar of his oversized coat, and walked to the edge of the woods. Small dark eyes peered intensely through the mist, trained in a steady gaze exactly on the spot where Joshua lay hidden.

"Who dere?" the soldier called in a whisper. He stooped his tall frame lower to the ground. "Who dere?" He came no closer. The soldier waited, half standing, for Joshua to make a sign. The other men at the fire turned on their haunches. Perplexed frowns crossed their faces. Joshua saw they were tense with curiosity.

"Show yourself," the tall soldier urged. With bony hands, he pushed back the lapels of his sagging jacket and thrust his long neck forward. "It be all right . . . come outta dere."

Cautiously, Joshua crept out of the woods, rising self-consciously in front of the lean black soldier who scrutinized him from head to toe.

"What you want? Why is you hidin' out 'round here?' the soldier asked as he thrust forth a square chin covered with matted hair.

Joshua said nothing, but walked to the fire and stood there looking down.

"Where you from?" the soldier probed again.

"West . . . just west of here," Joshua answered. "Been on the road all night."

"Sit down here, near de fire. Harge, give dis man a dipper o' water." the soldier ordered one of his companions.

Joshua sat on a log close to the fire, glad for its warmth on his feet and legs. He accepted the dipper of water and drank eagerly.

"I's Bill," the soldier introduced himself. "Dis is Willie, Fletcher, Henry, and Harge," he said with a sweep of his hands to indicate his companions.

Joshua nodded in their direction. Bill looked at him expectantly, creating a silence which Joshua felt warranted a response.

"I'm Joshua," he finally said. Then, he handed the gourd dipper back to Harge.

"Where you headed?" Bill asked.

"North," was all Joshua would say.

"North? Well, ain' nobody crossin' de San Jacinto River deese days. Too high. De Trinity, too. It be too dangerous. Reckon ain' no way fer you ta git north."

"I'll have to try," Joshua replied. "Is this Sam Houston's army?"

"You's right about dat," Bill answered. "We's been camped here three days now."

"Where are you headed?" Joshua asked.

"Dat's de question we's been askin' ourselves," Bill complained. "Don't rightly know how come de General don't move on." The tall soldier squatted near Joshua. "Dere's talk amongst de men . . . de white men, dat is . . . 'bout goin' on widout de General lessen he turns deese troops on Santa Anna's trail. Dey's gettin' mighty anxious ta fight. Reckon I can't blame dem none . . . I joined up wid dis army so'd I could git in a lick or two myself."

"You been with Houston long?" Joshua directed his questions to Bill as he seemed to act as spokesman for the group.

"Well, I don't rightly know how long, but it seems like a long time," Bill said slowly. "I come out from Kentucky wid Aaron Williams, my Massa. Jus' me an' him . . . rode all de way together . . . Massa Williams an' me. Den, soon as we gits cross de Trinity, he ups an' dies wid de fever. Mighty awful it was, him dying like dat. But, I gives him a proper burial near de river, so den I jus' keeps headin' West 'til I catches up wid Gen'ral Houston. Askt him could he use another man in his colored troops, an' ol' Master Sam says, 'Sure can!', so's I been marchin' wid him ever since." Bill locked his long black fingers together and placed them under his bearded chin. "I reckon I's ready ta fight. Yes, I's ready ta see what deese Mexicans look like."

Joshua watched Bill's tired eyes, noticing how the whites had turned yellow, flecked with brown spots. How his skin had withered to a puckered brown mask hugging his high cheekbones. Bill was old, probably too old to do more than travel with the troops and talk about fighting. No streak of raw courage was coursing through this old man. Joining the army was probably the safest thing he could do. A place to get food . . . for an accusation of vagrancy—especially for a black man—would certainly mean imprisonment.

Bill leaned closer to Joshua. "You gonna fight?" he asked.

"No. I gotta head north," Joshua answered feeling anxious to move on.

"You's gonna have trouble gittin' dere," Bill warned. "Travelin' north ain' gonna be easy."

Joshua took a deep breath, as if doing so cleared his mind and removed the obstacles he knew existed. "Maybe so," he said, "but I've got to try." He sat quietly, staring past the smokey fire as men moved around to dry themselves. They mumbled, complaining about the cool weather, the rains, and the ever-present mud.

Over the rumble of their low conversation, they heard a rapid pounding of horse's hooves. Joshua raised his head. A young boy on a large brown mare charged into the center of the camp. His floppy felt hat, pulled down over a shock of blonde hair, partially covered a naturally pale face now flushed a deep red. As his mare splattered mud in a wide spray through the camp, the boy yelled at the top of his lungs:

"I've a message for General Houston." He reined in the pawing horse. "I must speak with General Houston."

The dozing sentry, now alert, raced toward the boy, stopping in front of the restless animal.

"Who are you?" the sentry asked.

"Joseph Powell, from Fort Bend. I have news for Sam Houston."

"The general's still sleeping. What news do you have?"

"I'll only deliver it to General Houston himself." Joseph protested with a firm set to his jaw.

"Where did you say you're from?"

"Downstream . . . Fort Bend. I've got mighty important news for the general. Mighty important."

"Wait here," the sentry ordered.

Joseph dismounted, jumping easily to the muddy earth to stand panting in the center of the camp. His shoulders rose and fell as he gasped for air to stop the quaking in his chest.

Joshua crept closer, easing around the side of a wagon to hear what this boy had to say. His mind raced. Could this young messenger be bringing a warning to watch for a runaway slave who had killed a Texas soldier? Could he be the one to carry news of his own murderous deed? Joshua bit deeply into his bottom lip, sweat poured from beneath his leather hat as he nervously watched the boy.

The sentry returned, pushing through a crowd of soldiers now gathered in the center of the camp, anxious to hear this boy's message. Close behind him, a tall bearded man followed. He clutched a thin horse blanket around his broad shoulders. A pointed leather hat concealed more than half the man's brow and soft Indian moccasins covered his feet. There was a calm, inquiring set to Sam Houston's face. He had the look of a patient man, a thoughtful man, a man who did not decide things quickly.

"This is General Sam Houston," the sentry told Joseph.

"General Houston," Joseph acknowledged with a slight nod of respect.

"You got news for me, boy?" Sam Houston asked, pulling his draped shoulders back. He clutched the damp faded blanket close to his throat and looked curiously at Joseph.

"I'm from down the Brazos . . . Fort Bend," Joseph started. "Mexicans been at my ma's tavern . . . Santa Anna's been there."

"Santa Anna at Fort Bend?" General Houston's eyes flashed with interest. He stepped closer to Joseph. "You saw him?"

"Yes," Joseph answered. "Santa Anna and hundreds of soldiers."

"Are they still there? Tell me what you know." Houston needed to know how close the Mexican dictator's forces had come to his own.

"They're gone," Joseph said. "Left this morning. Headed to Harrisburg, they are."

"Harrisburg! Are you sure?" Houston wiped his nose with the back of his hand and leaned low over the boy. "How do you know this?"

"Late last night, Santa Anna came up to my ma's tavern . . . lookin' for food and a place to spend the night. My ma put 'em up . . . the general and about fifty officers. Talked all night long, they did. Kept me wake."

"What did you hear?"

"Santa Anna's set on capturin' President Burnet and the Texas Government at Harrisburg, that's the plan. They left out early this morning. I struck out the back of the place while they were saddling up."

"How many men you think he's got?"

"At least a thousand, I reckon. They were scattered all up and down the riverbank . . . as far as I could see," Joseph said.

"Mounted? On foot?"

"Don't rightly know 'bout that, General."

"Any artillery?"

"Didn't see any myself, but one of Santa Anna's officers, called himself Almonte . . . "

"Juan Almonte, yes, yes," Houston interrupted, musing over the name.

"Well, Almonte was talkin' about two big cannons, complainin' how hard it's been draggin' them through the mud."

"Two cannon, huh?" Sam Houston looked around thoughtfully, sweeping the ranks of his men with a serious stare. Then he spoke, "This is good news, men. This is the news I've been waiting for." He squatted down near a pile of warm ashes and picked up a thin stick. He began tracing a pattern in the gray dust.

"Harrisburg," he said to himself, drawing a curved line. He made a star at the end of the line, then circled it. "So, it's Harrisburg, then," he stated, as he rose to face his men. "Let's break camp."

At these words, the men whooped and cheered, throwing hats to the sky. It was time to move on. Time to close in on the elusive Santa Anna. They had a destination at last. As the soldiers rushed around saddling their horses, putting out campfires, and making ready to take to the trail, Joshua knew he had to make a decision.

Several thoughts came to him: If Santa Anna were headed toward Harrisburg, his next destination would be New Washington. Emily was now in danger, if she tried to leave Orange Grove, she would never get past the Mexican Army.

"You comin' wid us?" Bill's question brought Joshua out of deep thought. "Makes more sense to come wid us dan try an' cross de Trinity alone." Bill started piling gear into a high sided wagon. "Don't know what you might be leavin' Texas for," Bill went on, "but right 'bout now . . . it don't make no difference . . . whippin' de Mexicans is what be most important."

Joshua calculated his choices: Should he head north and take a chance of losing Emily? Join up with Houston's troops and risk capture, perhaps death? Or head back and try to find Emily?

"I've no gun, only my knife, and no provisions," he told the black soldier.

"Don't matter none" Bill replied. "We all share what little we's got . . . de colored troops have ta kind o' look out for demselves anyhow. You better come on wid us, dere's plenty o' time to git back north."

Joshua listened, knowing he could possibly blend into this group of colored soldiers and be safer with them than alone on the roads. But, his own safety was of little concern now, it was Emily he worried about.

By the time the morning sun had managed to break through the heavy gray sky, General Sam Houston, mounted on his huge white stallion, rode at the head of his ragged troops. As Houston and his men moved in irregular columns toward the city on Buffalo Bayou, Joshua Kinney followed, hoping to reach Emily before Santa Anna did.

--*-*-*-*-*

For the next three days, General Houston led his army of volunteer soldiers through muddy trails and swampy lowlands. The rain never stopped. Sometimes it fell in torrents, large wet drops soaking the men thoroughly. And when the driving rain eased, it dissolved into a heavy mist which hung on them like fog. They slept little, ate little, and conversed even less. The men pressed on in the rain, anxious to force Santa Anna to face the Texas Army. But this was not to be. Arriving at Harrisburg, they saw that the Mexican Army had moved through quickly.

Enraged at finding that President Burnet and the Texas Government had escaped, Santa Anna had torched and raped the city. And now, according to a few survivors, the Mexican dictator was headed for New Washington.

Joshua sat on the banks of Buffalo Bayou watching the remains of Harrisburg smolder in orange-red coals. Heaps of throbbing embers glowed as the town slowly turned into a pile of ashes. His desperation grew. He hated his inability to keep tears from gathering in his eyes. Pulling his knees to his chin, Joshua let his head fall back against the rough wagon wheel. Breathing deeply to still the quivering in his chest, Joshua inhaled gulps of the balmy night air and looked up at the surprisingly clear sky which stretched like an ebony curtain overhead. There was a moon. There were hundreds of stars. All the clouds had been pushed out to sea. The Norther had run its course, leaving behind a magnificent evening of crystal, clear quiet.

Joshua's sadness did not stem from the loss of Harrisburg, the town meant nothing to him. What brought these unwanted tears to his eyes was the knowledge that by morning Santa Anna would be at New Washington, at Orange Grove . . . and there was no way to rescue Emily.

He closed his eyes against the bright twinkling stars and replaced their brilliance with a vision of Emily, his yellow rose. The most precious thing on earth to him was now lost in the madness of this war. In a voice like a whisper sent down river, Joshua sang these words to himself:

> "Where the Rio Grande is flowing
> And the starry skies are bright
> She walks along the river
> In the quite [sic] summer night
> She thinks if I remember
> When we parted long ago
> I promised to come back to her

And not to leave her so.
Oh now I am agoing to find her
For my heart is full of woe
And we will sing the song togehter [sic]
We sung so long ago
We will play the banjo gaily
And we will sing the song of yore
And the Yellow Rose of Texas
Shall be mine forevermore."

Chapter Seventeen

A disquieting silence pervaded Orange Grove. Humid vaporous air pressed down from the heavens like calming tentacles brushing the land. And the atmosphere listed wet and heavy as bay waters sucked at sandy shores and morning dew glistened opalescent.

With calloused fingers, the Texas soldier rubbed his hairy chin, turning blood-red eyes in a piercing gaze on Emily. He squinted against this early morning light, jowls sagging, forehead tight from a night of watching, waiting, fearing the appearance of an advancing Mexican army. Other men slept at their posts. Leaning on huge wagon wheels, propped against stacked logs, wedged between high curved barrels, they nodded off in drunken stupors, snoring loudly among themselves. Tired of their vigil, the ragged Texans slumbered behind a feeble barricade stretching the length of Colonel Morgan's split log home.

Emily shifted under the soldier's stare. Her body ached from sleeping on the ground. Unable to leave the hastily constructed fortress, she had only dozed in a troubled sleep, sharply awakened every hour with demands for water, food, or cups of fiery whiskey. The men ate and drank in nervous gulps while arguing about Santa Anna's proximity.

Emily had served them all. Moving listlessly among the troops, she had given them what they asked for, her mind not at all on the present situation, but whirling with thoughts of Joshua. She wondered if he had made it across the San Jacinto River. Could she successfully slip away from Orange Grove to meet him? Worry numbed her to the painful reality that Orange Grove lay directly in the path of the advancing Mexican troops. An invasion was certainly imminent.

The night had passed without incident. Not a shot had been fired. No rumble of cannon fire had been heard. The silence of the prairie created tension.

Emily crossed her arms, hugging clammy flesh to her rough cotton bodice. Leaning forward from where she sat, she lifted her eyes at the soldier towering above her.

"Get outta here," he growled, kicking at her with the toe of a dirty boot. "Go on, get us some coffee."

Emily said nothing, cautiously sliding backwards, away from the man. Her eyes stayed trained on his hairy face, and though inwardly she trembled, her face presented an icy mask of non-feeling. Pride and anger kept her from giving him the satisfaction of showing her fear. Pressing the ground with the palms of her hands, Emily guided herself into the shadow of the open doorway. Only then did she stand and make her way hurriedly to the dark, silent kitchen.

Banked coals gave an orange glow to the room, threading the air with an odor of spent pine logs. In a corner opposite the too warm chimney, Hanna, Lydia and two slave girls slept huddled against one another.

Emily picked up a wide basket and set it quietly on the long wooden table. It was filled with the last available provisions; some dried beef, a handful of mud covered yams, and a chunk of dry, hard cornbread. With trembling hands, she packed it all in the pine needle hamper and turned toward the door.

"What is happening?" Hanna's voice came up from the shadowy corner in a hoarse whisper.

"Nothing," Emily whispered back, looking over at Hanna's sleep-lined face. "Nothing's happened."

"Good ta hear," Hanna muttered, standing to brush off her ragged striped skirt. She shuffled closer to Emily. "Shore good ta hear us is still in de hands o' Texans." Peering up at Emily's disheveled appearance, she cocked her head. "Where was you all de night? Looks mighty tired out, you do."

Emily lifted the oval basket with both hands, starting toward the door.

"With the soldiers at the barricade . . . all night . . . " She passed a dirty hand over her cheek, resting it in the tangled clump of hair above her ear. "They want more food," Emily said, shifting vacant eyes away from Hanna.

"What's de matter?" Hanna moved closer. "Somethin' powerful sad done happened. Ain' neber seen a face dat long on you."

Emily opened her mouth to speak, wanting to confide in Hanna, share her anguish of Joshua's departure, but she could not say anything. She let out a deep breath and stepped closer to the door.

"Did dem soldiers have a way wid you?" Hanna waited for an answer.

"No," Emily managed. "Nothing's happened . . . I'm just tired, exhausted." She brushed Hanna's arm in reassurance, blinking back tears she felt forming behind her lids. She forced a smile.

"I told you the Mexicans wouldn't get this far. I'll bet General Houston has already stopped them." Listening to her own words of comfort, Emily prayed it might be true, prayed New Washington would be spared the ravage of Santa Anna's troops.

"News like dat shore would be good ta hear," Hanna said. The young girl moved to the far side of the kitchen and looked out the tiny window facing the back of the plantation. "I see dem flatboats done pulled in. Gonna be a heap o' work loadin' dem heavy sacks what de Massa wants put on board." Hanna glanced back at Emily. "Guess you better go on an' feed dem soldiers. I gotta git down ta de dock 'fore Sam comes huntin' me." She dipped a rusty ladle into a small bucket, telling Emily as she sipped the warm water, "I be glad when all dis is settled . . . be glad when us can git back ta livin' like before. Dis war been a mighty long time comin'. Maybe you's right. Maybe we ain' gonna have no trouble on Orange Grove."

❋·❋·❋··❋·❋·❋

It was no cooler. If anything, the late morning air felt more hot and humid than the day before. Emily stopped and leaned for a moment against a single rough hewn post which supported the covered breezeway. No wind stirred the heavy air. Nothing moved around her. As she looked down the sloping grass to the edge of the bay, the only movement in sight was a gentle lapping of salty water curling in against shallow flatboats.

Emily wrapped both arms around the post and laid her flushed cheek on the scratchy pillar. Finally free of the soldiers' demands, she rested in drained exhaustion, letting her mind float free, and her eyes wander over the landscape.

Tom and Billy, the two fieldhands who had arrived at the plantation with her, labored under the weight of bulky crates as they passed cargo down the loading line onto the waiting deck of the vessel. Sam took his turn, heaving crates with a powerful thrust, then sliding them onto the deck. Sweat glistened on his upper torso, shining black and muscular under the heat of a sun which now beat down in force.

Colonel Morgan's aide, a man of overbearing size and presence, walked along the crude dock, watching the laborers carefully. With most of the settlers safely sequestered on Galveston Island, there was great need for more provisions to keep them comfortable. And as James Morgan had made clear on his departure, the task of loading and shipping supplies would be carried on by his workers at Orange Grove.

No word had come to the plantation regarding Celia Morgan's condition. Emily wondered if the frail woman was recovering or deteriorating. Galveston Island was not much more than a bleak strip of sandy beach, unpopulated and desolate. Emily had the awful premonition that her mistress would never return to the mainland.

Stepping off the low porch, Emily headed down to the water. As she approached, Sam looked her way and signaled with a cock of his head. She moved quicker, closer to where he stood.

"Where's Joshua?" Sam asked in a low voice.

Emily froze. She did not reply.

"Where's Joshua?" Sam pressed again.

Emily automatically took a place in the loading line, grabbing the next sack by a corner to hand it over to Sam.

"I haven't seen him since yesterday morning," she lied.

"Dere's some mighty sick folks in de cabins. Shore could use his help." Sam bent down to push a flat wooden box across the deck.

"Maybe he's in the stables," Emily said, rubbing the palms of her hands against the front of her skirt.

"Naw, I checked," Sam said. "I got a feeling somethin's powerful wrong."

Emily pressed her lips together, straightened her back and braced herself to catch the next piece of cargo passed down the line. They fell silent, working in a rhythmic motion, swinging crates and sacks on board while the sun burned down, heating up the land.

A seagull squawked and floated above them, darting out over the quiet bay, then circling back once more. Emily paused to gaze up at the wide expanse of gray-white wings spread out above her, envying the absolute freedom of the bird. Free to come and go as he wants, she thought. Free to go higher, dip lower, or fly away from this place altogether. Though Emily had been trying to keep her mind clear of thoughts of Joshua, she surrendered and let his presence fill her. Aching with his absence, she was consumed with plans to leave New Washington and meet him.

Would there never be a time for them alone? she wondered. Were they doomed to live their lives apart? Wounded by the sudden parting, Emily grieved for Joshua as if he were dead. Tears slid over her cheeks as she bent to the task of loading this boat for James Morgan.

The seagull squawked again. It beat its wings wildly, flapping off toward the huge silent house. Emily looked up as it passed overhead, then lowered her eyes to a sight on the horizon which stopped her in mid breath. A line of mounted men stretched clear across the prairie! Santa Anna had arrived at Orange Grove!

✦·✦·✦··✦·✦·✦

In the distance, a spectrum of red and gold glittered in vibrant flashes as swarthy soldiers brought restless mounts to a halt. Snorting horses reared tall on hind legs, tossing long silky manes from their eyes. Crashing hooves beat the land in thunderous vibrations, rising in a crescendo of stomping and pawing which bore down from the prairie, across the plantation, to the very edge of the bay.

Within a tiny fragment of frozen time, Emily watched in chilling horror as flank after flank of cavalry pulled in, one behind the other. The enemy waited, no more than one hundred feet from the ring of oaks bordering Orange Grove. They sat poised and sinister, assessing the strength of the rebel Texans.

No shots came from behind the barricade.

No soldiers moved to attack.

But when a surging scream rose up from the dark-skinned men who cried shrilly over the land, *la grita* was quickly picked up by one soldier after another. This high pitched cry, a blood curdling yell, sliced the air like a sword pulled back to strike. As the cry grew stronger, more men amassed until Orange Grove was surrounded. There were mounted men, some on foot, others driving high sided wagons heaped with valuable plunder. The Mexicans waited restlessly for their leader to advance to the front. And, in what seemed to be a very long time, but was only a matter of seconds, Santa Anna appeared at the head of his troops.

Dwarfed by his huge white mount, the general sat stiffly on an ornate saddle of gleaming inlaid silver, etched, and wrought through black leather. It reflected the white-hot rays of a late afternoon sun. In a haughty facade of pompous self-importance, Santa Anna tilted back his plumed head, lifted a gloved hand, and brought an instant hush to the massive gathering awaiting his command. Surveying the plantation spread out before him, Santa Anna lowered his short stocky arm.

"*¡Adelante!*" he ordered, giving the signal to advance.

Orange Grove was under attack.

Rifle fire exploded. Its sharp burst was nearly drowned out by the crashing sounds of soldiers sweeping down from the prairie. Too far away to execute a direct hit, the Texans' bullets fell to the ground, but they continued shooting, aiming rifles into the tangle of men and horses bearing down on them in a frenzy. The acrid smell of spent gun powder grew thick and pungent. The space between the Santanistas and the settlers was hung with small black clouds. The frightful boom of Mexican cannon split the air wide open. Terrified men and women fled in droves toward the cover of the forest.

Emily cowered behind a tall curved barrel, afraid to move. The others who had also been loading the flatboat, ran screaming into high swamp cane.

"Lawd, no! Lawd, no! Dey's here!" Emily heard Hanna's cries. She turned and saw the girl, skirts up past her knees, running with Sam toward the quarters. He pulled Hanna's arm brusquely, urging her faster, faster, to follow him closely. Sam looked back.

"Emily! Emily! Come on . . . git ta de woods." His eyes strained to connect with hers as he fumbled to hold onto Hanna.

Emily rose up, then crouched back. She could not follow. Sam and Hanna disappeared into a thick stand of live oak trees behind the quarters. From where she hid, Emily watched a swarm of uniformed men plunge toward the main house, bayonets raised, set on destruction. She cringed, thinking of Celia Morgan's plea for Emily to protect her home. It was too late, no one could do a thing to stop the Santanistas.

Flames suddenly roared from the tiny kitchen window, then flashed red-hot over the roof. The entire backside of the main house was next, quickly turning into a solid wall of fire. Horrified, Emily watched split logs char and crumble, watched them rapidly disintegrate into smoldering piles of ashes. Women and children trapped in the house, now ran screaming toward the bay, stumbling and falling in the path of ruthless soldiers who struck at them with the butts of their rifles.

Livestock ran loose. Lost in confusion, a pack of mules thundered in circles, not knowing which direction to go. Soldiers broke into the main warehouse. With cries of pleasure at their discovery, the men heaved James Morgan's provisions onto their wagons. Barrels of salt, casks of meal, and heaps of dried meat were rolled onto loaded flatbeds. Emily watched as the huge storage barns were stripped clean.

It was as if she were watching a play . . . one of those lively dramas acted out in a tiny church back home. She recalled sitting in the shadows of the drafty little hall, caught up in the reenactments of tribal wars and fierce struggles remembered by the elders. Their cries and grunts, moans and screams, all sounded very familiar to Emily. Even the frantic dashing around to try and find safety had its air of play acting about it. "This cannot really be happening," she thought.

In a disconnected haze of fright and surprise, Emily crouched low to the ground, her head pressed painfully against the dry splintered slats of the barrel. She prayed no one saw her.

As the looting in the main house came to an end, soldiers fanned out over the grounds setting fire to everything in their path.

Emily's heart beat faster, her mouth grew dry. Shutting her eyes to the soldiers' proximity, she pressed her palms together in a prayerful gesture, laying her forehead against trembling fingertips. And when the clanking of metal stirrups jangled directly above her head, she opened her eyes, then shrieked in horror. She was face to face with Santa Anna.

"Take her!" the general ordered, lowering his hand at Emily. "Strap her to my horse!"

Emily quickly darted from behind the barrel, stumbling blindly into shallow water at the edge of the bay. She had to get away. A large hand shot forward, grabbing her by the hair in a twisting brutal yank, and she screamed and plunged face down into the salty water. Unable to free herself from the soldier's grip, she clenched her teeth, holding her breath, trying to bear the pain. Emily felt as if her hair would detach from her scalp.

"You don't geet away from His Excellency. You coming with us." The soldier snorted in laughter, dragging Emily from the salty water onto the muddy shore. With a swing of his arm, the soldier bound her tightly with her own skirts, then secured her under his arm.

Emily felt herself being lifted, carried through the throng of shouting soldiers to be thrown like a carcass over the back of Santa Anna's horse. A piece of hard, brittle burlap was stuffed into her mouth, and with painful curt twists, the soldier bound a length of rope around Emily's hands and feet. The rough, coarse hemp cut deeply into her flesh, stopping the flow of blood to her limbs. She grew numb. She was terrified. She was captive.

Chapter Eighteen

He spoke rapidly . . . loudly . . . in bursts of staccato commands, answered quickly with, "*Sí, sí, Señor.*" No one disagreed with Santa Anna.

Bent on capturing the Texas Army, Santa Anna pointed his lumbering caravan in an eastward direction and slowly wound his way from the flaming ruins of Orange Grove.

The stench of sweating horse flesh sickened Emily. Strapped painfully over the rear end of Santa Anna's white stallion, she could not raise her head more than an inch from the animal's rough, coarse hair. It chafed and burned her face. Tied across the stallion, with her head toward the ground, she was unable to determine their direction. But one thing was certain . . . her hopes, her foolish persistent hopes of meeting Joshua, were now completely destroyed.

Emily's tears fell unnoticed. Her muffled sobs poured into the filthy burlap rag jammed so tightly into her mouth. In the wild confusion of this sprawling procession, she was just one more piece of plunder. When Santa Anna reached around to massage her buttocks with a rough thrust of his hand, Emily stiffened. His fondling turned her cold. His laughter brought a burning rage. The Mexican dictator was pleased with his conquest.

Following deep, marshy waterways, they continued at an unbroken pace. In time, the air took on the rancid smell of rotting vegetation. Forests thickened in larger patches. Spanish moss dropped down and brushed her face. Emily sensed they were nearing the San Jacinto River.

❊❊❊❊❊

Raising a large bony hand, Sam Houston brought his tired troops to a whispering halt. Unable to advance one step further, men collapsed on the spot. General Houston motioned for quiet, then jumped down from his horse to gaze over the broad plain before them.

Joshua pushed past the soldiers blocking his view and darted to the front. The scene unfolding before him was worse than he had envisioned. From where he stood, Joshua could see Santa Anna's Army strutting in irregular columns across the plain to the tune of a Mexican ballad. Trumpets blared as if they claimed a victory. Looking past the advancing enemy, Joshua saw streams of black clouds rising behind the troops. His chest tightened. Orange Grove was burning. And somewhere on the other side of this massive gathering of men, artillery and horses, he knew Emily was trapped.

Joshua did not know the size of the enemy forces, but he silently estimated they outnumbered the Texans by at least ten to one. Finally, face to face with Santa Anna's army, Joshua was ready . . . anxious to fight . . . impatient to cross the plain to find Emily. Finding her was all that mattered.

✦·✦·✦··✦·✦·✦

"There they are . . . to the left . . . lurking in the trees. See the artillery? See it?" Santa Anna talked excitedly to Juan Almonte. "We'll attack now!" the dictator ordered. "Move forward, men. Behind that stand of trees."

Almonte opened his mouth to protest this dangerous, ill-timed maneuver, but thought better of it and did as His Excellency commanded.

"Advance to the field," Almonte ordered. "Move the cannon out."

Santa Anna paraded in front of his men as they quickly pushed the heavy cannon into position. "Fire on the rebels!" he ordered.

An explosive roar drowned the rest of his commands. Smoke rose from the cannon's large barrel, but the Santanistas watched in dismay as their heavy black ball veered off into the bayou.

The Texans answered with a round of rifle fire and a blast of their own cannon.

Santa Anna rode onto the open plain.

"Fire away, men," he yelled.

The air vibrated with another volley of cannon and rifle fire, followed by screams from the Texans' camp. The Santanistas had scored a hit! Santa Anna laughed with pleasure and galloped from the plain to the edge of the woods, where Almonte stood watching in horror.

"Be careful, Your Excellency," he reprimanded. "You will be the next target." His words were barely spoken when a round of lead pellets thudded into the soft ground, only yards from where Santa Anna paraded.

"Nonsense," the haughty dictator retorted. "We are in an excellent position."

The exchange of fire was still going on as Santa Anna gathered his officers around him.

"We'll set up camp here," he said, with a sweep of his arm to indicate a slight rise on the prairie.

Juan Almonte stepped forward.

"I fear, Your Excellency, that setting up camp in such an unprotected area as this would be to our disadvantage." He bowed slightly as he registered his complaint.

"You're wrong," Santa Anna threw back. "We have the cover of heavy woods to the right and a clear front."

"But, *Señor*," Almonte continued, "we also have water to our rear and an open field to the left. This leaves no room for retreat . . . should it become necessary."

Santa Anna unsheathed his gleaming sword, raising it high above his head.

"There will be no need for an avenue of retreat. We will crush these pitiful rebels with a single attack." The general lowered his weapon, then, pointing to a small clearing, he ordered, "put my tent there." Then, spinning around quickly, Santa Anna lowered his shining sword at Emily and said, "put her inside, and two dragoons at the door." With a flourish, Santa Anna galloped to the edge of the battlefield, stopping to survey the vast plain stretched out before his army.

Content with his decision to set up camp in a location that provided a commanding view of the San Jacinto plain, Santa Anna smiled to himself, turned his white stallion, and headed toward his red silk tent and Emily.

✦·✦·✦··✦·✦·✦

More out of luck than accuracy, the Mexicans had managed a hit. Several Texans were wounded. Bill was among them, his leg shattered by a cannon ball. Crouched by his side, Joshua hurriedly wrapped Bill's leg with rags to stop the bleeding.

Joshua's hands were steady, but inside he felt like shattered glass. The ominous danger of an approaching battle brought a mixture of fear, anxiety, and restlessness to all the men. Joshua knew that for Texas to win its independence, many men would lose their lives. The finality of it all churned his stomach painfully, but his feelings of dread were tempered by a desire for revenge, and a determination to find Emily.

❈·❈·❈··❈·❈·❈

Within the shadowy rose-colored quietude of Santa Anna's tent, Emily sat atop a wooden crate staring at treasures gleaned from the parlors and sideboards of hundreds of Texas families. Crammed into the general's red silk tent were crates of silver, trunks of exquisite fabrics and leather bags of gold coins. An elaborately strung crystal chandelier, hanging precariously in the center of the tent, spilled its sparkling prisms over the blue and orange of a thick Persian rug. Emily caught a glimpse of her own distorted reflection on the smooth surface of a large silver bowl as she leaned over to pick up a small domed chest. The gilded box was heavy. She used both hands to steady it on her knees. And as she cautiously opened its curved lid, a mirrored interior caught the light and reflected the brilliant contents. Diamond necklaces, rings and brooches set with precious stones, and filigreed silver bracelets lay inside. Emily gently touched a square cut emerald, tracing its heavy gold setting with a trembling finger, then quickly shut the mirrored box and set it on the floor.

A package wrapped in brown paper caught her attention. The parcel, wedged between two wooden crates, had lettering on the front. Emily pulled it free, then gasped in horror as she stared at the handwriting—"Emily West, New Washington"—it read. Her grip tightened. She put it on her lap and gazed at it in disbelief. This was her veil! The veil she had put money on in Andrew Stephen's store. The veil she had hoped to wear for Joshua. Raked up with all the plunder of Harrisburg, this delicate piece of woven thread had wound up in Santa Anna's possession. Emily tore the paper open with shaking hands. The veil spilled across her knees in snowy white folds. Burying her face in them she sobbed for the future that would not be.

A shaft of daylight suddenly cut through the hot semi-darkness.

Emily shot to her feet, backing away from the entrance where Santa Anna now stood. He smiled at her from the open flap, his lips turned up in a sneer of delight, his eyes taking her in from head to toe. Emily crushed the veil to her breast and waited.

The general dropped the flap behind him. Entering the tent with two long strides, he went to a black leather trunk and threw open its humpbacked lid. Bending over the trunk, he muttered to himself while rummaging through its contents. Santa Anna tossed aside fringed satin shawls, heavy beaded capes, and gowns adorned with feathers. Finally, he turned, holding a red satin gown by the shoulders. A myriad of glass beads, sewn in a delicate rose pattern on the dress, sparkled in the dim light.

Santa Anna held the dress out to Emily, indicating that he wanted her to put it on. Trembling, she made no move. He came closer, finally pressing the gown into her arms. Looking at the white lace veil she clutched, he took it from her and shook it out. Then, he examined the diamond patterned lace carefully, nodded his approval and placed it on Emily's head. He laughed . . . a laugh of pleasure, approval, anticipation. Stepping back, Santa Anna picked up a bottle of wine, broke it open and sat on a crate and waited. When Emily made no move, he waived his hands in circular motions, indicating that she should undress. A grimace replaced his smile. Afraid to antagonize the general, Emily timidly pushed her dirty wool dress off her shoulders, over her hips, and let it fall to the floor. Bare breasted, she tried to quickly pull the red satin dress over her front, but Santa Anna stopped her.

Rising from his seat, he took the elegant dress from her, ran his hands over her full breasts, and continued down her stomach to unfasten her petticoats. He let them drop to the floor, standing back to take in Emily's completely naked form. His smile was wide. His pleasure enormous.

Emily kept her eyes cast downward, feeling Santa Anna's rough hands roam over her buttocks, down her thighs, and between her legs. She moved sideways. He clasped her around the waist, pressing his lips fully on hers. The white lace veil cascaded over the two of them, shrouding them under its diamond-patterned web. Tears slid down Emily's closed eyes as she resigned herself to Santa Anna's advances. He lifted her face to his, muttered something she did not understand, then, took her hand. With an urgent pull, he led her to the thick, soft carpet spread out in a corner of the tent.

He deftly unbuckled his wide silver-studded belt, letting it drop to the floor with a crash as his heavy sword struck the side of a trunk. Emily jumped back, startled. Then, he grasped both of Emily's hands at the wrist with one of his, keeping the other free to unbutton his shirt and tight fitting breeches. Impatiently, he pulled her down on the carpet beside him. Emily froze in his arms.

Uttering low moans of anticipation, Santa Anna slid his half-naked form over hers. Still clasping her wrists tightly with one hand, he pressed damply on her neck and shoulders with the other, leaving a burning touch on her flesh.

Emily squirmed and tried to pull away. She turned her face away from his. Santa Anna only stroked her skin more rapidly, moving his hand over the full curve of her breasts, along the soft roundness of her stomach, while his lips groped urgently for hers.

Trapped under the full weight of the general, Emily could do little to stop him from taking her. As the last rays of sunlight left the tent, Emily lay ravished and conquered among the treasures of Santa Anna's campaign.

+-+-+--+-+-+

No guards were posted around the Texas Army's camp beyond the ridge below the San Jacinto plain. Despite the brief skirmish with the Mexican troops earlier that day, Sam Houston and his force of nine hundred Texans remained outwardly calm. Sitting before burning fires, cleaning guns and sharpening their knives, they told each other stories about how they came to be a part of this fight for Texas' independence. They found comfort in knowing that together, they would soon face the elusive Santanistas.

Staying close to the colored troops, but remaining alert to the activity around him, Joshua busied himself by changing the bandage on Bill's injured leg. As he put a ragged piece of cloth over the bloody open wound, Joshua's mind began to fill with troubling thoughts of Emily's uncertain situation. Where was she now? Was she hurt? Wounded? Was she wandering the roads alone trying to catch up with him? His determination to find her strengthened.

By chance, Joshua now found himself in the midst of preparations for an impending battle, but all he had ever wanted to do was find Emily and, perhaps, to head north, away from this troubling business. Now, faced with the uncertainty of the approaching conflict, he resolved himself to get through whatever these next

hours would bring, to survive, and once again embrace his Yellow
Rose.

✦✦✦✦✦✦

The absence of noise and movement in the Mexican encampment
struck Emily as very odd. She knew it had to be late afternoon,
though Santa Anna slept at her side as if it were midnight. She
looked over at the small dictator, repulsed by the pinched features
and frail appearance of the man who commanded an empire. His
thinning brown hair stuck wetly to a sweating forehead, and his
child-like arms lay in a listless embrace across Emily's chest. She
moved slightly, testing his consciousness, inching herself slowly
away from his grasp. He did not stir. Fortunately, the many glasses
of wine he had downed through the night, along with the startling
amount of opium he had chewed, had taken the general's senses
away.

It was stifling hot in the tent. Emily needed some air. Throwing
her woolen dress over her body, shoving her feet into muddy boots,
she crept cautiously toward the tent flap. Emily breathed a sigh of
relief and lifted the silk back to receive a rush of cooler air.

All over the camp, smaller tents stood with their flaps down.
Rifles, stacked in spiky pyramids nearby, lay against crates of wine,
piled shoulder high, throughout the campsite. It was siesta time, a
tradition that even the Mexican Army refused to abandon. A feeling
of security pervaded the camp.

Emily glanced around. No one was moving. The dragoons,
usually stationed at Santa Anna's side were missing. She looked
back at Santa Anna's sleeping form and knew that now was the time
to escape.

Crouching low to the ground, Emily moved through the opening.
She had secured the tent flap and was starting to rise when the
piercing crack of rifle fire split the air. The high barricade around the
camp shattered, and the Texas Army descended on the Santanistas
with shouts of "Remember the Alamo," "Remember Goliad."

A bugle sounded in the Mexican camp, and directly in front of
Emily, a soldier leapt from his tent in confusion, charging weaponless
toward the advancing Texans.

"Hold your fire. Goddamn it, hold your fire," Sam Houston
shouted to his men. But no one paid any attention, all discipline was

at an end. The men waited for no orders, but fired wildly into the camp, reloaded, and fired again.

Unarmed, Joshua picked up a rifle left stacked by the fleeing Mexican soldiers and plunged through into the tangle of men fighting hand-to-hand wielding crudely fashioned weapons. The Texans fought with clubs, picks, knives, rifles, and anything they could use to strike the enemy. Scores of Mexican troops fell to the ground around them while many more dropped their highly polished swords and European weapons as they fled in terror from the relentless Texas Army.

Emily screamed at the sight of the ensuing slaughter. The Texans pursued the fleeing Mexicans with a vengeance. Bayonets snapped off at the hilt in many bodies. Lead balls riddled any who tried to run away. Many were run through by lances, plunged through by mounted Texans.

Finally, awakened by the tumultuous invasion, Santa Anna pushed past Emily knocking her into the fray. He looked around wildly, trying to comprehend what was happening. Wearing only a pair of silk drawers and a silk shirt, the general ran excitedly into the middle of the fighting.

Shouting orders to which his troops paid no attention, Santa Anna clawed his face and pressed his hands to his mouth, angry and terrified that he had lost control. Realizing there was no way to regain command, Santa Anna flung himself onto a big black stallion and rode off into the swampy marshland. Emily watched him disappear into the woods.

Rushing back into the tent, Emily grabbed the general's ornate sword. Tugging frantically with both hands, she shook it until the sharp blade loosened and slid from its snug fitting sheath. Lunging forward, she thrust the weapon through the back wall of the tent, pushing downward with all her strength to rip a gaping hole in the blood red silk. Without ever looking back, she threw aside the sword, gathered her skirts up around her knees and stepped through the ragged opening. Screams and cries of terror echoed over the tent and down the marshy field rising sharply as the hellish massacre continued just behind her.

Emily ran, too frightened to scream. She plunged blindly through the tangle of prairie grass and mud, putting distance between herself and the blood-letting on the battlefield. Shrieks of dying men and slaughtered horses resounded in chilling waves through the air. Cracks of rifle fire, coming in a continuation of staccato bursts made Emily wince and press her eyes closed with each new round.

Taking deep breaths to calm herself, Emily stopped to assess her situation. Suddenly, a riderless horse charged in her direction. Without thinking, she grabbed its reins, pulled it toward her, and mounted the wiry gray mustang. Heading away from the carnage and death, Emily pointed the horse toward the only open road in her path. She hoped it would take her to Orange Grove. There was nowhere else to go.

＊-＊-＊--＊-＊-＊

In time, the thunder of cannon finally ceased. The air began to lose its acrid smell of spent gun powder and seared flesh. Joshua saw the ornately uniformed bodies of the Mexican soldiers strewn throughout the area lining the edge of the swamp. The Santanistas fled into the woods as the Texans routed and secured the enemy camp. In a frenzy, Joshua frantically searched each remaining tent hoping to find Emily alive.

＊-＊-＊--＊-＊-＊

When Emily emerged from a thick stand of oaks, she came upon the remains of James Morgan's split-log house. Like a charred skeleton, it lay starkly black against an unusually magnificent sunset. Within its familiar ring of leafy oaks, the sprawling house smoldered in a pitiful heap of destruction. Riding down into the quarters, Emily passed row after row of cabins that lay smoking and charred. The sight frightened her more than the memory of the sinister red silk tent from which she had just escaped.

Dismounting, she stood with arms pressed across her chest, doubling over in grief and exhaustion. Emily watched, through a blur of tears, as the only home she had known in this new land slowly reduced itself to ashes. All her disappointment, anger, and regret about coming to Texas seemed to culminate with the burning of Orange Grove. Life here had been a continual struggle to remain one step ahead of the insidious forces which never stopped bringing her sadness. Joshua was gone. Orange Grove was destroyed. Her future in Texas seemed lost.

As the shadows from giant oaks deepened and the sunset faded into the bay, Emily found enough strength to slowly make her way past the pile of rubble that had once been her cabin. Walking toward the edge of the water, she sensed another's presence. There was the muffled sound of low sobbing, deep sobbing, as if a man were crying. Emily stopped to listen. Above the crackling and snapping of burning wood, she was certain it was crying she heard.

Winding her way through the narrow spaces between burning cabins, Emily came to the beginning of a thick cane brake. Stepping cautiously forward, she parted the high brittle reeds. When she looked down, she saw Sam . . . kneeling in anguish over Hanna's bleeding form. The young girl lay in a twisted mass of blood covered canes, still and lifeless, the side of her head split open.

Sam looked up. He made slight squinting movements with his tear-filled eyes. Emily felt the pain which gripped him. She dropped to her knees beside him.

"Oh, Sam. Not Hanna," Emily moaned, stroking the girl's smooth brown hand. "Not Hanna." Emily choked on the words, her own flood of tears now coming forth. She covered her face with one hand, pressing the side of her head. She fell heavily against Sam. Her grief mingled with his.

"Don't know, Miss Emily," Sam's voice cracked. "Don't know why dis chile had ta die. Neber did wanna come out here. Neber did like dis place. An' she didn't want nothing but a little bit o' happiness. Don't know why de Lawd done took dis chile so soon." His words were choked with loss, floundering for answers that did not come. He turned and put an arm over Emily's back, drawing her nearer.

"Ain' a soul left on de place 'cept us. All de others done run off inta de woods. I stayed ta try ta help Hanna, but wasn't nothin' I could do . . . nothin' 'cept watch over her till de end. I's fixin' ta bury her, now." He squeezed Emily's shoulder. "I's glad you's here ta see her put away. Woulda meant somethin' ta Hanna, knowing you's alive. We seen you strapped ta dat horse, dragged 'way like a sick ox. Didn't think you'd be comin' back . . . thought I'd seen de last o' you."

Emily wiped her face with a grimy hand, feeling sand and dirt on her skin.

"I got away . . . in the middle of the fighting. I cut a hole in Santa Anna's tent, stole a horse, and made my way here." She stopped and looked deeply into Sam's eyes. "It was awful. Horrible. The

Texans cut up the Mexican soldiers like pieces of dead horse flesh. There were bodies all over the place, thrown for miles from the battlefield. In some places, the dead were four feet deep, one on top of the other." She swallowed hard, wiped her eyes with the edge of her skirt, then went on. "They were fighting to the death out there. It was a massacre."

"Who won?" Sam wanted to know. "Is dis place in de hands o' de Texans, now?"

"From what I saw, I think most of the Mexicans are dead, but I really don't know, Sam," Emily answered.

Turning her thoughts away from the battle, Emily began to question Sam. "Have you any news about Joshua?"

"No. I ain't seen him, but I heered they's a bounty notice 'bout him posted up in Harrisburg," Sam replied.

"A bounty notice," Emily said in horror. "That's serious, Sam. You think he's been caught?"

"Naw, I doubt it, Miz Emily. Joshua be too smart for dem men what hunts him. He knows deese parts. He'll be all right."

Finding little consolation in Sam's words, Emily turned and walked away, lost in her own thoughts of Joshua and the love she knew would never be fulfilled.

❋❋❋❋❋❋

Flaming torches staked into the soft sandy soil gave off enough light for Sam to dig a grave, but left sufficient darkness to mask his grief. He tried to be brave, to hold back his tears, but his grief was much greater than even Emily suspected.

A hard working, silent man, Sam had never hidden his attraction to Hanna, but then, he had never openly displayed affection for her, either. Their relationship had been jovial and friendly; a friendship that had unexpectedly deepened into love.

Now, as she watched him line the shallow grave with boughs of pine and gently lay Hanna's tiny body inside, Emily felt more like an intruder than a comforter. Kneeling, Sam's shoulders began to tremble with heaving sobs as he laid his forehead against the damp earth. Emily spoke in a thin voice. "She'll rest in peace. The pain she's suffered here is over." Emily moved closer to Sam and knelt beside him. "She's gone from us now, Sam. But who's to say she's not the lucky one?"

"Maybe she's better off dead," Emily said flatly, the terrible ordeal of her own capture, rape, and losing Joshua spurred her words. "What's left for us, Sam? Where do we go from here? Out here alone on the prairie, the Mexican soldiers only miles up the road. Who knows what will happen to us?" Her words, a torrent of fear and anger, suddenly stopped. She pressed her cheek to her shoulder to avoid Sam's look of surprise. Emily was ashamed of her childish display of self pity.

Sam turned away from Emily. He started pushing handfuls of dirt over Hanna's still body.

"Folks gonna come back," he mumbled, his voice husky with grief. "Dey's gonna build Orange Grove back up again. You see."

"No, Sam," Emily's tone was resolute, "there's nothing to come back for. There's no reason to return."

Footsteps crunched the charred grass behind them.

Leaves rustled nearby.

A tree limb snapped.

"You're wrong, Emily," a voice floated out of the darkness. Icy pangs of hope soared through Emily. She spun around, eyes wide.

The ragged circle of light widened as Joshua lifted a torch high above his head, casting an amber glow across his bronze face.

"Joshua," Emily gasped, rising as he came forward, one arm outstretched. He clasped her firmly around her tiny waist.

"Joshua, you're . . . " He stifled her words with his lips, kissing Emily with the tender urgency she remembered. And as she buried her face in the familiar crook of his neck, she heard him speak softly against her rumpled hair. "I had reason to return . . . I had to claim my yellow rose."

Epilogue

The bloody massacre on the Plains of San Jacinto destroyed Santa Anna's army. With six hundred thirty soldiers killed, over two hundred wounded, and hundreds captured, the main Mexican forces began their retreat from Texas.

✦·✦·✦··✦·✦·✦

General Santa Anna was captured by the Texans and returned to Mexico. In his own country, his military career continued to flourish, and he remained an explosive force along the Texas border.

✦·✦·✦··✦·✦·✦

General Sam Houston went on to be elected the first, then, the third President of the Republic of Texas. He was a prominent figure in Texas public and political life until his death.

✦·✦·✦··✦·✦·✦

In May of 1836, William Bollaert, a writer traveling through Texas, came to New Washington. He listened to Emily West recount her tale of capture at the hands of Santa Anna, and documented her story in his book, *William Bollaert's Texas*. When Emily's tale circulated throughout the settlement, she was called the heroine of the Battle of San Jacinto for the part she played in Texas' independence.

✦·✦·✦··✦·✦·✦

In July of 1837, Emily West petitioned for a passport from the new Republic of Texas to return to her native New York. The original petition, housed in the Texas State Library Archives, verifies the fact that Emily not only survived the Battle of San Jacinto, but also, that she had become disillusioned with life in Texas and wanted to return North. It is not known if she left Texas.

✦-✦-✦--✦-✦-✦

The first known copy of the lyrics to the song "The Yellow Rose of Texas" was copyrighted in 1858 by William Pond Company in New York. It is believed that the work may have been used by Charles H. Brown, a vaudeville performer in New York, as part of his act. On the vaudeville circuit, Negro music began to replace English music as slavery proliferated in the South. The anonymous, original manuscript with the lyrics to "The Yellow Rose of Texas" contained only the initials J.K. The author of this love ballad remains a mystery.